SHAKESPEARE'S
CLCK

A NOVEL ABOUT GIRLS IN A LINE

JAN MORAN NEIL

CRANTHORPE
—— MILLNER ——
PUBLISHERS

First published by Cranthorpe Millner Publishers (2021)

ISBN 978-1-912964-63-5 (Paperback)

www.cranthorpemillner.com

Cranthorpe Millner Publishers

Other titles by Jan Moran Neil

Novel:

Blackberry Promises – *Creative Ink Publishing*

Collections:

Serving Bluebird Pie

(*Creative Ink Publishing*)

Red Lipstick & Revelations

(*Indigo Dreams Publishing*)

When This Is All Over … Anthology

(*Creative Ink Publishing*)

Plays:

Blackberry Promises

Brave Hearts & Baggage

The Deadly Factor

A President in Waiting …

www.stagescripts.com

About the Author

Jan Moran Neil was trained at the Royal Central School of Speech and Drama and the National Youth Theatre. She spent many years in the professional theatre before forming Creative Ink for Writers and Actors. Her plays have been performed on the London Fringe, Guga S'Thebe Theatre, Langa and Masambe Theatre, Baxter, Cape Town. Her short story and poetry collections include her winning story 'Death by Pythagoras'/BBC Writers and broadcast on Radio 4 and her winning sonnet 'Silver Surfing'/Bloomsbury Publishing which was also published by the Royal Society of Literature, as well as other highly commended poems. Jan has a Masters' degree in Creative Writing from the University of Cambridge. She is available for readings from her collections and novels.

www.janmoranneil.co.uk

For my school chums: Alison, Jan, Hazel and Caryl – who never saw sixty.

And for Madeleine Lily and Eleanor Rose – who have it all ahead of them.

'Aphorisms speak to suit their occasion.'

1

Jayne (53)
December 20th 2005

The undertaker's clock on the Milton High Street has been repaired. For years we thought it was half past four when our double-decker school bus rattled by. In reality, we were always earlier than half past four but we never realized we had extra time until someone pointed out that the hands were stuck. Oh, my. That was thirty-four years ago. They've had time to fix it.

Right next door to the undertaker's is the jeweller's. The clocks are fringed with tinsel: clocks which look like old, oak school clocks, plastic kitchen clocks, children's character cartoon clocks, clocks without cuckoos, Spanish mahogany grandfather and grandmother clocks; clocks beating to the pace of a living heart. Bracket clocks trying to square their unbeatable circle, ticking time to ... waste, clocks thieving time so make ... haste. Catch cold clocks out. My dry breath quickens, sand grains of time beneath the feet of passers-by shift like this drifting snow. All those watch faces, all those clock faces. Tick tock, but I, the dead wooden stick of I, I the deathwatch beetle: I. Am. Always. On. Time. And Time terrifies me.

Tick tock: all those watches reading different times. I will

1

make my way to meet you at the department store when the correct watch reads eleven-thirty am. But which is the correct watch? I will choose. This will then give me time to go the toilet … sorry, I mean *lavatory* and brush up, find a quiet table for our midday appointment. Should I choose the silver watch with the square face or the gold strap of a bracelet hiding a tiny oval face: a face with tiny, trim white arms and numbers you cannot read but which looks beautiful? Like yours.

Or will it be the men's watches that tell the true time? Classic, Sports or Ultra-Thin? Oh my, it is then that I see you. My heart skips. (My cumbersome teenage legs never could.) I see the back of a woman who is selecting from a black velvet tray of men's watches. Could it be you? Backs … so many alphabetical school lines: my surname having begun with a 'T' and yours a 'W'. There was, of course, the infamous full-lipped 'V' sandwiched between us. 'V', the sign for two fingers up to the world. Fuck Off or Victory. But there you are. Except there was, alas, no 'U'. No neat Miss Underwood to protect me from the wretched 'V' at my back. How I had longed for any 'U' between my 'T' surname and those insistent fingers belonging to Miss 'V' behind me, prodding my left scapula for always. I am sure that is why I am round-shouldered. It could have been all so different if there had been a Miss Underwood between my Miss 'T' and her Miss 'V'. I do, of course, know your back well, Miss W: you turned it on me so often.

For now, you turn to the glass counter on the left and I shift behind a huge tray of diamond rings so my own readable face cannot be seen. But then I really see you. Shock. You look … familiar. There is something so familiar about you but just at this freezing moment I cannot put my own jewelled fingers on this familiarity, like there's something on the tip of my lisping tongue which will not give. You look at your watch. You don't want to be late for me either? How strange that you should look at your watch when surrounded by so many. You never did see what was in front of you …

You are still an assisted blonde. When I first glimpse you, you look like a regular middle-aged woman, but within all those dark and tinselled thousands of seconds your teenage self emerges from the trays of diamond rings. Or is my clear and certain bell of memory ringing out of that last time I saw you in the school crescent? Wearing the prized diamond ring hidden beneath your buttoned up neck. (I saw the hint of golden chain, golden girl.) The last time I heard your voice, you delivered your head girl speech on final prize-giving. Prizes were your thing.

Are you buying your husband Danny a Christmas present, lucky girl? Or maybe not so lucky. My icy index finger which can't quite place your familiarity touches the iris blue envelope in my right pocket as the jewelled fingers of my left hand touch my mobile phone. What will I do if I get the call before midday? What timing! Alas, timing was never my greatest skill, was it? Even though I am always, always on time. For very good reasons.

What do you know, Mrs Danny Diego? You probably won't answer the questions. You didn't then. You won't now, having been schooled, I'm sure, by your Right Honourable husband. I'm not sure he has been either right or honourable though. Through the jeweller's window I can see my own smooth forehead and I can also see you have selected two men's watches. You hold a leather strapped watch in your right hand and a gold in your left. Your once creaseless brow now shows the signs of fifty-three years. You don't do Botox or something like then? You look so ... familiar. You frown slightly like you used to at the school Biology laboratory stick insects. You frown again and then ... take both.

2

Thirty-Two Minutes, Twenty-Nine Seconds
Later

'*Jayne Thornhill.*' You are clutching a small gift bag with a sprig of tinsel. Oh my, all those minutes ticking away therein.

'*Shelley Witherington,*' I say. Your backdrop is this store's Garden Furniture department. The assistants will be having a light day. '*Doing some last minute Christmas shopping, Shelley?*'

You ignore the question, nothing much has changed then, and place the gift bag on the floor by our restaurant table. Had I not known better I might have thought the gift was for me: some kind of gift of forgiveness! I'm glad I snooped. You have a PVC handbag.

'*Diego,*' you say quietly. '*Diego, Jayne. Shelley Diego.*' A short gap; your glance sweeps the parquet flooring and then, '*I married him.*'

There's another gap. Amongst the noisy bric-a-brac of this restaurant I can almost hear the ticking of those two watches in the gift bag at our feet. You go on. '*But should I call you by your pen name Rose Good?*' A waiter swoops upon our table, looking only at you and I have tried so hard over these years, so very hard to be, well … you.

'*A wine without the mull,*' I say to the black-eyed waiter.

'*And you, Shelley. What will you have?*'

'*Oh,*' you say. '*But it's only midday.*'

'*Three minutes past to be exact,*' I say quickly, checking my watch. '*So that makes it just cheeky. It's Christmas and we're fifty-three, not twelve.*' I try to smile and then add, '*And you are no longer head girl.*'

You nod and the waiter smiles at you, places laminated menus before us and says with an Eastern European accent, '*My name is Sebastian.*' He will want a tip.

'*Bring us a bottle, Sebastian. A Chile Cab Sav. It's Christmas,*' I say.

'*I go home to Budapest tomorrow. In time for Christmas. I have two gels.*'

Oh, my. One of those waiters who talks. His Hungarian accent pronounces 'gels' just like our headmistress used to. You engage with Sebastian. You ask the ages of his 'gels' and how long he is going home for and how long he has worked at Milton department store, '*Like we used to,*' you tell Sebastian, so we're all on the same level playing field. When Sebastian finally leaves, I say, '*Call me Jayne. It has a 'y'.*' I am trying to tap into that dark past.

You just say, '*I know.*' Quietly. '*How could I forget?*'

We look around. We haven't met for thirty-four years but I'm not going to ask if you have children. In 2005 we hadn't started Facebook sharing or even mobile phone galleries. I know you don't have children so I'm not going to ask for snaps. I strongly suspect from experience that your husband wanted children very much indeed. I say, '*I chose to meet in the Milton department store as we both worked here on Saturdays, didn't we, Shelley?*' I give the word 'Saturdays' an italicized emphasis. I mean, as if Shelley Witherington, now Mrs Danny Diego would ever have worked in a

6

department store on a permanent basis! *'I worked on Books,'* I say. *'I read all of 'Aesop's Fables' and some sections of Jane Austen's 'Sense and Sensibility' whilst waiting for customers.'*

'I read all your books, Jayne ... or should I call you by your pen name Rose?' you say. You've already asked me this. Your tone is surprisingly apologetic and I believe you are nervous. How much then do you know? This dead stick is swallowing very hard at the mention of those books and losing landing power.

'The Book Department has become Garden Furniture.' I look up to the next level of Rattan sofas and remember how I swallowed Aesop very easily on that patch above the short flight of steps some thirty-four years previously. *'What once was Garden Furniture is now Ladies Hosiery,'* I carry on. *'You worked in Ladies Hosiery, didn't you, Shelley?'*

You nod and we both look upward from the open-plan seating and stare at a hammock. *'I recall you introduced me to the concept of pantyhose when I told you that my white ankle socks had become ribald.'*

You smile for the first time and your face is so familiar ... what is it about your face that is so familiar?

'I think I meant 'ribbed,' I say. There is another gap but this time we look at each other before I add, *'It was one of the nicest things you did for me.'*

'We were on commission,' you reply softly.

Then just as softly I say, *'At least you didn't try to sell me blue stockings.'* Because that's what I was: a Blue Stocking, frumpy and flowery, frowsy and bookish. You know exactly what I mean. Biting my lip, I see you watching. We both look away and up at the garden furniture when thankfully Sebastian arrives and you give him your full attention.

7

Sebastian's fingers make hard work of the corkscrew. He wears a wedding ring. The ensuing pop of the Cab Sav cork comes as a relief. I swallow some wine quickly. I've had to swallow a lot in my time. And after it all happened you barely swallowed anything at all. My icy fingers make sure the sacrosanct, iris blue envelope is still in my right pocket. I know it is there but I keep checking, having lost some pretty precious documents in the past. But not this one. To sit on such information for over twenty years, since Friday 31st May 1985 on Daisy's half-term to be exact, has been … uncomfortable, to say the least, and now this sleeping dog will have her day. This iris blue envelope is my trump card. It's a jolly good job in the end that I kept the blue envelope and its contents because otherwise you would say I had made the whole thing up, told a big porky pie. I always told the truth but, unlike the fate of the school's faded hockey pitch sidelines, my truth got painted over.

'*I've been reading your Young Adult books for years,*' you say. I say nothing so you shrug your pretty shoulders and say, '*Oh, well, maybe I never grew up.*' I raise my eyebrows. You go on. '*I can't help but think of you as Rose Good. I mean Rose Good is just so funny …*'

'*But my Rose Good Young Adult series is deadly serious,*' I say without a smile.

Sebastian comes to take our laminated orders. We quickly order duck salads because I really want to know how much you know.

'*What did you do when you left school?*' you ask changing the topic and smiling up again at Sebastian as he whips off for the duck. '*I mean before your books became successful.*'

I pause. I pause for quite a while before answering. '*Well, I didn't go to university like you, Shelley. If you recall, I*

8

didn't get a school reference.'

You lift the laminated menu to mask your reddened face. Sebastian has left menus in case we want dessert. Are you considering a Battenberg? I don't think so. *'What did you do after Cambridge, Shelley?'* I know, but then you say something to surprise me. Well, you always surprised me. You always did things I never expected you to do, like the wrong things. You say something which probably is going to change the course of events because you say something I didn't know. You say softly again, *'I didn't finish my studies at Cambridge, Jayne. I fell pregnant.'*

It's at this point that the duck arrives: they must keep the duck plated on the counter. From the look of your PVC handbag and fun faux fur coat, I don't think you could have afforded the Milton hotel although you can obviously afford two men's watches. And you don't look as though you have much fun. Sebastian asks you how far you have travelled today and you tell him you are moving soon, retiring early, you say giving a girlish giggle, moving to the midlands but I know all that. What I didn't know was that you 'fell' pregnant. What a strange turn of phrase: 'fell'. These days I am falling all over the place but not from being pregnant. I drain my glass of Cab Sav. If Sebastian is not giving us time to digest the duck, he is certainly giving me time to digest the fact that you were once, was it just once, pregnant? This is a whole different kettle of fish to mix my metaphors. I can feel my empathy for Shelley Diego burgeoning even if I have none for Sebastian and give him a half-smile combined with raised eyebrow. He exits.

Then I hear myself sounding like the Jayne Thornhill that used to be, because out comes, *'Why? Why did you want to meet me, Shelley?'* Refraining from using that old cliché, why now. I think I know 'why now' anyway. All those withheld numbers on your landline. All those calls the not so honourable Danny Diego has been receiving since September...?

You take a deep breath and surprise me once again. '*The Tree Project.*'

Tree project? Tree Project? What the hell is the tree project? But I don't say this. We may be reading from the same menu but what plot is Shelley Diego on? I had been expecting so much more: anger, remorse, questions. '*Tree Project?*' I ask.

'*Teaching. I teach now,*' you say.

I give you a cold hard stare. This prompts you, I know, to say, '*I thought I might be able to make a better job of education than they did then ...*' Your voice shakes but you go on. '*I thought that you must be inundated with requests to give talks, through your website, and that if I mentioned the Tree Project based at the college in the website email I sent to you, I might get no reply. You see, the Tree Project is very important to me. It's a place people can come to trace their roots ... a kind of refuge for young people who have recently traced blood parents from whom they had been separated at birth ... how, and I know, that you, Rose, I mean, Jayne, you Jayne, were adopted and I felt from your first book 'Girls in a Line', the one with the strange pen name, that you may have traced your mother ... I mean your birth mother ... by the clues and hints you made in your narrative ...*'

'*Do you know who my birth mother was?*' I interrupt you.

But you carry on; don't answer my question. '*It's just that if you could see your way to coming to talk to a group of project members and then endorsing, being a patron ... I mean that would involve only a little time. We would*'

10

understand that your time is limited, but to have a name like yours attached ... connected with the project would be ... well, it would make a success of all that we have been doing all these years ...'

I am astonished. Astonished. Because now you would like *me* to help *you.* You were always so good at speeches albeit this was rushed and breathy. Milton High School gave you such an opportunity springboard. But time is on my side now so I take it. I take my time before asking, '*You would like* me *to help* you?' With these words the whole meeting has been turned on its head. I put my hand in my jacket pocket.

'*Life has put spaces between us,*' you say. You haven't touched your duck salad. I wonder if you still have eating issues.

'*Oh my, I think you did that, Shelley. Can you blame me for saying that?*'

But you don't reply. You just look awkward and upward.

'*Does Danny know you are meeting me?*' I ask. This is the first time I mention your husband.

'*No,*' you say. '*I suppose you knew I married him from my email address ...*'

'*I see the Milton local papers from time to time.*' A tune emanates from my jacket pocket. '*Daisy. Daisy. Are you all right?*' Well I know Daisy is panicking as soon as she says, '*Hi Jayne.*'

'*I'll be there in a couple of hours. I'll order a car to bring me home. Call a doctor. I'll be there soon. Very soon. Take care and remember your breathing.*' The phone is switched off and placed back in the left pocket. Then I say something which reminds me so much of my former self: Jayne Thornhill. '*I'm so terribly sorry to have to truncate our meeting. I had so looked forward to seeing you, Shelley, and*

11

you look so well but I have to get to a hospital in the midlands.'

'*Oh, dear,*' you say. '*Is someone unwell?*'

'*Having a baby,*' I say.

'*Your daughter?*'

'*Not quite.*'

The duck has been abandoned. The blue envelope is about to be delivered. Then you suddenly ask, '*Why did you try to contact me via my sister-in-law Lydia in the autumn? Lydia said that you phoned her landline and asked for me. How did you get my brother's landline number, Jayne?*'

I hesitate and then, avoiding giving an answer, say, '*I thought you left a message on my website email because I had phoned your sister-in-law. But it turns out it was because of your Tree Project, is that right?*' I'm not about to tell you why I contacted your sister-in-law Lydia.

You don't reply but stare down at your wedding ring.

'*How can you meet me after thirty-four years, to be exact,*' I say, '*and not mention her name?*'

Such pain on your still-pretty face. You were and still are pretty. Prettiness can be more attractive and longer-lasting than beauty. '*You mean Rachel?*' you say.

'*I mean Patricia, Shelley. Patricia Vickers. Tricky Vicky. Miss 'V'.*'

And then you do the most extraordinary thing. You rise from the table abruptly and picking up your PVC handbag you say, '*I'm sorry, Jayne. I'm so sorry.*'

At first, I think you are saying you are sorry about having to leave. But then you say, '*About all that. I'm sorry. Danny and I ... well, we are so sorry.*' And then you leave. Just like that.

I stare at my mobile phone and think of asking Sebastian

for the number of a cab company, as these are the days long before Uber, because I must get to Daisy quickly. I finger the blue envelope that I didn't have a chance to give you – I mean it's the reason why I came! My lack of timing overwhelms me and then my foot brushes against something under the table. I see the jeweller's gift bag with its sprig of tinsel. But you are gone, Shelley Diego née Witherington. Scared off by the name of Patricia Vickers. Time changes nothing. I look at the gift bag which I know contains two watches and wonder who the lost time is for. Then I do something which is so 'Jayne Thornhill'. Because I never knew you had once been pregnant. I do it because of that or maybe I do it because of your request for forgiveness. Or do I do it because Sebastian comes to clear the table and says you have settled the bill? I take the iris blue envelope from my right hand pocket and I place it between the two wrapped gifts which I know are watches, but I do not know for whom they have been bought. This iris blue envelope contains a very telling photograph, which I have sat on and guarded for over twenty years. I get up and place the gift bag and envelope in the restaurant bin. I chuck the envelope and contents away, Shelley. I chuck them away with the lost time because you know something? I feel sorry for you. After all these years I feel sorry for you and your lack of Botox. But I also bite my lip and chuck the proof away because I am, and always will be, still 'Jayne'. No one ever really changes.

Part 1
July 1984 – May 1985

3

Still Jayne (31)
July 1984/Tuesday/Just before Lunch

Dear Shelley,

So this is my story.

When Mave O'Leary came into Milton Library on a gush of wind to borrow some books on Interior Design it was a foreboding. Or was she a foreshadowing? Probably both. Mave O'Leary always lay the breadcrumb trails to whatever nasty would happen in my pre- and post-pubescent school life. 'For home improvement,' she whispered, her left hand sweeping back those dark bobbing curls. 'New house,' she added. Those hands ... very busy hands ... always doing hands. She was both light and right-handed but the left hand was particularly busy today with its diamond on the correct finger ending in a spiky, varnished nail: iridescent red of course.

'Oh my, are you marrying Paul Witherington?' I said bringing the dating stamp down on *Innovative Ideas for the Modern Home.*

Mave's eyebrows knitted together in a cross stitch and my spectacles misted over with perspiration in the same way they did at school. 'Oh no,' she said. 'I absolutely dumped him years ago. At Charing Cross, to be precise.' She batted away a bluebottle. 'But someone told me he was marrying his sister's best friend this summer. A woman called Lydia who comes ready-made with a dowry. From Cambridge probably. They always clustered around Cambridge that lot, didn't they?'

There was a library pause where one could hear the thumping of books on the counter, the stamping of due dates, Doreen Dawe stamping her foot and the buzz of the bluebottle. Mave had never acquired the skill of whispering and this annoyed my head librarian. Mave's eyes settle on my bent head, for I was trying to disguise the deep reddening of my cheeks as a result of hearing these names once again. And I wanted desperately to wipe my moist spectacles. Mave never expected answers from me anyway but finally, I mumbled, 'His sister?' then bit my lip.

'Oh, come on, Jayne. Don't give me that crap about not remembering. We could hardly forget all that business, now could we? How could you not remember Shelley Witherington? Head Girl and Bottle Washer.'

I couldn't imagine you ever washing anything apart from a fair bit of whitewashing but Mave prattled on. 'I heard that she worked in a shoe shop. And not Saturdays either. That's a turn up for the old schoolbooks, isn't it? Oh,' then she gave one of those familiar gaggle of giggles as she was flicking through *Self Build and Renovation,* 'a turn up for the books. How fitting. Like shoes.' And she giggled again. Mave laughed a lot, I recall, and I could see Doreen Dawe didn't like her. Neither did I. Mave then looked up at me and said, 'I thought you were working as a telephonist when you left school. What are you doing here working as a library assistant?'

Actually I wasn't an assistant, I was a librarian, having

done my training some years after doing a typing course. 'I got my wires crossed at Milton Corporation so they sacked me one Friday lunchtime,' I said and took the *Self Build* book from her to stamp.

'That sounds like Jayne Thornhill.' And then she said very breathily glancing up from my stamping hand, 'Oh. I do believe you are married! How on earth did you do that?' It was an O'Leary rhetorical question, so onward she rattled. 'When did you get married?' This implied a response as she gave an unusually decent pause.

'Just a few months ago. Our courtship was lengthy. We started courting in 1976 when the summer tomatoes flourished.'

I could see she wasn't interested in the tomatoes. 'Courtship,' she whispered giving a small smirk down at *Innovative Ideas* and shaking her black curls. It was the only time she whispered. Loudly she said, 'What's your surname then?'

'Tips,' I said.

'Oooh, change the name and not the letter, change for the worse and not the better, Jayne Thornhill.' She sounded as though she was making many mini-discoveries this Tuesday lunchtime. And then opening up *Self Build* she said, 'Paul Witherington is getting married in his old college at Cambridge and then there's a big do in the gardens.'

'The backs,' I said and then immediately wished I hadn't corrected her use of the word 'gardens' because her eyes narrowed at me. I looked quickly down at her *Self Build and Renovation,* took the slip, wishing I hadn't made such a big one of my own, and placed it in her green-coloured for non-fiction library ticket; this would then be placed in the index file. She took the book with her left hand, sighed deeply and opened the shiny pages of *Innovative Ideas*. 'Oh, Jayne,' she said. 'This is such a lovely book. Do you have to stamp it? Would the library *really* miss it? Aren't I an old mate?'

My answers to her questions were 'yes', 'yes' and 'no' but I would never have said. What I did say was, 'It is a lovely book, Mave.' I made sure Doreen Dawe wasn't watching and said, 'I don't suppose the library will miss it.' I took the book and checked the price trying to give her a smile. 'For an old mate.'

She tucked *Innovative Ideas* and *Self Build* under her arm and said, 'You're still Jayne, aren't you, after all these years? Still got that lisp then. You never change. Bit of the old rumple dumpling around the middle. Hope marriage doesn't get me that way.' Off Mave's blackish curls bobbed through the swing doors. Sighing, I took three pounds ten shillings from my own purse under the library till and paid it into the library. We would never see either of those books again. I then turned my thoughts to my pregnancy leave and the possible merits of hair dye.

Doreen called to me and said that Edwin was on the line. He phoned to tell me that the government had just abolished dog licenses. We don't have a dog, but Edwin had been given to phoning me with miscellaneous messages, and then enquiring as to my state of health. Doreen Dawe was getting irritated by these constant telephonic interruptions and as I replaced the receiver, I had the distinct feeling that Mave's visit was leading up to something. She would keep the other damn book and ignore the reminders. The concepts of 'borrow' and 'lend' were anathema to her. Mave just stole. It surprised me that she had a lending library card and a ridge of high pressure descended on my spine. Missing items at the hand of Mavis O'Leary were commonplace: an odd plimsoll, a silk scarf, a diary …, and the loss was always, always the precursor to something much worse. I touched my wedding ring; I touched my stomach and felt that old nausea rise to the back of my tongue. Someone was watching me from the balconies overhead, a shadow at the swing doors, a footfall behind the bookshelves. I had felt it for weeks now. No one was ever there. I didn't tell Edwin. He would have insisted I take my pregnancy leave early.

As I left the library office, a dark shadow passed over me. Then there was that unmistakeable smell of rosewater mixed with something sickly sweet which swept across the library counter. I took a deep intake of vanilla fragrance before looking up, my spectacles misting over, fully expecting to see the smile of the hyena who had finally found what she had been looking for.

But it wasn't like that at all. There was no hyena: only the skeletal image of someone who had been, in the forests of the night, more fully-rounded in my head than this shadow. When she spoke, there was no power in the voice (and oh my, oh my, there had been power in that voice) or in the attempted smile or in the sunken, almost misshapen and hollow eyes. What had once been dark, solid, impenetrable to me was now … almost fragile, biteable even: Miss 'V', Tricky Vicky, Patricia Vickers. She said with a slight crack, 'Hello, Jayne. I believe my library book is long overdue.'

I couldn't eat anything that Tuesday lunchtime.

4

Jayne (23)
The Long Hot Summer of 1976

It was actually an overdue library book that brought Edwin and me together and nothing from then on was going to tear us into separate pieces. But considering Mr Tips's frequency of visits to the Milton Public Lending Library in the tomato-flourishing summer of 1976, it was odd that he should be in the possession of an overdue library book. I had noticed the offending slip in one of his buff-coloured for fiction library tickets.

'An oversight,' he had whispered, clearing his throat and touching the knot of his tie. 'I do beg your pardon. How much is the fine?' Mr Tips's accent was undoubtedly a midlands one and there had never been even a smidge of his roots in the 'thank yous' he had been giving me over these past few months. He had been borrowing for some time, you see. The queue would be long and if Doreen Dawe was free, Mr Tips would raise his eyebrows at the ground as if, at that moment, the carpet had asked him a question. Or he would blow his nose on a large white handkerchief to avoid taking his turn with Doreen. Once, he even blatantly stepped aside allowing a mother with twin toddlers to take his place. Doreen, with her dumpling cheeks and dumpling hair bun, would grimace with impatience and tap her foot.

I pulled myself together quickly. 'Three new pence,' I said.

He patted both his pockets and then looked at me with dismay. 'I'm afraid I have left the house without change,' he said as quietly as possible. (Unlike Mave O'Leary he had learnt the art of *sotto voce*.) He reached into his trouser pockets and pulled out a note, flushing with embarrassment. 'Do you have change for five pounds?'

I made a bold statement. It was one which would ensure the continuity of our relationship but very much in keeping with my demeanour. 'Let me lend you the fine money,' I whispered back. Being a librarian had given me authority. I added, 'I'm sure you will visit us again.' And then I believe I turned crimson. To allude to the frequency of his library visits was thoughtless and rude.

But he said, 'I am most grateful, Miss …?'

'Thornhill.' I noticed that a few borrowers were giving us both nasty looks for being so disruptive.

'Tips,' he whispered back, blatantly ignoring the outsider reaction. 'Edwin Tips.'

As I now remember back on our first proper verbal encounter, I fancy that he said, 'At your service, ma'am.' But then maybe he didn't. Edwin was certainly in my service for a long time after that. When Mr Tips had exited through the swing doors, I noticed that the overdue library book was in fact Jane Austen's *Sense and Sensibility* and I took this to be a sign of synchronicity: a word I found tricky to negotiate at the best of times with my lisp. My novel narrative was highly Austen influenced. I also noticed from his registration form that he was old enough to have served during the Second World War. Just.

23

When he swung back through the revolving doors that next midsummer's day to return the three new pence overdue fine, he suggested coffee as a 'thank you'. I accepted both. Over coffee, I discovered, strangely, that Mr Tips could remember none of the plots or characters of the books he had been borrowing: Dickens, D.H. Lawrence, Jane Austen. He remembered one of Sidney Sheldon's books in great detail. But no matter. As we walked back through the Municipal Park, on hearing that I was, 'working on an oeuvre of my own over these last few months, with the flavour and influence of Jane Austen', Mr Tips asked what my typescript was entitled.

'*Soap and Synchronicity,*' I said, lisping badly.

Passing the bench dedicated to Alistair Jennings, Mr Tips laughed out loud. 'What a wonderful title,' he said, seeming oblivious to my lisp. And then … 'A comedy?'

I frowned at a rhododendron. 'No,' I said softly. 'It's deadly serious.'

Mr Tips, in time, taught me to smile at myself but for now he became excited … or rather moderately enthusiastic. 'This may be an area where I could be of some assistance. Parentheses and colons, and the like.'

I stopped, took hold of the green iron railing and gave Mr Tips a look of confusion. A brass band in the gazebo was playing a marching tune, sunlight reflecting from the hardworking trumpets and saxophones.

'Forgive me. I worked on trade magazines; plumbing and installation and the like.'

'I'm sorry?' I said, my spectacles beginning to moisten on this blistering summer's lunchtime. The brass band was playing 'Land of Hope and Glory'.

'As a copywriter, I worked as a copywriter before I was given an earlyish handshake. Forgive me again, but I did not mean to infer that your powers of punctuation were limited … In fact, my contact with the publishing institutions is limited but I may be able to offer assistance … by the way of full stops and the like …'

But I was not listening. In the distance I had caught sight of a family of three: a small child and parents seated on the park bench. You see, Shelley, that's why it was important to tell you this part of my back story. Maybe you thought I was going off-piste. I did not know then why I had been so mesmerised at that time but there was a degree of familiarity I felt but could not place. I do, of course, know now. Hindsight gives one a clear landscape of vision even if like me, one has acute astigmatism. The father was now dancing on his knees with the little girl. They were both swaying in time to 'Land of Hope and Glory'. Who were they? The answer seemed on the tip of my lisping tongue and I shivered involuntarily. My mind must have been playing tricks. Mr Tips immediately removed his suit jacket and swung it around my shoulders. 'Are you catching a chill?' he said.

My attention and gaze were diverted from the family to the man standing in front of me. The jacket lay heavy on my damp back and I would have to shoulder it for the rest of the stroll back to the library but it was a chivalrous act and few had cared about my health before now. In that moment, a future was conceived and I forgot all about that family of three until reminded much later.

From then on, in 1976, the courtship progressed at the rate of my novel: steady and slow. I would love to have been swept off my big feet but there were gentle compensations. These years were fertile with the future and Salmon Surprises. Mr Tips was a keen cook of healthy foods, so out went the high cholesterol of my former years and in came a new, toned shape that was as foreign to me as was the Romanian speech therapist Edwin employed to streamline my s's which remains to this day a dodgy sibilant. I finished my first novel in 1984, and we married, although neither factor was dependent on the other. It was just synchronicity. Mr Tips, having satisfied himself that every full stop was in the right place, set a date for despatch and our marital match. I speedily acquired diamond and gold rings on the correct finger. 'Change the name and not the letter, change for the worse and not the better,' Doreen Dawe had said, concerned about the age gap but I was only concerned with the last letter of 'Tips' and how I was going to negotiate my married surname for the rest of my life.

We had a small wedding: Doreen Dawe gave me away. Both my parents were, by this time, dead and that choice was probably adventurous for those days: a quality I rarely displayed. The overpowering scent from the gardenia table arrangements on my wedding day made me think of Patricia Vickers. Anyway, I proceeded to haul my novel around the publishers and haul Mr Tips around estate agencies. Then something happened to irrevocably change our lives. For all our lack of courtship urgency, I discovered in the late spring of 1984 that I was pregnant.

Mr Tips shed tears of joy. His life, he said, at fifty-seven, was now beginning. 'Our common bond makes all those colons and commas worthwhile,' he said, in his mild-mannered and self-effacing way. 'This is not just a fresh page or a new chapter. This is truly another book.'

Indeed I needed to start one as my first one was going everywhere but nowhere. 'Our new book together will be called either Rebecca or Joshua,' I said, having a penchant for biblical names. These proposed names had been conceived long before foetal conception. I thought how satisfying life was: to have long-term plans and then see those plans shape into reality. It was the same way I felt about my writing. But Rebecca or Joshua would not be mine alone. She or he would belong to Edwin and me, would be genetically fifty-fifty of each of us. This idea was thrilling. I was also thrilled with the small piece of land we purchased with our neat little Milton house. (Edwin liked things to be just so, insisting that the chicken carcass and fish bones should be wrapped in yesterday's newspaper.) Together, Edwin Tips and I built a rock garden, working side by side, knees to knees, embedding the beautiful miniature plants in the rich warm soil we had placed between the rocks. I have always loved rockery and alpine plants, their diminutive charm reminding me of the seed tray gardens I loved making as a child, recalling the small plot of land which was assigned to us all behind the school prefabs. I was so happy to see my rock garden grow with the size of my stomach, that the words on my second, more serious novel grew and flourished too, although publication at that time always eluded me. I wanted you to know this. I wanted you to know how happy I could have been if things had turned out differently, if I had been left alone. I was not always in search of a website. You can see how happy I was, can't you? Can't you, Shelley? Oh, I know people would think that Edwin and I were a couple of nerds. I was always the Blue Stocking School Nerd but I had found my soulmate and no longer saw the world as brittle and unfair. I considered, in the quiet moments at work, how happiness could be found in the most unlikely places, like a rock garden.

All was going so well, that, like the old cliché, I felt something had to go wrong. Since I had become pregnant,

27

there were moments, only at work in the library, when I experienced a dark foreboding. I was tempted to leave work, Edwin would not have minded. But a few more weeks would allow us both to enjoy maternity leave pay. Oh, my. Why did I worry about the maternity pay? Why, Shelley, why, oh, why?

5

July 1984/Tuesday Evening

The day she turned up at the library, Patricia suggested, 'A late afternoon walk in the park, Jayne.' My life with Patricia had been far from it. Then she added, 'I like flowers.'

The pale blue veronicas in the park gardens were beginning to flourish. The willows, the roses and raised banks of grass absorbed the resonance from voices, giving them a muffled, ethereal quality. Patricia's voice was reedy, lacking its former booming volume. Walking awkwardly through the gardens on this warm summer's day, it reminded me of the women in my novel who took a turn about the park to discuss their lives and I wondered if Patricia would aggressively explode into song, the way she used to on top of the 366 bus. You could tell which way Patricia's wind was blowing when she opened up to song: she made up her own words to the songs in the hit parade, didn't she? But we were grown-ups now.

She suggested we go the quick route to the bench and I was also reminded of the garden allotments which lay just beyond the school toilets ... sorry, I mean *lavatories*. Milton High insisted that fifth formers learnt to cook and garden when we were taking O-levels. The cooking would prove useful in future family life (although Edwin cooked with a passion which almost equalled his passion for me, so that had been a waste of time). The creation of a garden, given a small patch of land, had been a happy experience for me. It was probably the only fresh air we received bar hockey, and I told the PE staff that I was menstruating whenever possible to avoid sports lessons. My small patch of garden was, of course, adjacent to Patricia's, having been assigned, alas, alphabetically. I chose to plant vegetables. Patricia chose flowers. 'One is closest to God in a garden,' I said aloud on this balmy Tuesday evening.

She turned to stare at me and I didn't feel grown up anymore. I was right back on the top of the 366 bus, not knowing what I had said that was wrong. What had I ever said to change her moods so abruptly? There were some quick, aspirated breaths, before she said, 'This is a park.' She seemed to flinch. Sorry if this is all a bit of a detour, Shelley, but we had walked a fair way.

I tried to smile and shrugged my shoulders, asking, 'How did you find me?' as if she had spent her adult life in search of me.

'I hazard a guess.'

It was an odd phrase to use when I knew Mave would have tracked me down for her. But just why, I didn't know and didn't like to ask. Patricia's face was gaunt, but the will was still there, flittering somewhere around the set of the jaw. The memory that had always lived in my head was, as I said, more fully-rounded like the kind of bosoms I never possessed; a kind of richly dark and sparky attractiveness that leaders seem to have even if they aren't classically beautiful. Oh, yes and my, Patricia had always been synonymous with sex as far as I was concerned. I knew next to zero about the subject but a great deal about Patricia. We had studied each other far

30

more than the syllabus. For now, she was dressed in a tee-shirt and denim trousers, very informally, as though she might be about to participate in some painting and decorating. But she still smelt of vanilla even though she never was. She looked upward, and, as if testing the early-evening air, her nostrils twitched. An early season wasp hovered around Patricia's wispy eyelashes. She barely reacted, the wasp and she seeming in some kind of harmony. There were creases at the corners of her sunken eyes and her skin was yellow and papery. I had never wanted to see the face again. Why had I agreed to come to the park? There was a strong recollection of wanting so desperately to move forward, to put all that behind me and I had, up until now, done so successfully. This woman was here to hold me back, pinning me to my past, like the slug or deathwatch beetle she had always seen me as. Suddenly I felt thirteen again: humiliated, cornered … fat. Those cumbersome adolescent feelings returned with unwelcome familiarity, rushing down the inside of my elbows and thighs in the same way as Miss Simkiss's voice or Patricia's songs used to. Why have you come back, I wanted to ask.

The wasp was now crawling slowly along Patricia's left hand: hard, coarse hand. No wedding ring. I notice rings. The wasp hovered above the knuckles. Patricia sat down and motioned for me to sit also. We sat. Patricia began to speak slowly in this new thin, reedy voice from this new diminished body. 'I have not been well. Not well.'

'Not well. You're not well?' But what did 'not well' have to do with me?

'The tumour inside my head has grown,' she said, the wasp now tracing the seam of her denim trousers. It occurred to me that I had only ever seen Patricia in school uniform

31

before today. I couldn't think about tumours you see, only school uniforms.

'Sometimes I have dreams of being compelled to attach my brain to a chemistry examination paper, but it is impossible, because my brain has become a treacle pudding.' She spoke seriously to the veronicas, not me, and I had this embarrassing compulsion to laugh. Maybe it was nerves. This was a grave situation and it would be indecent to laugh. Patricia was not laughing. She was glancing sideways at me. The wasp was now tracing the outline of Patricia's big toe. Her sandals were dirty, her toenails neglected. An early-evening ripple of breeze reminded me that time was moving on and so could I. Mr Tips would be preparing a fish supper: cod in white wine sauce and maybe a half-bottle of Liebfraumilch for him and elderflower for me. I looked at my watch. Patricia caught me looking. I felt it a sin to worry about my time when Patricia may have so little. A powerful rush of guilt suffused my limbs, but Edwin would be, by now, more than concerned. Patricia closed her hooded eyes and took in a deep breath as if wanting to inhale life. 'Que sera,' she whispered. The sun retreated behind sharply-defined grey clouds.

Then she began to hum an old Doris Day song, quite suddenly starting to sing in a broken, faded voice about being a little girl and asking her mother what she would be in the future. Doris Day and Patricia Vickers. I ask you.

Patricia would be seeing no long term future. Her singing voice was lifeless. She shrugged the now bony but still broad shoulders. Momentarily, just fleetingly, I considered if this was some kind of hoax: Patricia in a park, singing Doris Day. Had the girls a plan? There had always been a plan. Maybe this was one of those – *You look pretty today, Jayne. Come*

32

and be on our team, Jayne. Why not come and be on our team, Jayne?

They would sometimes pretend for days that I was on the team: had a place in their corner of the class, was part of the bunched, summer, red candy-striped school dresses, not apart from it all until:

Thank you kindly, dear friend.

Just a joke. Fuck off, you pathetic bitch.

I wanted to slip away. To say: 'I'm awfully sorry you are where you are, Patricia, but my cod is waiting at home for me. I have another life waiting for me which has nothing to do with you. You are not part of Edwin or our rock garden or the nursery in Happy Daze lemon we are intending to paint together. I don't need to be in your team anymore, you see. Boo. Be gone. You have no power to come and write your story.'

Oh, *why* didn't I say it? *Why* didn't I just go home?

Rachel would have said it, for Rachel had always treated Patricia like an annoying insect. Once Rachel likened Patricia to an unwelcome parasite and said I should not play host but I was never quite sure what she meant until I looked up 'host' in the dictionary. Rachel Sherman: always in front of me; petite, dark as a caramel salted nut, brilliantly bound for splendid days. But my hand went to my belly and I said, 'I can't think of any greater hell than to not be here for my baby. I couldn't imagine …' *Why* did I say that? This was an allusion to her tumour, which may well not have, after all, been terminal. I was making an assumption and this made me embarrassed. My words trailed off with the rising wind.

'Your baby?' Patricia looked sideways at me, quickly. She seemed hurt as though I had been keeping a secret. Should I have said this earlier? Should I have informed her earlier of this fact? Patricia looked down at my hand, still placed on my belly. 'You are pregnant?' Perhaps I shouldn't have been. Shouldn't be stacked with life and the future, when this woman (it was so hard to reconcile the fifteen-year-old Patricia Vickers with this woman beside me) was decaying inside. This woman, her elbow brushing against mine now, had stage-managed and directed my executions. How many times had I died before those executions? They had been tiny deaths preparing me for some bigger ordeal which lay ahead; clusters of candy-stripe observing my dread from a distance. Patricia Vickers had once been the small tyrant who had set out to disturb my dreams, blotting any scrap of peaceful landscape. For no sooner had Patricia departed than, the die being cast, other heiresses inherited the title of tyrant and my executions were, of course, endless and then finally ending. As things of course always do. But this girl: this one had been the most feared. Her removal had temporarily brought a false drop of relief.

Poised to rise from the park bench, my landscape now green, promising and abundant, I owed this woman nothing and I should have left except she then said, 'Did you ever discover who your real mother was?'

Thrown off-piste, and this is what Patricia would do, I know this now, bewildered, I said, 'I … no … I … you remember?'

'You went through hell being adopted. It was what distanced you from us.'

Who was 'us'? How ironic that Patricia should be sitting on this bench, fifteen years on, saying that my adolescence had been hell as a result of being adopted. This woman had been the author of that hell, but I was now forced to reconsider my past. Had I unknowingly contributed to that hell by cutting myself off from the team?

'Are we forced to face our demons or are we given a choice?' Patricia then suddenly turned her face towards me with an uncanny leer and she looked above the top rims of my spectacles. This was the closest one was going to get to a smile. Her bottom lip scrunched up and I felt she was looking inside my head. What did she mean by that?

'What do you mean by that, Patricia?' I said biting my lip with nerves.

Patricia explained, although she seemed to be tiring. 'You have a choice to discover your real parentage. Your baby does not. You owe it to your baby. That is fair.'

I contemplated at that moment what Patricia Vickers had ever known of 'fair' for you see, at this juncture, I still retained a dash of suspicion about this scenario. My adopted parents were my *real* parents but I didn't like to say.

'You could trace your mother, yes you could,' she went on. 'I know all about bloody social services. I can help you because it is your duty, your duty and responsibility to your unborn child. Your baby should have its ancestry to hand.'

Edwin was forgotten.

Patricia could do this: get carried away and forget who was listening, like that séance. 'You must do this for your baby.' Then she did something surprising, which I would never forget. She placed her left hand over my stomach and I shivered in the early-evening sunlight. But what she was saying seemed rather appealing. I had always been more than curious about my roots. I had felt guilt for wanting to discover, but more to the point, I was frightened. Frightened that if I discovered less than my hopes and dreams, the fairy tale expectations which had carried me through my early years would have been a sham. My exalted image of my real

35

mother had been a sanctuary to which my young Jayne had turned in times of trouble. Patricia was still speaking. She was saying that this was a mission. Patricia liked this word 'mission'. She repeated it several times. 'I have been so driven to find you. It was a mission.'

'Oh, my,' I said under my breath. Maybe this was the catalyst which was needed to inspire me to action. It was synchronicity. Patricia was the catalyst and Patricia was giving me permission to trace my real mother. But as I watched the wasp finally vacate Patricia's body and crawl slowly to the gravel on the pathway, I realized that I had almost forgotten the question I had wanted to ask from the very beginning of the reunion. 'But why were you driven to find me? What caused that initial urge? Why have you contacted *me*?'

'I have been in and out of remission for years but now I have months, maybe only weeks.'

I could have walked away at that moment. Turned my back on Patricia Vickers and got on with the rest of my life. I was free. I was about to do so, for I knew Mr Tips would be checking the kitchen clock, calling the library, maybe even legging it up to the bus stop, or evaluating if he should do so, in fear that he might miss my emergency telephone call. I would have taken Patricia Vickers right off the table but for her next half-dozen words. 'A need to square the circle.'

These five words, no sorry *six* words were about to pin me to my past, like the butterfly stuck to the lepidopterist's canvas. No longer a makeweight this meeting was going to give me the opportunity to go back, re-trace and somehow redeem the past. Square the circle. For here was Patricia Vickers, the girl who had paraded Jayne Thornhill; humiliated her when she was physically and emotionally naked, here she was, vulnerable and defeated beside me, wanting to *square the circle*. The notion that I could go back to page one and re-write that story, give it all some purpose, was just irresistible. The past's furniture was being re-arranged and I was hooked, especially as she suddenly said, 'What are those flowers?'

I looked ahead of me. 'Veronicas,' I said, reminded of the only time Patricia had ever conversed civilly with me when we were at school: it was when we were kneeling at our allotments. When no one else could hear.

'You were always so clever with flowers,' she said. 'I like flowers.'

Clever! Patricia had called me clever!

Looking back, I would always remember rising from that bench with Patricia, in hope. But I wished I had got up and walked away … for how could anyone forgive me for what I eventually did, Shelley? I certainly have never been able to forgive myself. I would, of course, also remember Patricia's foot landing firmly on the parasite which she had seemed to entertain for the duration of that conversation.

In later years I came to judge this meeting to be as ill-fated for Patricia and me as it was for the wasp.

6

'You have written a book?' Patricia narrow-eyed me sideways.

We were seated on our park bench. During the course of those stretched summer weeks, we would come to see the bench as ours: Patricia becoming irritated if others paused upon our small sanctuary. She would glare at usurpers, moan at them quietly with fatigue, forcing them to vacate the resting place, leaving the two of us to take up counsel. *The two of us ...!*

It was a kind of counselling: a forum where we could come and reorganise the past, make sense of the present and avoid the future. I was feeling very altruistic about it all and was reminded of the very few times when Patricia had spoken to me alone. This had been at those plot allotments, when on our knees she had sought advice from me about the correct way to plant flowers, how one should tend for them, what soil cultivation was best for daisies and how she adored roses. We had talked about the petal formation of roses, their brilliant lipstick pinks and reds and I had told her eagerly of their romantic names and associations: dog roses, damask roses, china and tea roses. In those quiet adolescent and autumnal moments, elbow to elbow, she had secretly become my friend. I had thought my torture was all over, until the ghastly

New Year of 1969 arrived. I had only been in remission.

'What kind of a book?' Patricia asked me again.

In the furrow of Patricia's eyebrows I realized that the hours spent writing a book might seem selfish to others: others who might have to work hard for a living. 'A novel,' I replied, reddening slightly at the thought of ancient compositions ...

'Why have you not mentioned this before?'

When this particular conversation took place it was our third meeting in the park. It was mid-July. Why I had not mentioned my novel before? Was I trying to hide something? 'I'm writing a second one.' Maybe this was why I had not mentioned the first.

'Is it published?'

'No.'

Qualification was needed, I could see from her raised eyebrows. 'But my husband has some publishing contacts.'

There was a silent space of time whilst I eyed the bobbing passage of a bumble bee. It was during these spaces that I would come to feel a sense of discomfort. I knew I owed Patricia nothing, but I felt compelled to sit with her. Apart from flowers we had never shared social intercourse at school even though Patricia was doing plenty of the other kind of intercourse. I suppose I had just got used to doing what Patricia told me.

'Husband.' Patricia mouthed the word at the trees; mouthed the word again, as if handling the novelty of the notion before play. 'Do you love your ... husband?'

The sun was shining on my spectacles and I could neither see nor think clearly, surprised by the intimacy of the question. It was rather like being sent impersonally, a very personal questionnaire. The moment turned vicious as I suddenly remembered Patricia Vickers singing, *singing* the love I had embedded in my diary on top of the 366 bus. I remember writing that I had desired Danny Diego to be the father of an invented 'Rebecca' or 'Joshua' and I still liked these names very much. It was probably one of the many reasons I had no desire to see you Diegos again. Silly, I know, but you were both a painful reminder of all that had been very silly about me and all that I had desired to escape from. And here I was, seated next to Patricia Vickers! I felt that familiar embarrassment right now deep within my loins as I did then.

'Of course.'

Patricia seemed to read my mind now in the same way as she had done in the past. Like the time she said she and the girls had made up a nice story for me and I didn't know how they all shouted either 'yes' or 'no' or 'not sure' all together when I asked a question. Patricia hadn't joined in; just watched but seemed to determine the responses by some magical remote control.

'Remember the hysteria we had together on top of the bus coming home,' she said. It wasn't a question.

We? Together?

'When I used to tease you about loving that boy,' she continued.

Tease? That boy? I thought these strange words to describe the past which was being re-written all over the Municipal Park. Had Patricia seen it that way? I had not expected this kind of restructuring of the past. I suppose, initially, I was expecting some kind of apology on her behalf.

'Did we call that boy Benny or something?'

'No. We called him Danny Diego,' I said biting my lip so hard I drew blood and sucked a little.

Another vacant space of time. There was a sweeping wave of breeze in the trees, an ambulance siren to remind us we were in the town before the reply came. 'Ah ...' The 'Ah' being packed with possibilities and then lost swiftly in the musky aroma of the Municipal Park flowers before she whispered the surname softly, 'Diego,' ... and then ... 'You do not love your ... husband.'

'Why do you say that?'

'You thought too long before response.'

**

Loving Danny, Shelley.

Danny was one of those young boys who knew he just 'had it', didn't he? The power to be loved and he took up space. He took up so much of my thinking space as an adolescent but he also owned his own space. People who swell in the space around them often encroach upon that which belongs to others, as though the bits surrounding you is territory which belongs to them. Danny and Patricia always had that in common. The two times I did speak to Danny Diego, he moved in so close to me that I felt I would faint. The Players No.6 nicotine on his breath was intoxicating.

I first set eyes on Danny Diego when he played the dashing Cassio in *Othello*. I went to each one of the three performances at the geographically adjacent but remote boys' school. Cassio was concerned with losing his reputation by being drunk and the allegations of doing 'other things' with Desdemona. Danny was particularly good in his 'drunk' scene and I remember the line '*what wound did ever heal but by degrees?*' Cassio needed a surgeon and I felt for Danny. It was after you, Shelley, skimmed the stage with lost and found white handkerchiefs that you started going out with Danny Diego. Indeed: what wound did ever heal but by degrees? Unfortunately I never got a degree.

**

Patricia embraced the idea of my tracing my bloodline. She came stacked with all sorts of information: telephone numbers, names of people in social services who could help trace blood mothers, leaflets on coping with the possible rejection on first contact. Patricia unloaded it all like packed lunches. I assumed that the whole business of tracing blood mothers was a huge, lengthy project: something like writing a novel. But, liking short cuts, Patricia was anxious to move things along. The truth was that social services had not got involved when I was adopted in the fifties. We had drawn a blank, until Patricia suggested I did something as simple as ask my adopted mother.

'Oh that's rather like the clicking of the wicked witch's skinny fingers in *The Wizard of Oz*. Hey presto and we are home,' I said. 'But alas, my mother is dead.'

Patricia looked at me long and hard. As though I was making light. 'I'm sorry,' I said. 'But where do we go from here?'

'Did your adopted mother not have any friends?'

Maybe more than I had ever had, I thought. 'She was in the Sally Army.'

Patricia said nothing. It gave me time to think even further. 'Doreen Dawe,' I suddenly said. 'Doreen Dawe. She is still with the Salvation Army. It was how I got the post as assistant librarian in 1976,' I said. 'I am useless at interviews but Doreen Dawe knew my parents from the Salvation Army.

Nepotism.'

**

Doreen Dawe had been so useful. She had given me a job and, not having had me for very long, she had given me away. In loco parentis. Except she told me, 'The Salvation Army didn't arrange your adoption.'

'How do you know that?' I asked the back of her bun when she was locking up that evening.

'Because you were seven when your parents left the Church of England and came to us,' she said, handling a Martin Amis novel which was on top of a pile as if she might catch some kind of virus.

'Do you not have my birth mother's name?' I asked.

'No,' she said flatly and placed the Martin Amis down in the same manner. And then added, 'Your adopted mother did mention a name but I don't recall.'

I thought that would be the end of it until she said when she put her raincoat on – she always anticipated rain – 'But I'm a librarian.'

I knew this.

'So I would have made a note.'

It was an agonizing few days' wait. Female workers in public institutions are very busy. But Doreen Dawe eventually found me a name saying, 'Miss Crawford. Your adopted mother referred to her as Miss Crawford and I made a note on Christmas Eve 1952, the month you arrived at the Thornhills. Your mother had probably had a spoonful too much of the festive sherry and let the name slip. I don't believe Miss Crawford was ever mentioned after that. The woman could be married by now and women get lost with their married names. And anyway,' she said with a shrug of her shoulders, 'why go digging over old ground?'

'Raking, Doreen?' I said.

'Pudding?' she replied, meaning 'pardon'.

'Raking. Don't you mean 'raking' over old ground?'

She gave a small smile. 'Take care, Jayne,' she said softly, picking up a pile of books and hugging them into her tummy for distribution.

That all tallied with my October birthday. It took August, a few telephone calls to several spinsters of the same name in the directory and several stomach upsets. When my birth mother's surname was first mentioned, even at that point, I heard the distant tinkle of the school bell. Patricia was fascinated by the whole story. She suggested that my meeting should be our bench in the Municipal Park Gardens: the bench which was dedicated to Alistair Jennings, Mayor of Milton 1964. Amazing coincidence, synchronicity even, the year we started High School. I had read the square gold plaque many times. I was standing staring at it, in early September; the mop-headed hydrangeas were just beginning to adopt their dark red, autumn colours. I was thinking it was a good time to pick them for drying and wondering what my birth mother and Alistair Jennings looked like. I was also adjusting to reading and seeing the world with some new contact lenses as I suppose I wanted to impress my new birth mother.

Sitting on Alistair Jennings's park bench, I felt I was not alone. I felt 'on camera' – as if the world, or at least someone, was out there peeping around a sycamore, viewing this monumental occasion. This was the stuff of soap opera and World News. My birth mother would say, 'Not a day goes by when I don't think of you with regret in my heart.' The scene had been playacted in my head for as long as I could remember.

During that twenty-minute wait (I always arrived first, on time, if not before) every approaching female figure was imbued briefly with a life story which ended as soon as they simply passed the Alistair Jennings's park bench. My life was about to change – any one of these female park strollers could be my mother and my stomach was upset. Mr Tips felt that this could be doing nothing for the baby at all.

And then quite suddenly, as if from nowhere, a small-boned woman in her sixties stood at a distance in front of me and I had that overwhelming scent of familiarity. I had seen her before.

7

Saturday 8th September, 1984/Just After Three pm

She took a tentative step forward, as though requesting permission to sit. In fact I had this weird flashback in thinking that this woman never sat. We were acting out a scene in a film. Someone was out there with a camera on their shoulder watching this improvisation. I did not like to say 'mother' for fear that this was a park stroller (the woman looked too small to be my 'mother') so I shifted up the bench and gave a socially-acceptable half-smile.

The small-boned woman sat tightly to one end of the bench as though she didn't wish to take up too much space. Her eyes flitted briefly across to me and then away to the nearby veronicas. I did the same: we then studied the small rock garden with a baby fountain trickling into a Municipal Park pond. It was one of those dry, dusty September days which is fed up with summer and anxious to move on to true autumn. The air was thick with the pollution of nearby passing vehicles.

'Are you going to have a baby?' She spoke.

With a six-month mound rising from my best Laura Ashley maternity gingham; palms moist, breathing shallow and armpits prickling, I swallowed hard. This was the voice on the end of the telephone; the voice which had, at first, been silent and then quivered, faltered, cracked into agreement to meet. Even the voice was familiar, now it was attached to the body. I *knew* this woman. This woman was my mother. I nodded. 'Yes, I am going to be a ... mother.'

It was on this last word that I began to cry. Often given to tears, it was no big surprise but this moment marked the end of a long, imaginary road. 'I could never, ever, imagine giving my baby away.' I didn't know why I said that. I went to apologise but possibly the tears were unearthed from all the anger I had suppressed during my lifetime. It was the kind of comment I had heard when watching soap operas. I just said that; and then carried on crying. The woman opened up her handbag and, taking out a handkerchief, she passed it to me. Our eyes met over the handkerchief, which was clean, and I accepted it yet again with some odd sense of familiarity. Then blew my nose.

'I seem to know you from somewhere,' the woman said.

I considered this to be an odd comment for a mother to a daughter she had abandoned but I knew her from somewhere also. I dried my eyes which were itching and then placed my contact lenses in the woman's, sorry, I mean my *mother's* handkerchief. She had one long line of unplucked eyebrow. It creased up as she spoke. 'Did you ever go to the High?' Her vowels were coarse and flattened: a bit like Edwin's when he had had a touch too much Blue Nun wine and his midlands roots escaped.

My eyebrows creased up too. I nodded. For me, the spaces between the words held a lifetime of emotion and missed moments but the woman lifted her head to the sky as if searching intently for some lost information in the clouds. 'In the sixties?' she said, looking upward again, this time as if doing mental calculations. I nodded, not sure where all this was leading. 'I'm sorry for such an emotional outburst, Miss Crawford,' I said.

'Call me Margaret.'

Margaret Crawford. This woman's name was *Margaret Crawford.* Now I had the Christian name those school bells once again were ringing in my ears. How did I know that name: *Margaret Crawford?* I noticed a mole on the woman's nose. A long grey hair protruded from it. Then just as my memory was flickering so was there a shadow flickering behind the trees. Miss Margaret Crawford. My mother. And it was then that she said it. 'I was on the buses then.'

The 366 bus. Of course. The mole, the handkerchief. This woman, I mean, my mother, had lost her job as a bus conductress because of me. Me. Her birth daughter. She looked at me as if trying to piece together what had happened in that dark past, and forgive me, Shelley, for using the phrase but I do have a bullshit detector. Miss Crawford didn't realize at that moment exactly *who* I was: there had been several girls and I was just one fat one. Although I do remember her singling me out to pass me that handkerchief across her ticket machine. How could Miss Crawford recognise me now? I had contact lenses. She had been kind. But of course it had been my adopted parents who had been there for me when it all went dreadfully wrong. I was seeing the irony of what happened when we were fifteen, culminating on Mother's Day of all days. It was as if some Higher Being or Little Greek God from the Heavens had planned that timing back in the sixties, now that I knew Miss Margaret Crawford was my *mother.* And then the dreadful dawning happened. I felt sick to the gut. *Someone* had planned this meeting; had known exactly who this woman was and I to her. Margaret

48

Crawford, our bus conductress, was rattling on, in the same way that she rattled that ticket machine every morning and night of my mid-adolescence. She had her reasons, she was saying: a one-night stand, little money and her family was devoutly religious. No trace now of my father if that was what I was after. Nursing home, having me for six weeks and letting me go during the Great Peasouper Smog of December 1952. Never got married, never had children. Had I been happy? And something about caring for your rose that is important, not just the planting of the seed, but all I could think was: those girls who were now women must have known who Margaret Crawford was and they had planned this meeting. Shelley, I even wondered if you were in on it. *Why, why now?*

'366,' the woman finally said with a degree of triumph which was then followed by the darkest of despairs. She seemed to slump, round-shouldered, further to the end of the bench, taking up less space than she did before. She was embarrassed now; I could tell because she bit her lip. 'Rum do,' she said, shaking her head. 'Rum do.'

8

The Back End of Summer/1984

Eventually the winds with a bite tumbled through the park and swept Patricia and me indoors. Confronting Patricia had never been an option. Any contretemps with her was out of the question so I thought I would store that one up, shrugging off any details she asked me about Miss Crawford and making it clear I was very, very grateful to her for pushing me to find my birth mother. She gave me a dusted down look. 'I did *not* push you. You wanted to do it.'

'I'm sorry,' I said. 'That was just an unfortunate turn of phrase.' And as far as Patricia knew, I need not have made the discovery of my birth mother's previous occupation or what part this woman, my birth mother, had played in our past.

Patricia lived a good distance from Milton; at least an hour's journey so she obviously hadn't just been filling in time seeing me. It occurred to me that I was in some way important to Patricia as she had been making a huge effort to meet me. I was convinced that she had known all along that Miss Crawford was my birth mother. And Mave had known too. But how and why *now?*

Picking my way in my new boots from the train station to the estate where Patricia lived, I had to cross a children's swing park and dodge all sorts of debris. There were some bald boys with big boots eyeing me suspiciously. One of them even jeered. When I reached the estate (a council estate, I think) I noticed that some of the houses were uninhabited. There was broken glass at the windows, paint peeled from doors shut tight to the world and litter hugged the kerbsides. Even the billboards looked tatty. This was such a long way from the train station and my life: I had said I would be there by three o'clock. Patricia's house had net curtains laced with grime. I swallowed hard and held back a tear. I wished I had not come. I would not stay long and besides, washing net curtains was probably not the biggest thing on Patricia's mind at this time. I might be able to wash them for her.

'I'm sorry I'm a few minutes late.'

When Patricia showed me into the kitchen, I couldn't see a washing machine. A utility room was not in sight. I could take the net curtains home and wash them, returning them crisp and ironed just as Edwin did ours. There was a pungent smell of cat in the kitchen. Half-eaten meat lay in a dish on a floor muddied with paw prints; half-eaten cereal was abandoned on the kitchen table. The refrigerator door was so filthy I shuddered momentarily to think what might be decaying inside. It was, altogether, a miasma of despair and well, it was just so … dirty. What would Edwin have thought?

As I shuddered, I was reminded of you, Shelley. You would shudder quietly in that subtle, silent way, attempting to hide distaste. Like the way you did when you came to my twelfth birthday party and was surprised when you had to go upstairs to the toilet … I mean *lavatory*. Patricia must have detected my feelings as I looked about the kitchen because she said, 'I am doing scientific experiments.' She didn't

51

smile. 'Coffee?' she asked.

I refrained.

Lionel Ritchie's 'Stuck on You' solo was emanating from the lounge radio. Flies stuck on squares in a spider's circled web came to mind, the glue probably of my own making. Maybe I didn't realize then that the glue was self-made. I looked for a clock, not wishing to look at the gold watch Edwin had given me; that would be obtuse. There was no clock in the kitchen and no clock in the lounge, which Patricia, I noticed, called a front room. She had waited for me to pass in front of her before entering the front room. The moment produced tremors. Patricia Vickers – behind me.

One of the tabloid newspapers on the coffee table displayed a beautiful photo of the Prince and Princess of Wales with their son Prince William and their new baby boy Harry. I placed my hand on my growing stomach: six months, going on seven. The journey had been quite an effort. I was tired and my legs were aching and heavy. I waited for Patricia to offer me a seat. She went to turn the volume down on an old transistor radio which had been stuck on a shelf to the left of the mantelpiece. Her tee-shirt was the same one that she had worn several times at the park and I wondered if any washing was ever done in this house. Or maybe that was a scientific experiment to do with water rationing. Above the mantelpiece, where a clock should be, was the stuffed head of some kind of deer, buck, springbok or whatever, with strange and beautiful horns reaching out into the room. Was this wide-eyed beauty imitation or real? I was beginning to feel altogether uncomfortable and rather like this stuffed prey when the latch on the front door clicked open. 'That will be Daisy,' Patricia said, settling into an armchair in the corner of the room by the window. 'They want me to take chemotherapy now.' She said this lightly, as though it were an invitation to take tea.

'Who's Daisy?' I asked.

'Hazard a guess,' she said.

The door opened and I was shocked. I was shocked because I had not been prepared for anyone else to be living with Patricia and I hate guessing games. It reminded me of that ghastly game of 'Yes' 'No' and 'Maybe' the girls had all made up for me. I felt like this now. How could I guess who Daisy was? I might guess incorrectly. Or I might hazard a guess, as Patricia would say, and then Patricia might simply agree to my guess. Altogether I felt I should not be here.

Daisy entered and at once she seemed familiar but she didn't remind me of her mother Patricia. She was strawberry blonde and podgy. Maybe it was because she looked about fifteen and, like Lionel Ritchie, I was stuck on that age group. She had a double lower lip. On closer inspection I could see that there was a sore below the child's mouth. The teenager pulled down on her overstretched jumper and sucked on her quasi lower lip, flashing me a look of suspicion.

'She is not a social worker,' Patricia said quickly to the child. 'She is an old friend.'

I was touched.

'I've got a composition to do and Miss Pit Bull Terrier'll fucking castrate me if it's not done by tomorrow.' Daisy slumped into the sofa.

'This is my daughter.' Patricia sighed and raised her eyebrows and eyes to the peeling ceiling.

Ah. So this was 'the baby'. I then realized that Patricia had mentioned the chemotherapy before Daisy entered the room because the child did not know about the severity of her mother's condition. In fact, I wondered if Daisy knew the illness to be … terminal. Terminal: end of the line, end of the flight. Patricia's baby had not been terminated then.

Daisy's language shocked me and I wished I could sit down for my six-month pregnant legs were giving way. The cat slithered through the door and jumped across Princess Diana's smiling face on the coffee table. Patricia, Daisy and their cat observed me standing by the fireplace. 'Daisy has balls,' Patricia said, a shaft of autumn sunlight piercing through the dirt-clogged window. 'Metaphorically.' Patricia even half-smiled. 'She was a very close friend of mine when I was at High School,' Patricia said to Daisy without using my name again.

I felt flushed with pride, fifteen once again and on the road to redemption but just then a hard-backed book was flung across the coffee table at the sofa. The cat screeched and sprang for the door. Daisy yelped, the book having hit her mouth.

'Do not use foul language and stop biting your lip. You look like a bloody clown,' Patricia said, basking in the fading sunlight and an old malignant streak of power. 'I told you I would throw the book at you.'

Familiarity pervaded the air. I looked back at Daisy who only responded with a faint moan and a sideways look at me to clock my reaction. I wanted to go to the child, to place my hand on her pudgy knee and an arm around her shoulders which dipped between the blades. I wanted to give Daisy some comfort. But this was Patricia's house.

**

Daisy was pleased with my editing assistance to her composition entitled: *Her Burning Desire*. She chose to write about a young girl who wished to be carried away and quite frankly so did I. 'Daisy Jacobs' was scrawled on the front of her exercise book, the handwriting immature for a fifteen-year-old. 'Daisy Jacobs 5P' on the front of the child's exercise book made me realize she was fifteen: she told me she had just had a birthday although not a birthday card was in sight. However, sums were in order. There had been rumours when Patricia left Milton High as to why. That séance slipped back into my mind: Patricia screaming, 'Who is the father of my baby?' I remember thinking, how could she not know? So who was Jacobs? Jacobs. Jacobs. Something flickered in my mind. Of course, I had always known more than most on account of my trips to the toilets ... I mean *lavatories*. When we finished, Daisy looked up at me and smiled with her three lips and said, 'I like your boots.'

'They're new,' I said.

'Can I have them?' Daisy said abruptly.

'Well ...'

'Oh, please.'

I felt sorry for Daisy having had the book thrown at her. 'If they fit,' I said.

I didn't notice the autumn night wrapping in around us. When Patricia told Daisy to, 'Go to the fish and chip shop,' I suddenly thought of fish and remembered Mr Tips insisting. *Don't be late home for I'm preparing Stuffed Fillets of Plaice in Prawn Sauce. Friday night, stuffed fillets and a bottle of Liebfraumilch – milk for my dear wife.* Although I wouldn't be drinking the Liebfraumilch. Patricia, it seemed had rather a taste for wine, but cheap Spanish. I had seen the bag of bottles when I had entered the house. Patricia would not hear of me going home and whispered confidentially, as she took a pound note from her purse, 'This is my treat. I am taking chemotherapy tomorrow and I am slightly apprehensive.'

'I can't imagine you ever being apprehensive about anything,' I said, and then, in order to raise Patricia's smile, I added, 'You have such … balls.'

The comment failed to raise anything. I wished I had not said that word. It did not sit as easily on my lips as it did on Patricia's.

'I need you. Stay,' she said.

So that was that. I looked at Patricia's hair. It was still abundant. In that moment, I felt something for Patricia she had never spared on me: pity. 'I should phone my husband. Let him know I won't be home for … tonight.' I was about to mention the stuffed fillets of plaice but I stopped myself. There was not a Bakelite or alternative handset in sight. 'I'll accompany Daisy to the fish and chip shop and make my call from a public telephone box.'

Patricia and Daisy exchanged what might have been some kind of knowing look, but I didn't know. I didn't know anything.

**

'The phone box gets vandalized,' Daisy explained to me as we crossed the road. It was now so late the streetlamps spilled neon light on to grey tarmac. There was a fine drizzle in the air. I said nothing but I was worried, desperately needing to explain to Mr Tips, and I was becoming very, very tired. He would understand my dilemma … if I could get through. But what if the public phone was out of order? We didn't have mobile phones then. I could hardly go back on my promise to Patricia. I looked at my gold watch. Eight-thirty. Edwin would be mad with worry as I was never late.

'I didn't see any clocks in your house.'

Daisy tightened, shuddered even. 'Mother *hates* clocks. Grandpa has two in every room. Mother says she's served time enough. She doesn't want it in the house.'

'But how do you know when to get to school?' I asked.

'You've got a funny 's'.'

Daisy had detected my old lisp. The Romanian speech therapist had convinced me that he had shot that down.

'Did you get ripped off at school for that?' she asked.

'Yes.'

'So do I. For having red hair like yours,' she said.

We were now approaching the parade of shops and the phone box was in sight: my communication cord to Edwin. The rain was falling fast as I entered the booth. I picked up the phone and heard the comforting purr of a connected line. 'Hello … hello … Edwin,' I said as the beeps signalled for coins in the slot.

'Where have you *been*?' His voice was ambrosia but he emphasized the word *been* accusingly. It was unlike him, but he was concerned.

'I'm still here. At Patricia's.'

The booth door swung open. Daisy mouthed the word, 'Raining,' and moved in to share the small space with me.

'You're almost seven months pregnant,' Edwin said.

Daisy was closing the door to shut out the rain. I felt crowded and nauseous. Daisy smelt of wet dog and they didn't have one. 'Seven months and it's my body.' I had no idea why I said that. I had never spoken to Edwin in that way before. There was a pause whilst I could not help but see a sense of surrealism in this situation. Here I was, almost seven months' pregnant, squashed into a phone booth in the middle of, I think, a council estate, miles from Milton, with Patricia's teenage daughter, who was sniffing back phlegm. The connected line scratched into my ear. 'Edwin, I can't desert her tonight.' Then, knowing what I needed to say to him, I said to Daisy, 'Lovely, go into the fish and chip shop whilst I speak to Edwin.'

Both of Daisy's lower lips crumpled, but she responded to my request.

'Who are you speaking to?' he asked. 'And why are you patronizing a *fish and chip shop?*'

'That's Patricia's daughter … Daisy. Edwin, Patricia is having chemotherapy tomorrow.' This was a responsible thing to say and I hoped to appeal to his sensibilities. There was another pause. I looked out through one of the square glass panels in the public telephone box. Daisy's bottom lips were now arched upwards in a smile. Poor, sad Daisy was being bullied now and not just by her schoolmates but by my own tormentor: her mother. That was one of the blessings of having once been a victim. Empathy was abundant when you recognised another. It was raining hard now and Daisy, dressed in only that overstretched jumper, would get drenched. The child smiled again, opening her mouth. There was a gap between the front two green teeth. She reminded me of me, when I was her age.

'Well,' Edwin was saying, 'if your friend really needs you. It's just that particularly, tonight, I had a very small surprise for you.'

'Edwin. Freeze the Stuffed Fillets for next Friday night.' The high shrilled pips were bleeping and I had no change left. 'Patricia will be recovering from chemotherapy tomorrow night and I'll need to stay.' But the line went dead. The purr of the telephone line was no longer comforting. I was not even sure if Edwin had heard those last words, but Daisy needed me and my fate for the short term future was as hermetically sealed as that jar of gherkins we carried home.

9

Autumn 1984

I could not leave until the following Wednesday: Patricia's first visit to the hospital resulted in consecutive daily visits. She said that Daisy had become attached to me. Neither Edwin nor Doreen Dawe were happy. Two more trips to Patricia's after that initial September visit were made. The following month in October, Patricia was taking chemotherapy again but Mr Tips was reluctant to let his wife go. 'Seven months pregnant, maternity leave now due and you should be resting.'

I had given him a kiss on his furrowed forehead and he had said, 'Fish Florentine on Friday night. No staying for the weekend. It's your birthday!'

Closing the front door firmly behind me, I was on a mission and Patricia could be in remission. At this point, I was thinking of Daisy, suspecting that the teenager was more a victim at her mother's hands than ever I had been. Daisy and I shared her bedroom and she had displayed more than just teenage modesty in covering up her own body. My suspicions were justified, when, on the Thursday evening following the usual visit to the hospital, and during the soap opera *Crossroads* Patricia threw not a hard-backed book but the cat at Daisy.

The claws of the cat had drawn blood from Daisy's neck. I sighed. Patricia had always managed to draw blood by proxy. I had carried the snapshot of blood on my school shoes and Patricia's malevolent smile throughout my life. Patricia was not smiling now. Drenched with fatigue, sucked of life or energy, she looked defeated. She put on a Chopin waltz tape and told Daisy to clear out of the house and let her breathe.

Daisy was crying. 'I only said the actress had beautiful eyes,' she sobbed.

'At times there is something in your face I see and do not like,' Patricia said. The obvious anger at her own condition was being turned towards her daughter. What point was there now, in reporting a dying woman to social services? Besides, the authorities had taken no notice of my statement all those school years ago. Why should they now? No. It was best to pace our way through Patricia's remaining weeks and focus on Daisy's GCEs right now. Patricia never sat any and I didn't do that well so a scheme of work for Daisy was essential.

'Can't you stay until I get home from school this evening?' It was Friday morning and Daisy's back was burdened high with haversack. She was combing her long red hair in the musty hallway mirror and at that moment I planned to bring some cleaning materials on my next visit. Where was Patricia in the daughter's face? I had never asked Patricia who Daisy's father was – I had a good idea anyway – but I wondered now if the apparent dislike for her daughter stemmed from a hatred of him. It must be hard to see someone you hated in the face of someone you should love. I opened the front door on to a cold, darkish October morning. My voice was shaded with guilt when I said, 'My husband will be waiting for me. I must go home. It's my birthday this weekend.'

Daisy's reflection and three lips scowled back at me from the hallway mirror. A draft of wind swept doorstep leaves through the hallway and Daisy and the cat skulked into the morning leaving me at the front door, hand on the latch. She turned at the crumbling gate at the bottom of the pathway. 'Promise you'll come back next month.'

'Promise,' I said. 'We'd better be thinking about Christmas then.'

Daisy half-opened her mouth displaying the gap in her front teeth. Then she said, 'Ooooh, don't mention Christmas to Mother. She hates it.'

I felt I had to ask. That name 'Jacobs' kept swirling around in my head: on the tip of my lisping tongue but I couldn't put my cold finger on whom he exactly was. 'Do you ever see your dad, Daisy?' I asked.

Daisy's head nodded vigorously and she smiled displaying that gap in her front teeth. 'He's lovely, my dad,' she said. '*He* never forgets Christmas like Mother. He visits.'

'Does he have a Christian name?'

'He's not Christian. Don't ever mention the word to Mother.'

'I meant his first name, Daisy.'

'Dad,' she said, turning her laden back and shuffling towards the bus stop in my new leather boots as they were rather too big for her. Bus stops. *Jacobs.* Bus stops. Patricia had been pregnant with Daisy all those years ago but my thoughts then ran to this possibly being Patricia's last Christmas: a time when I would be giving birth to a baby who would need me. A time which would be my baby Rebecca or Joshua's first Christmas. Poor Patricia.

Patricia called from the upstairs bedroom, faintly. 'Jayne. Jayne. Come ... Do not leave us this weekend. Do not leave us.'

I sighed deeply. Oh, my. Daisy, Edwin, my unborn baby, Margaret Crawford: my birth mother, whose telephone calls I had left unreturned, and ('Jayne ... Jayne ... where are you?') even Patricia Vickers desperately needed me. My birthday this weekend would have to go on hold.

'Come on, Cat,' I said, for this appeared to be the cat's name. 'Let's get you and Patricia fed.'

**

I had absolutely no intention of visiting Patricia and Daisy when I was eight months pregnant. But in preparation for my last visit before the baby was due, I went into Milton to buy Christmas presents for my two friends which I planned to place in the post. It was late November and the department stores blazed with decorations in purples, ochre and cardinal scarlets. The shopping precinct, which was being extended, with its central tinkling fountain, was redolent with chestnuts, spices and custard pies. I was feeling buoyant: the new Band Aid single was drifting from the nearby record shop and the lyrics reflected my own sentiments. Did Patricia and Daisy know this was Christmas at all? Earlier that month I had tried to talk of fir trees and cinnamon, searched some downstairs cupboards quietly for some remnant of decoration but Patricia was having none of it and Daisy didn't seem to have knowledge of Father Christmas at all. Here, I had my whole life ahead of me whilst Patricia, alas, had little. I passed through the cosmetic department of the department store and remembered Daisy eyeing my lipstick enviously. Patricia might not approve and maybe it wouldn't be too good for those lips, so I bought some Jane Austen novels instead. And for Patricia? Well, Patricia was losing hair, so maybe a Kashmir scarf would be appropriate. I was horrified when the shop assistant told me how much the scarf was, but this would probably be the last present the dying woman would receive. And anyway, scarves are light on postage. I smiled to myself. The thought of buying Patricia Vickers a Christmas present would have previously been inconceivable, but here I was, selecting her favourite colour: blue.

It was in Mothercare that I bumped into Mave. Two bumps together. How we laughed. Although Mave said, 'I'm barely there.' But she had a small ridge so she must have been even quicker off the mark than Edwin and I had been, having married only this past summer. Mave had not been seen since her since her library visit in the previous July, as needless to say, she had not returned her borrowed books. I had decided to buy some lemon babygrows and was admiring an irresistible fluffy rabbit with a lopsided ear when our bump happened. 'I thought you looked rather more podgy than usual when I saw you in the library,' she said. 'You never let on.' Maybe neither had she, I mused.

I apologised for the omission and in my buoyant mood I disclosed to Mave how close I was to Patricia and Daisy, bobbing up and down with all that redemption for the past. Here I was, happy with my husband, pregnant and turning the tables on that putrid past. I was, quite suddenly, taken aback by Mave's response, 'You haven't bought her anything?'

I was holding on tightly to the carrier containing the blue Kashmir scarf. 'Would Patricia feel patronized by a gift?' I asked.

Mave threw back her bouncing black curls and laughed. 'Patronized? That's Patricia Vickers's profession – seeking out patrons.' Then she looked up at me seriously and said, 'You have. I can tell. You've given her money, haven't you?'

'Only a little. Her daughter, Daisy, is in need.'

Mave groaned. 'You've fallen for it. You never change, Jay.'

Had she forgotten my name? She had remembered it at the library some months before. Or had she just lost the last consonant? Mave never lost anything at all. But then I thought this might be an affectionate and warm abbreviation whilst there was an undeniable nasty vocal attitude edge towards Patricia. 'She tries to fleece everyone. She uses everyone she touches as a conduit for her own purposes, especially you.' Mave was fingering some frilly dresses with those spiky, red fingernails. Mothercare was playing a piped, 'Little Donkey'.

'What do you mean?' My heart began to pound a little.

'Patricia either wants money or information, mark my words. Whenever she contacted me, after we left school ...' she said, plucking a pink polka-dotted dress from the rack, 'she wanted something. She asked me to find out where you were working and sound you out. I refused of course.'

'But she came into the library a few hours after you left last July.'

'She *stalks* me,' came the reply.

'But she wants to square the circle,' I said without thinking.

Mave snorted down her nose and her eyebrows lifted in two perfect upturned 'U's. 'Square a circle, my arse,' she said. 'You were always a nice fat round sitting target for Patricia. You must move on.'

This woman, Mavis née O'Leary, had possibly stolen my schoolgirl diary, probably read most of the contents and had certainly seen me naked and in tears. All of my redemption washed away. I felt foolish, I felt fifteen. Facing the demon in Patricia had been about sweeping away the past and growing up. Now here was Mave telling me to move away and move on. A familiar embarrassment rose within my loins, but to make everything much worse, Mave then said, 'She came to me not long ago, asking for money, when she first got out of prison. I told her to sling her hook.'

'Prison?' I was horrified. Patricia had never mentioned this before. And here I had been relishing how close I had become to Patricia.

'She went down for a year. I think Benji Jacobs was involved somehow. Well, she should have served longer but Benji got her off lightly, I think. She told me Benji would always *see her all right.*' Mave shook her bouncing black curls and held up two dresses: one striped, one checked. She obviously was hoping for a girl.

'Benji *Jacobs*?' I said. I could hardly believe the words I was hearing in Mothercare. 'Benji Jacobs?' I asked again.

'Jay, where *were* you in the fifth form? He's Daisy's father. He wanted to be a dentist. But then he may have become something big in the City. They earn well which is just as well …' And those hands with the long red nails kept flicking and whipping through the babygrows. 'Because he's supported Patricia and Daisy all these years and you'd better watch out, or you and your husband,' she quickly looked at my wedding ring, Mave liked rings, 'will soon be doing the same.'

'But Benji Jacobs was …'

Mave wasn't listening to me, for she had now progressed

to cot duvets. It had always amazed me how much Mave had liked 'things'. 'Daisy has spent her little life in care. The Jacobs's family won't have anything to do with Patricia or Daisy, although I do believe Benji Jacobs has been terribly good about it all. Patricia always said Benji had *seen her all right.*'

How was Mave privy to all this information? She knew so much, I knew so little. Times did not change. Mave had always been the source of rabble knowledge. Tut, tut. Mave raised her full, rounded eyes to the Mothercare ceiling. How could I be so naive? This was the measure and drift of her dialogue and body language.

'But she was your *friend,* Mave,' I said.

Mave widened her eyes in disbelief. 'I was *never* her friend, Jay. How *could* you say that?'

Had I invented the past? But Mave, I remember, changed her mind according to the colour of the environment. So then I was about to turn the school tables with my own information, feeling a tad guilty that I might be using it to gain ground. 'Patricia's got a brain tumour.'

Her wide eyes widened even bigger. 'So she says. Do you believe everything that woman says to you?'

I felt foolish. 'I've accompanied her to chemo.'

'Have you been *in* the chemo hospital room?'

'Well …'

'Just make sure she's not attending the clinic for an ingrowing toenail.' Then she held up two cot bedspreads: lemon and lilac. 'Which colour do you think?'

'I'd take the lilac,' I said.

Mave frowned at the cot spreads. 'That's pink. Not lilac.'

It was true: nothing had changed. My eyes could not be trusted. My contact lenses had misted over and Mothercare was too much.

**

Mave went to pay for the lemon cot spread. I had half-expected her to pop it into her bag and walk out in the same way she used to pop those shop-lifted, plastic-cased block mascaras into her school satchel. Had Patricia really stalked Mave or was there something Mave was not telling me? I kicked myself for not asking if she had known the identity of my birth mother but then, maybe this hadn't been the time or place. And was Patricia really ill? I tried to recall if there had been anything wrong with her toes. I had accompanied Patricia to the hospital, expecting to take part in a drama, but she had always told me to amuse myself in town on every visit and return some hours later with a taxi which yes, okay, I had always paid for.

I decided to buy some lavender room spray for the Christmas package. Patricia had obviously given up on disguising bad smells which she was always careful to do at school: all that nicotine in the lavatories had been overpowered with the scent of sweet vanilla. Her present lavatory drains probably needed a plumber. I sighed. How different were our lives. Had Patricia wanted my company for the money I was able to give her? When I got home, I placed the fluffy bunny with the lopsided ear in the cot for Rebecca or Joshua. Mr Tips had decorated the nursery in a brilliant yellow wallpaper with smiling suns and crescent moons. A single divan had been installed for 'Mummy' beside the cot for night breast feeds. A mobile of wooden horses, more crescent moons and clowns had been hung above the cot and an alphabet frieze decorated the nursery's girth. The room smelt of fresh paint and a clean future. Virgin room and a future where Mr Tips would dance on his knees with our perfect little Rebecca. Something flickered in my mind: a mother, a small child and a father on his knees dancing to stirring brass band music: a family and the Municipal Park, 1976. I looked at my reflection in the long mirror. Eight months of pregnancy bloomed and bulged. Both my peachy face and poodle perm were filled out and I would have been contented enough had I not seen Mave. And contented I might have remained if the phone hadn't rung at that moment.

**

It was Daisy breathing heavily.

'Breathe, Daisy,' I kept saying. 'Breathe. What is the matter?'

'We need you, Jayne.' Daisy was crying now. 'Please come.'

'Daisy. I'm about to have the baby very soon. It would be foolhardy of me to travel now.'

'Oh, please, Jayne. Please come just once more before Christmas. Mother is so sick and she ...' Daisy's voice trailed away into a bundle of sobs.

I heard myself saying, 'I will call a taxi, Daisy. I will be with you in a couple of hours.' I could hear Edwin's car pull into the driveway. Placing the handset on the receiver I went from my bedroom and into the nursery, pulling out my suitcase from the cupboard.

Edwin's footfalls could be heard on the stairway. He popped his head around the door. He was holding a brown paper package in his left hand and Samson, our new

69

Yorkshire Terrier pup in his right. Samson had been my small surprise a couple of months previously, when I had been expecting only Stuffed Plaice. 'Alas,' he said, 'your book has been returned from the publisher.'

Edwin and Samson both looked across the nursery at me with sorrowful and regretful brown eyes.

'Oh.' I was devastated.

Edwin seemed momentarily taken aback. 'I must call my contact and see what can be done. I don't want you upset at this time.' He quickly looked to the floor at my suitcase. 'No, Lovely, not this weekend,' he said and let Samson carefully down to the floor, keeping a watchful eye out for spillages.

I sighed. 'It's the last time.'

'No,' he said. 'Not at eight months.' It was the same tone of voice I had heard in the public phone box when the line had crackled and spat back at me and Daisy stood smiling through the pane of glass, gap in the front teeth needing me to stay. I remembered the promise I had given the child that cold October morning, even though I had actually stayed the whole of my birthday weekend that month. I didn't break my promise to her then and I wasn't going to do so now.

'Our last visit to the hospital was harrowing,' I fibbed. 'There is no way I could allow Patricia to go to the hospital on her own and have treatment.' Actually on a number of these hospital visits I was left to mind Daisy which is why I had suspected that Patricia had needed a Daisy minder. We both watched cautiously as Samson sniffed at the contents of my suitcase. 'Besides,' I went on, 'Daisy would not be able to cope with her mother's reaction to the chemo.' I was now familiar with these medical abbreviations. 'So please, give me strength and support me whilst my friend is undergoing treatment.' I was surprised by my speech and with the tear

70

which sprang to the corner of my eye, especially as Patricia had said that her blood count was too low in the previous month to take the treatment at all. But I suppose I have a fondness for fiction and I knew that Edwin's delicate sensibilities would be upset by such stringent terminology as 'chemotherapy'.

'You said last time was the last visit before the baby was due. What has changed?' he said.

'Daisy has called me in distress,' I said. Then I added, 'I'm needed.'

These last words provoked a hefty reaction. 'Forgive me, Lovely,' Edwin said. 'You are strong where I am ineffectual. I know too well your ability to cope in a drama ...' He went on, 'But I'm thinking of our baby and how much he and ... I ... need you too.' He scooped up Samson with one hand, because we had agreed that the pup should never be allowed into the nursery. 'Patricia is lucky to have such a loyal friend as you.' He raised his palms to the ceiling. 'But you said yourself, you hadn't seen her for years. So where are her friends and family in her hour of need?'

Challenged twice in a day! My charity towards Patricia was being challenged once again and I needed to defend myself. I had had quite enough. 'Her family has disowned her,' I said, having discovered this information from Mave only two hours earlier.

'Why?'

'Because she has spent time in prison.'

'Teaching?'

'No. She was serving time for ... I'm not sure what for ...'

There was then a very long pause. I stared down at my sensible flats. Suddenly I caught sight of Edwin's reflection

71

in the long mirror. He was still clutching my rejected typescript and Samson. 'No,' he said, at first quietly, and then louder. 'No. I am not at home with you visiting this … lady again. Allow me to accompany you on your journey and stop with you.'

It was a chivalrous thought and initially I thought this a very good idea, until I realized that Patricia didn't have a phone. 'Edwin, how can you turn up unannounced and uninvited?' It might have been a different story if we had mobile phones. But then again, her house was very dirty. Edwin would be shocked and anyway there were only two bedrooms. He went to mumble something about booking into a guest house.

'And what about Samson?' I said.

Edwin had to agree but then he stood firmly in front of me. 'No. No. Something is not right about all this and I am not happy, Jayne. I am not at home at all with this situation.' This last word circled the room with the alphabet frieze and his words increased with intensity. 'No. I forbid it. You will not go. I forbid it, do you hear?'

I could do nothing but hear. Samson looked at me and cringed at the tone of his master's voice. Edwin's words fell heavily amongst the fragile lemon paraphernalia. I put my hands to my flaming cheeks. I had never seen Edwin like this and it worried me. He was very angry.

'It is only until Monday. The last time until the baby is born.'

His voice came crashing down. 'No. You are my wife and you will do as I say.' Edwin threw the rejected typescript on to the single divan bed and placed Samson in the hallway. These words were fatal. There was now no going back. I had read all the right articles in all the right women's magazines.

72

A strong, independent woman should not be treated like this. Stooping to pick up my suitcase, I brushed past him and almost tripped up over Samson. And as I placed my hand on the bannister rail, I thought I heard him say, 'Let this be on your head, Jayne. On your head.'

Maybe he did and maybe he didn't. This dialogue was the way I sort of remembered it, Shelley: I was, however, heavily into the style and flavour of Jane Austen at this time.

**

It was a silly quarrel. In time I would come to see that. I cried for all of the taxi journey and wasn't sure what the driver must have thought. If only I had told the driver to turn back. I would get to Patricia's and then walk up to the public phone box in the evening when I would hopefully be feeling a bit better. I would phone Edwin and he would apologise for having been so unreasonable.

Why did I need so badly to return to Patricia Vickers? I tried to persuade myself that it was for Daisy Jacobs's sake, knowing what it had been like to be bullied by her mother. But I also knew that in truth my motive had always been to return and square a circle: put the past right. And then there were all those unanswered questions. Edwin was paying for what I most desired.

When I got to Patricia's she opened the door and exclaimed, 'How can you afford to pay for a cab! All the way? You must have more money than sense!' But I just burst into tears and said, 'I don't wish to burden you when you have so much to cope with yourself, Patricia.' I had hardly ever used her name.

Patricia agreed with the women's magazines. 'No one

these days has to take flack like that from any man,' she said, flattened vowels ever more pronounced in her anger. She was defending me. When she took out a bunch of tissues from the sleeve of her cardigan and handed them to me, my mind was blurred and dizzy. I cried into the tissues and almost fell upon Patricia's bony shoulder but refrained. The last time I had ever been in physical contact with Patricia was when I was sixteen. I had not wanted that contact then. I remembered that heavy, firm push from behind. *'Patricia, stop. Don't.'* I shivered. For now Patricia was stroking my fur coat and plying me with some bitter-tasting coffee. 'There, there,' she was saying. 'There, there.' To be honest, I had clean forgotten why I had come: to protect Daisy or to help Patricia in her sickness.

And then I had to say it. 'Tell me about Benji Jacobs,' I said.

Instantly I knew that despite the 'there theres' we were not intimate enough to share that, for I saw the look on Patricia's face.

'How do you know about Benjamin Jacobs?' she said sharply.

I was about to say I saw Mave who told me he had become a dentist or maybe something big in the City but it was then I felt a sharp twinge in my abdomen.

10

November 30th 1984

Food had not been a priority when I left Edwin that Friday lunchtime. I always brought some for the three of us. I mentioned to Patricia that I had not eaten lunch.

'A sandwich, then?'

'Don't worry. I'm not feeling that hungry.' I didn't really want to sample any contents of a decomposing refrigerator, but in truth I was feeling quite ill.

When Patricia went through to the kitchen, I took my lodging money from my handbag and reached up to place the ten pound notes on the mantelpiece. I felt more than a twinge in my abdomen: it was a sharp, wrenching pain. 'It could be Branston Hicks,' I said to Patricia. 'But I need an ambulance to get me to the hospital, or at least a doctor and especially Edwin. Please call 999 and then call Edwin.' I was suffering at the mantelpiece, bent over in pain when Patricia did something which altogether surprised me. She threw back her head and laughed uncontrollably. 'Not *Branston*, Jayne. *Braxton* Hicks. It is not pickle, Jayne.'

It was strange behaviour when I was in such pain. I was back on top of the 366 bus for Patricia's behaviour was, at this time, wholly inappropriate. I needed to convey that a sense of urgency was required. 'We're not on top of the 366

75

bus now, Patricia. Please call the neighbours for help.'

'Your memory is excellent for detail. How do you remember which number bus we travelled on?' She waited for a response and repeated to herself, 366, as if this was some distant but important memory. I was being engulfed in another wave of pain.

'Patricia, the contractions are coming too quickly. You need to contact the neighbours.'

'I fell out with them a long time ago. The cat shat on their lawns. Lawns,' she scoffed. 'As though we have lawns on this estate.' She tutted to the ceiling.

I was becoming breathless with pain. 'Take the purse from my handbag and ask the neighbours to go to the phone box. Please, Patricia. Please phone Edwin, anyone.' My head was swirling.

She put her head on one side. I remembered the twist of the head from years ago. Patricia would set her human Alsatians on to me and then sit back, place her head to the side, as she was doing now and watch with detached interest. She moved towards me at the mantelpiece. I was concerned. But Patricia picked up her pierced earrings and put them in her ears, her eyes and mouth tightening in concentration.

I thought I might be sick. 'Patricia, hurry. Hurry,' I moaned.

'Give me your jewellery,' she said.

'What?' I was clutching my abdomen. What on earth was she saying?

'If you are swelling up with childbirth, wearing jewellery is dangerous. And contact lenses.'

I was relieved that Patricia was showing some level of concern. At least some semblance of normality had returned. I was seeing white stars in front of my eyes, but I managed to remove my engagement and wedding rings, the gold necklace Edwin had bought for me on our wedding day and my gold watch. 'Good thinking, Patricia,' I said.

'Your contact lenses,' she said.

I did as she said then she left without a word. Thicker and thicker the pains were coming. A resounding pain came faster, faster and angrier in my belly. I tried to remember my breathing exercises and placed my palms on the wall with the peeling wallpaper. The memory of the breathing exercises reminded me of the comfort of group Childbirth Trust camaraderie. For a fleeting moment, I was back in the world of the sane and sheltered. All would be well.

There was no pause between pains. I couldn't help feeling that something was drastically wrong. How I longed to be in that fresh lemon nursery and not here because my astigmatism was so bad that I could barely see. I wanted … needed … Edwin but the only company I had now was a dysfunctional cat which yelped and bared its needle-like teeth. Oh, silly, silly Jayne to get myself into this situation. And the pains came again in rushes. Why did I have the feeling I was being watched? Patricia had been gone for some while. I looked at the mantelpiece for a clock. No clock. Just that poor and stuffed, wide-eyed deer. Patricia had taken my watch. No watch. Why had Patricia taken my watch? Patricia had said to remove my jewellery. I would swell. What was the time? These waves and rushes of contractions were searing and violent. I was perspiring profusely: hot and then prickly cold. Then a gush of water. I began to yell in desperation. Still no Patricia. I tried to see in the half-darkened room. My spare pair of spectacles was in my bag. Where was my handbag? There was a flicker of movement at the window. I called out for help. But nothing. Oh, why had

I not stayed with Edwin? He would have phoned for the ambulance straight away. Eight months. I was only eight months pregnant. This was not good. Delivering at seven months would be better than at eight, I knew. My palms were still pressed against the wall, but it was becoming difficult to remain standing. The cat rubbed its arched back against the back of my calves. Where was Patricia? Oh, how could I *be* in this situation? At my utmost need, here I was, at the mercy of the person I had feared most in my life. What was I doing here? What is the time? What is the time?

I stumbled to the sofa and collapsed in a mound, burying my head into the dank brown of the cushions. They smelt of cat urine and neglect. I felt nauseous, retched as the front door slammed. Oh, thank God. Help was coming at last.

'Jayne? Why are you lying like that on the sofa?' It was Daisy in her school uniform.

I peered upwards in the dying light of the tiny lounge. The child looked frightened. 'Daisy,' I whispered. 'Go to the neighbours and ask them to call an ambulance. My waters have broken. The baby is coming.'

'Mother's here,' she said.

I watched as Patricia entered the room. 'They are all on their way,' she said.

'Oh thank God, thank God,' I cried.

'Daisy, get me some sheets and blankets from upstairs.'

'I'll have my baby at the hospital.'

'That baby is going to be born any minute.'

But the baby was not born any minute. The pain went on for what seemed to me like hours; an unnatural pain; a pain without relief. Then someone was saying, 'The baby will be here soon. Very soon. Bear down. Bear down. Let me mop your brow.'

Where was dear Edwin? I wanted Edwin and my spectacles. I wanted to see my baby being born the way we had planned. When I felt the baby come, I was too exhausted to greet it; too exhausted to realize that the baby had not screamed; too exhausted even to react when, in a dripping haze, I saw a woman coming towards me with a pair of scissors. 'Let us cut the umbilical cord,' the woman said.

Then I saw Patricia pick up the baby and wrap her in a towel. She smiled. 'She looks like those flowers we saw together in the park. Those pale blue things. Violets you said. You should call her Violet. I love those flowers.'

She meant veronicas.

11
Out of Time – 1984

In and out of consciousness I drift, dreaming of vegetable patches where the hardy purple-sprouting broccoli has come too soon. Winter is waiting for adolescence to push through but I have planted the seeds too early and someone has disturbed my carrots. I will not win, for the violets and daisies, which I planted for a 'friend', will be blossoming at judgement time. And I smell something strange nearby …

There's a stench of my own sweaty heap and bloodied sheets on the bedroom floor; now a distant clatter of someday milk bottles, then a dog barking, sometime the siren of an ambulance which is never calling for me. Days merge. Late November dusks fall quickly into December; the ubiquitous voice of the radio tells me so. The outside leaves scrunch beneath footfalls, threatening to enter the house but the bedroom door only opens on Patricia and Daisy.

Once, I fancy I hear Mr Tips's voice. At nightfall: gentle midlands vowels against the backdrop of a harsh wind. Wasn't there a tapping at the door? I am sure I heard a tapping at the door. 'Patricia, Patricia …' I moan with the wind. I wake up now and then but it is always this same dream: the dog is lost, the bad witch has me, the good witch wants me to walk; the room is full of bunny rabbits. I can't get back to the house and it is November. It seemed to me, Shelley, that when I awoke from that bad dream or nightmare, that I was truly never going to be the same again. And it seemed also, that the nightmare was not only about my past, but strangely prophetic.

Another voice tells me it is now December. Is this the voice of a friend or is it that man on the radio? When I awake fully, I will be back in the lemon nursery with Mr Tips and the rabbit with the lopsided ear. This is a dream: just a dream. 'Violet' lives in a drawer removed from a chest in this, Patricia's bedroom. Blinking at the drawer, I wonder what my baby looks like and I remember the Moses basket which sits in our Milton hallway. A basket which protects is a Moses basket. There is a white cot in a lemon nursery, a rabbit with a lopsided ear, a divan for night-time breastfeeding. Why have I not fed my baby? And then I hear Patricia's voice whispering, 'There is something strange about this baby.'

**

When Patricia left her bedroom, I found the strength to crawl my way to the armchair. The drawer was at my feet. My hand made a tentative move towards the drawer. I noticed my rings had gone. Where were my rings … my watch? Patricia had taken my jewellery because of … what was it, she said? Oedema. What time was it? No clock.

'Violet Tips,' I said out loud to the fireplace, practising.

I took a deep breath. What did Patricia mean? *There is something strange about this baby?* I had an overwhelming urge to take the baby up, take her to my breast. My hand moved to the drawer again. Should I pull the towel back from

81

the face? Or should I pick the baby up with both hands? I had never held a baby before. We – the prospective mothers (of course, I was now a mother!) – had been taught at the classes, to hold the baby's head in the palm of the hand. I could try. I stooped down, picked up the towel and placed it on my lap. It was hard to believe that anything existed in there. As I sat in that corner armchair, I tried to think what my baby might look like. My hands shook. My lap shook. Something living lay in my lap: something living which came from me ... and Edwin.

My fingers tugged at where the face should be. My right thumb felt something hard, cold, stiff where a cheek should be. I opened the towel up and was unprepared. There before me were tiny ears of my ears, tiny eyes of my eyes, a sweetie honey button of a lip. My hand shot up to cover my own mouth in wonder at such smallness, which belonged to me, was made from me. I took the baby to my breast, realized I was still wearing the same maternity dress I had worn on my day of arrival which was when...? Days ... weeks ago.

The baby's mouth did not catch the nipple. The baby's head fell against my breast, like the lopsided ear of the bunny rabbit I had purchased in Mothercare. I cupped the baby's head with the palm of my hand, cushioning her into the breast. I placed my nipple to the baby's mouth. But the mouth did not open. I looked into the eyes. But the eyes did not look into mine. I looked again into the eyes. The eyes did not focus. Babies' eyes sometimes do not focus. I looked into the baby's features. I tried hard to see myself or Edwin in these features. Where was the genetic fifty-fifty? But no one can be seen in newborn babies, can they? Silly me. The eyes were dumb. The features were featureless. I cupped my hand to my mouth again, but this time it was not with maternal pleasure, but with horror.

What had Patricia done with my baby?

12

Still Out of Time

'She is perfect in every way.'

When I awoke, I was in Patricia's double bed and flanked by my two friends.

'I ironed sheets for you, Jayne.' Daisy beamed at me from my right.

'She is perfect in every way,' Patricia repeated from my left and smiled down at the 'baby'.

'But she's a doll,' I said. I had seen a doll. I *knew* I had seen a doll.

'Is she not just?' Patricia said passing over the bundle with her rhetorical question.

I looked down at …

'Violet,' Daisy said. 'A flower name like mine.'

I looked down at Violet. She was breathing. I tried hard to breathe. 'She isn't a doll,' I said.

'But she is. A beautiful blue-eyed doll,' Patricia insisted, smiling and leaning across to look into the baby's face. She was almost blocking out any dull, grey light from the sash window.

'I don't understand,' I said. 'I saw a doll. I know I saw a doll.'

'Well,' Patricia said. 'I expect you saw a good many

things. You have been delirious throughout Violet's birth and for the past twenty four hours.'

'Twenty-four hours? Isn't it December?'

'It's December 1st today. Saturday,' Daisy said.

I must have heard December being mentioned on the radio this morning. 'White rabbits,' I said, which I always said superstitiously on the first of the month before midday but Patricia must have thought me delirious because she said, 'Daisy. Get Jayne something to eat and a cool flannel for her forehead. She is still hallucinating. Listen to me, Jayne. You gave birth quickly. We helped you stagger the stairs early this morning. Your baby needs to feed from you. I had sent Daisy out for formula. But eat and feed your baby.'

I looked down at Violet. She did not seem perfect. There was something wrong about her. 'What has happened to me?' I said to no one at all.

But Patricia answered. 'You have had a baby, Jayne. You have also been talking about radios and carrots and bunny rabbits and Edwin.'

'Where is Edwin?'

Patricia took my hand in hers and smoothed over my knuckles with her forefinger. 'Jayne. There was no time to call him even if we had his number. We needed Daisy to help deliver Violet.'

'But he was here.'

'Yes, you called his name but he has not been here since you arrived yesterday.'

I was confused.

'How were you able to deliver a baby?' I asked her.

'The midwife came, Jayne. She delivered your baby. She said you must not be moved for some while.'

As Daisy entered the room with soup and flannel I said, 'I

thought to call her Rebecca.'

Daisy at once cried, 'But we have been calling her Violet. She knows her name now. Please, Jayne.'

But at that moment I was distracted. Patricia was placing a pink dummy in my baby's mouth and I … I flipped, Shelley. Can you blame me after all that had happened in the past? I screamed. I screamed and shouted at her. 'Stop it. Don't you dare do that to my baby! How dare you!' And I lurched from the bed and wrenched the pink dummy from Patricia's hand.

I thought I saw a tear in Patricia's eye. Had there ever been a tear in her eye? But she simply said, 'I was only trying to help you, Jayne. I have only ever tried to help you. I am tired now. You need help. You need help.'

**

'No,' Daisy said. 'You live *here* now. Mother says she is going to bed to die and you are going to help and look after me and Violet. And anyway, the midwife said you could not be moved!' The strawberry blonde hair was flicked across the shoulder, the green eyes deliberate in their intention. We were all in great need of help.

'Violet and *I*, Daisy. Not me and Violet,' Patricia said.

Did grammar really matter now? And I wasn't sure that was the right grammar.

'I will die in my own bed,' Patricia said. 'So unless you want to get into bed with me, Jayne, you might move back into your own room.'

What a thought that was. 'It's not my room, Patricia. I have been sharing Daisy's room and I do need to go home.'

'I'm looking after Violet until you get better. Mother told

me to do that,' Daisy said.

I sighed deeply. Daisy's emotions were heightened. Hormones. Pre-menstrual, I expected. And after all, she had seen a baby born. Goodness knows what would be happening to any GCE study and I suspect she was studying the lower grade CSE but this had never been discussed. Now I had recovered from that wretched pink dummy experience – my baby would never ever have a dummy – no never a dummy – I would stagger to the neighbours, or even to the public phone box and call for the taxi, despite Daisy's protestations. I would leave the Jane Austen books I had bought for Daisy and … I looked at Patricia. She obviously did not believe in keeping presents for Christmas as the Kashmir scarf was already on her head. She saw me looking. 'The splendour of blue,' she said and as if she could read my mind she added, 'Presents are for the present.'

The map of escape was inside my head. Map to freedom which I hoped Patricia wasn't reading. I could then return to the safe domesticity of a glass of Liebfraumilch on a weekend when I wasn't breast feeding and the clear running water of sanity. Oh, Edwin, I am returning.

**

'The taxi is here.'

Daisy was going with her mother for the final chemotherapy session that Monday morning. I had spent two nights in Patricia's bed and said I would move to Daisy's room today. Patricia had spent the nights in Daisy's room and kept Violet. I knew I had only been at Patricia's for two days and had lost time when I had given birth to Violet as the radio had told me so. I had asked Daisy on the Sunday to please go

87

and phone Edwin from the telephone box and tell him he was a father. But she said it was out of order. Everything was out of order.

'Goodbye, Daisy.' My eyes rested a little longer on the child's than perhaps they would have done had I not made the decision to go that day. I did not say 'Goodbye, Daisy' with a final emphasis, for fear that the child would refuse to accompany her mother to the hospital. Or worse still, Patricia may not go if she smelt my desperation which she so deftly always had. No, Daisy should not predict our parting in my inflection.

Patricia shuffled down the hallway, down the pathway and into the awaiting taxi. I watched from the upstairs front window. It was a misty view: Patricia believed as much in window cleaners as she did in Christmas. 'My final session of chemotherapy,' she had said. 'I will have no more.'

And as the taxi started up, I said to my baby, 'That will be us next, Violet. And I may even re-name you when I leave here. We will have no more. Goodbye forever, Patricia. Goodbye, Daisy.'

I needed some change in case the neighbours were not in. Change for the public telephone. No purse. Patricia had my purse. Patricia had my bag and spectacles. Patricia had my jewellery. I would find the purse and the jewellery in Patricia's bedroom. Forever the thief, Patricia had stolen my diary, stolen my clothes and schoolgirl dignity, stolen my wedding ring, my time. What was left? My husband, my baby. I must keep both safe. I placed the baby in the middle of Patricia's double bed. I must find my purse. Still there were nagging daggers. What was wrong with my Rebecca? I meant, my 'Violet'. I staggered to the sash window to open it. How in God's name would I ever make it to the public telephone box if I couldn't make it to the window? I looked around. There were no photographs on the bedside table, only rows of plastic bottles filled with tablets. There were no framed photographs of Daisy as a baby, toddler or child; no smiling mothers on seaside piers as it would be with my own daughter. I scanned the room. I would seek out my purse and jewellery and then I would be gone. I opened the bedside drawer. There was nothing. The drawer fell to the floor. I opened the freestanding wardrobe, and pulled down a bag from the shelf above, then another, and another. I threw scarves to the ground, tore nasty wire hangers from the rail, chucked all those blue and more blue clothes to the ground, kicked shoes across the room, ripped into Daisy's well-ironed sheets – but had they actually been washed? (They used the launderette.) Then with the sweep of my hand the bottles of medication on the bedside table clattered to the floor. 'Where is my purse? Where's my jewellery, Patricia? Where is my husband?' I opened up the remaining drawers in the chest and dumped the contents on the floor and then screamed, 'You bitch. You bloody bitch. Why did you come back into my life?' Then I sat on the double bed and wept in huge, wet spasms of grief. And so it seemed did Violet. 'What more can you take from me, Patricia?'

As if nuzzling in response at my feet, and it wasn't the cat, a large brown envelope lay on the bedroom carpet. I searched the maelstrom of mess I had made in Patricia's bedroom and spied my handbag. I reached for it and took out my trusty spectacles which I had missed dearly and then looked closely at the brown envelope. It was marked: *Private and Confidential.*

Inside the brown envelope was a hefty bulk of papers. I was about to find out what more Patricia had taken from me.

13

December 3rd 1984/Five Hours Later

When the latch on the front door clicked open that evening I was sitting on the dank, brown sofa in the lounge or front room, waiting, fuelled by adrenalin. Daisy rushed into the room, and on seeing me, there was a look of relief on the child's face, as though she had detected a note of finality in the words, 'Goodbye, Daisy'. She took Violet from my arms and to her cheek. Patricia stood at the door. 'I feel as sick as a bloody dog,' she said. 'That's the last time I am going there.'

'You would know all about time, wouldn't you, Patricia? Controlling it. Serving it. Reversing it,' I said.

There was this gap. It felt like a long lost molar in the back of one's mouth as we stared knowingly at one another. She knew what I meant. I had confronted Patricia for the first time in my life. You have to understand, Shelley. Finding what I did marked *Private and Confidential* was like digging up all I had buried in the past: all that I had wanted to forget. But finding it made forgetting impossible. And that anger fired my adrenalin, as wretched as I was feeling. The grey, December wind rattled at the letter box.

'Mother. The hospital said you were to return tomorrow and the next day,' Daisy said, looking at me accusingly and feeling the baby's nappy. 'She's soaking.'

I apologised.

**

Patricia's room was chillingly cold. I had left the sash window open all afternoon and the early-evening December dark was descending. Patricia was sitting on her double bed, the sky blue coverlet neatly spread before her. 'You found your jewellery then.'

'Yes, yes I did.' I looked at my watch. Four-thirty. Time would re-enter this household. I hadn't managed to get my rings back on to my fingers. I must have been still more swollen than before the birth but I had done an excellent clean up job on the room, despite my physical condition and the way I had been feeling. Every drawer was back in place, every far-flung shoe returned to the freestanding wardrobe. Everything was as it had been: even lots of Daisy's birthday cards, from her 'father', which I wager had not been opened by her. A lot of letters from this so called 'father' written to Patricia. I would read them later. At my leisure. All was in place except for the pen I had placed on the bedside table and the brown paper envelope which had been strategically set on the neatly spread, double bed's coverlet.

'And you found your handbag,' she said.

I was wearing my spectacles: my contact lenses had gone with the whistling wind.

'It is cold in here. Shut the window,' she said. Wearily, she placed her head back on the pillow and then she retched. 'I am finished,' she said.

'No, Patricia. You're not finished. You must have *hope*.'

Patricia looked across the murky room at me. 'Shut the

91

window,' she said.

'I will shut the window, Patricia, but I need you to do something for me first.'

'I can do nothing.'

'But you must, Patricia.' I took a few steps toward the bed, picked up the brown paper envelope and withdrew the sheaves of paper. 'The book is really good, Patricia.'

Patricia stared fast at the papers which lay in my hands. Her eyebrow twitched upward, fractionally. Her eyes gleamed with the kind of fury I had seen once before: the séance. Those séances the girls used to do in the Biology lab. But there had been a particular séance: that last one, when she had screamed at the moving glass demanding the spirits to tell her the identity of her baby's father. Patricia had gleamed in fury; just before she had smashed the glass. I knew that she could do nothing with that fury now. There was now no energy left to ignite the emotion. Not like the energy that was igniting *my* fury. 'You have been writing ...' I was barely able to breathe, 'about me.'

She lay on the bed. She heaved her head slightly on the pillow and sighed heavily.

'You seem to have understood all that I was going through.'

She looked out of the window.

'What I was going through when I was a teenager.'

She drew her once full lips together.

'You seemed to be able to express my feelings as a teenager better than I could now, myself.'

She closed her eyes.

'But it's not finished,' I said. 'We are going to write the next page and the ones after that. Because, Patricia. This is *my* story. Taken from the diaries you stole from me all those years ago.'

'Shut the window,' she said.

'Yes, I will shut the window, Patricia, but listen. And listen well. You are going to give me the rest of the story and when you dictate, I will say 'yes' or 'no' or 'maybe'. Get it?' I said. I wanted, you see, to find out if she remembered that game. The one about the nice story she and the girls had made up for me. But had ended in my tears.

Patricia's jaw tightened, as if she were about to retch again. 'I am not amused by your silly games.'

'Games, Patricia?' I said whooping us back to our adolescence. 'We both know about games, don't we? Only this time I am controlling the game and our time.'

'Where is Daisy and where are my medications?'

I came to sit on the side of the bed. I took hold of Patricia's hand. Tightly. I had never taken hold of Patricia's tiny hand before. Her hands were oddly small for someone so tall and well-built. The hand I was holding was freckled and bony and very, very cold. The sheaves of the typescript lay upon her lap. 'Your medications are in the bathroom. They are safe there. Patricia, with my help you will get through this just in the same way that I helped my mother when she was,' I was going to say 'dying' but stopped myself, 'when she was suffering in my sixth form years.' I nodded at Patricia. 'My mother and I became very close at that time and we can spend time together now as a family. Daisy can look after Violet and we can write a story … *together*. It will give our lives such purpose because we are going to re-live the awfulness of my adolescence.'

She lifted one nostril.

'Now, let me close that window,' I said.

'Thank you,' she said.

I think it was the only time Patricia ever thanked me for anything. She must have been very cold. I took up the typescript and stroked the A4 sheets of paper. Then I stroked the faded, creamed paper where once my adolescent ravings and scrawling were exposed to the world: my 1969 diary, stained and smeared with a trail of her blood, from cutting her thumb on my diary all those years ago. Rachel called it 'divine retribution' and I didn't understand then but I do now. 1969 was smeared with blood. I flicked through the pages and found what I had written as a fifteen-year-old. These pages had not been given back to me, when I had been made to beg for my writing and so these words had probably never been 'published' on top of the 366 bus. But she had kept them.

I read my words to her. '*I like the sounds of voices in the street when I am trying to sleep in the afternoon and the sun comes in through a slit in the curtain and the curtain is flapping in the wind. That sends me to sleep. And I like the sound of the waves on the sea and running on a never-ending shore, barefoot with hair that flies behind me and does not stick to my head. And I run and run and run ...*

The curtain moves in the cool evening breeze. The trees seem like huge black giants as night sets in. I hear voices, unfamiliar voices laughing, murmuring, being carried away by the breeze and I smile. I smile because I know no one can touch me or stretch out and reach me. I'm alone and the world is far away, unaware of time that presses heavy on my lids or the breeze on my hot cheek. I watch the world grow darker and think and then sleep, and I'm still smiling because here, here, no one can touch me but the breeze and my dreams.'

I just looked at her. I never before possessed the courage

to eyeball her. I stroked the red and white silk scarf which you, Shelley, had bought me for my twelfth birthday: the birthday party to which only you, Rachel and taut Tamsin Prew had accepted invitations. You remember taut Tamsin Prew, don't you? Oh you do. You did her out of being head girl. But for everything that happened, Tamsin Prew would have been head girl. For some reason Patricia had kept my things which Mave had stolen on her behalf. The scarf I had given to Mave as a gift but Patricia had strangely kept that too. The only reason I could fathom was that Patricia had always needed me as I much as I had needed her: the victor and the victim.

Finally she said, 'What are you waiting for?'

'I will tell you what I have been waiting for, Patricia.' I paused here for dramatic effect and then lifted my eyebrows. 'To tell you some home truths.' I paused again. 'When you have no option but to listen to me.'

If she had possessed the energy to shrug her shoulders she would have done.

'I know what you did on the 366 bus.' Then from the brown envelope I drew out my birth certificate with the name Margaret Crawford clearly registered as my mother. And for Father? Father Unknown. Blank. I placed it on the coverlet next to her. 'I know now you knew who my birth mother was all along. What a game that must have been to you in the Municipal Park. When you could have given me my birth mother's name with the click of your fingers. How did you come to have my original birth certificate in your possession?'

Her lashless eyes flickered.

A scoop of anger welled up inside me. '*Tell me* how you have come to have my original birth certificate.'

You know what she did, Shelley? She just smiled like she was still in control. But she wasn't and she never ever would be again because I then took out Daisy's birth certificate.

'I know who Daisy's father *really* is.'

That got her. It was the first time I ever really saw terror in her eyes. It seemed to concern her more than her brain tumour.

Then I picked up the pen which I had previously placed on the bedside table. 'So you had better do as I say if you don't want me upsetting any apple carts. Because I know the man named on Daisy's birth certificate isn't her father either. You've obviously not only been screwing Benji Jacobs but screwing this man too.'

I pulled up the one-and-only chair in the room and said, 'Excuse my pun. Now. Let's get on.'

14
Into 1985

And so it went on.

When Daisy was out to school and Patricia was sleeping, I found the house keys, locked the doors and carried Violet to the public phone box. Not that Patricia could now walk anywhere but I wasn't taking any chances. Edwin was overwrought but delighted to have a daughter. I made him promise to purchase me an old typewriter, a pushchair, a cot and some clocks: six wall clocks with a very loud tick. He spent a lot of time in the Milton department store. On his very first visit to Patricia's, Edwin fully understood that I could not leave an isolated friend in need, even at Christmas. And once he had left I nailed the clocks on to Patricia's bedroom wall.

The Olivetti I installed in the corner of Patricia's bedroom. Her bedside cabinet became my desk. Oh my, how I loved turning the tables. Happy to care for Violet, Daisy kept visits to her mother's bedroom to a minimum. Patricia was becoming sicker by the day; the sand grains in the timer were accelerating through at such a rate. These were some of the words that I had found, words that Patricia had written about me.

'*She is behind me; skimming the hem of my school skirt,*

thrusting a foot at the back of my fat knees which buckle beneath me. Forever the stabbing finger which lunges into my broad shoulders like the urgent angry jabs of vaccination needles. She must have studied my back so well. She is at the back of my journey – always – singing the story of my life. My growing womanhood becomes her public exhibition; my private thoughts are exposed to an unruly audience. I am never alone.

Let alone. I wish she would leave me alone. I try to draw up some strategy to avoid her. I keep my eyes low to the ground. I do not ask for this attention, but the more I wish to disappear, the more she sharpens the point of focus upon me. I am always reluctantly conspicuous. In the blackest moment of night, she is there. When I ebb into dawn, she is there, dancing on the fringe of my dreams, ever constant. I cannot lose her. She is always there, watching me. She says she will return. I believe her. I believe in her power over me. I live in terror of her.'

How well Patricia had understood me – and I had only ever wanted to be understood.

And so, we spent the last days before the end of 1984 in this way, working side by side, Patricia bedbound, me typing dutiful sheet after dutiful sheet, in the corner of the room: click, click of the typewriter teeth against the carbon paper, clunk, clunk of the heavy hands of the clock. Click, click, clunk, clunk chattering away and hastening Patricia and the book to our ends. She would sigh at the ticking of the clocks whispering, 'I am finished. I am finished.'

And I would say, 'Have hope, Patricia. Have hope and anyway you are not finished until you tell me how you came to have my original birth certificate and *why* you insisted I find Margaret Crawford.'

And she would whisper, 'Why, why, why, Jayne? Why always a 'y'?'

It infuriated me.

Edwin and I missed that Christmas together. First of all there was the dog to be cared for but he also more than understood when he saw the beginnings of our typescript. Patricia was my dying muse who had to be cared for and whilst I was so doing, the pages were flying off of the old Olivetti typewriter in my fury. After all, I told him, I was squaring the circle of the past. She was helping me and I was helping her. Edwin visited regularly, bringing provisions and realizing how attached Daisy had become to her protégé Violet. I could tell he knew something was wrong with our baby. But just for now I didn't tell him what the district nurse had said. Only that neither I nor Violet should be moved. That was a porky pie.

As I read through the letters Daisy's 'father' had sent Patricia, I suddenly had a recollection of a sunny spring day in 1976: of what I had seen in the Municipal Park when I first walked out with Edwin, and spied what I considered to be a family of three: a small girl, a mother and a father on his knees, singing to the brass band. I knew now who they were.

Patricia was lying on the bed. She was half-asleep. But she looked up one frosty January afternoon when I had been working hard and spelling out the story of my adolescence and said, 'You have read my private and confidential letters.'

'I didn't need to read your letters to know who Daisy's father *really* is,' I said, taking off my spectacles to indicate that I would stop working. 'Because it's not that nice Jewish boy called Benji Jacobs who wanted to become a dentist, is it? Daisy believes Benji is her father and he does, too, but I know better.'

Patricia stared at the wall but never at the clock.

'When they said you left school, I'd hoped you had been expelled for what you did on the 366 bus. But then I heard you were pregnant. I knew things, you see.'

Patricia did not look at me. She seemed involved with the wall. I went on. 'I knew that you weren't going to incriminate Mr Brody.'

Her eyes without lashes fluttered at that name.

'Mr Brody.' I repeated the name. 'Daisy's father was never a schoolboy, was he, Patricia? Not Benji Jacobs or Danny Diego. I know Daisy's father is Mr Brody who came with his boys to paint our school that winter. Mr Brody 'had' something on you. I know this, Patricia, because I used to spend a lot of time in the school toilets. *Sorry.* I mean *lavatories.* Do you remember when the school lavatories were being re-painted?'

Patricia, bedbound and wearing the blue Kashmir scarf I had bought her, looked past me and through the sash window.

'You used to meet Mr Brody, the painter there, didn't you? Do more than meet.'

She eyed me suspiciously, with contempt even.

'I used to sometimes hide in the toilets during sports lessons, especially swimming.'

She didn't react. She gazed again at the outside brick wall.

'I read nearly all of Jane Austen's *Persuasion* behind a locked door, and *Jane Eyre*. Once, just before a Biology lesson – we were studying frogs and tadpoles – I was about to come out. I heard your voice and stopped myself from pulling the chain ...'

15
Jayne (16)
Monday 10ᵗʰ February, 1969/Two Thirty-Two pm

Patricia needed to know I *knew* who the father of her baby was. This is the way I told it to her, more or less.

I can smell the nicotine from Mr Brody's rolled cigarette; smell it as the smoke drifts above the tops of the open cubicles. I spoke to him once, Patricia; could smell the nicotine – and the whisky on his breath then.

'You on the pill?' I hear him say to you.

'You never asked me that question *before* Christmas,' you say.

It was February, 1969. How could I ever forget that month?

'I said – are you on the pill?' His voice is insistent.

'Of course,' you say.

You weren't on the pill were you, Patricia? That was a porky pie.

'Are you sixteen?'

'Why are you suddenly so interested in my age?'

'You know why … I said are you sixteen.'

'Of course. O-levels this summer.'

You weren't sixteen were you, Patricia? Another porky

pie.

'You won't be passing any O-levels the way you've been skiving lessons since last term.' I can hear him exhaling nicotine. I am terrified that you both might hear me. I'm in a toilet ... *lavatory* I mean, at the end of the row, so I can sit on the seat without my feet being seen. My big knees are bunched up under my chin; my thighs are cold. These outside lavatories are freezing.

'You have an interest in my education?'

I hear you both now exhaling, so I think you are smoking too. I've smelt the nicotine on you in the Science lab and in the Geography room when you asked me what I was doing on this planet. The smell has lingered upon you these past few months. I have even smelt it on you when we were kneeling together planting violets and daisies and roses for your garden patch during the autumn term. You've even stopped smelling of vanilla.

'I've taught you a thing or two.' Mr Brody laughs. His accent is ... a little common.

'You were hardly starting from scratch.'

I don't understand.

'Two of a kind, we are. Bet you can't wait to leave school.' He laughs again. His laugh is full-bodied.

Now I think I can hear the shuffling of cards and I'm right because I hear you say, 'Let me tell your cards for the future. Let us see what the dreaded cards foretell.'

'The birds I meet down the Cat's Whiskers,' he says and I remember this is a club I don't go to, don't go to clubs, 'they can't wait to leave school either. What have they got to look forward to?' I can smell Brody's aftershave lotion from a distance. It's mingled in with the nicotine. We could all smell his aftershave. It was the scent of man, so different from the scent of female adolescence. It was a nice but scary kind of smell.

'Is that a rhetorical question?'

He goes on. He is unusually talkative. I have spent time reading in this toilet whilst he has occasionally whistled but painted alone. 'On the till at Woolworths, punch your card in at nine, fifteen minutes' break in the canteen, pay day on Friday and ten bob extra at Christmas. Pocket money to purchase knickers they can't wait to have ripped off after they've danced around their handbags at the Cat's Whiskers on a Saturday night.'

It sounded awful. I'm hearing the click of the Tarot cards and the beat of my heart, for Brody is a big man and all of twenty-three. What would the two of you do to me if you heard me, found me?

'Skirts up their arses,' he goes on, 'smelling of hairspray and catch some poor sod with a pink positive on the pregnancy test. Leaving school? You'll exchange the school bell for the factory one, that's all.'

'I organise the ringing of the bells,' you say. And I know you do. You get Brenda Baker to change the times of the lessons by a few minutes to give you longer in the toilets. Bell Ringer Brenda Baker. Nobody notices but me because I keep my eyes firmly on the correct time on my watch. Recently I've had to hide in the grounds during swimming lessons because you come here so often and I don't want you to catch me in the toilets listening to what you are doing right now.

'You're no different from those girls in the clubs,' he says.

'My father is on the board of governors.'

'Oh, la. Does he know you're *fraternizing* with an ex-con or what you get up to at lunchtimes in that Biology lab?'

103

There's a pause before you say, 'How do you know about that?'

'Brenda has a big gob,' he says.

'Let me read the cards for your future.'

'I've already read the writing on the wall. I paint enough of them to know.' I wonder what Brody is referring to and then I realize it's all the things you scrawl about me on the lavatory walls.

'What do your walls say?' you ask him.

'Walls. I strip them. I paper them. I paint them. Most days I can't get the boys to turn up and do the job, so it's me, a room, a tranny, Radio Caroline, the Kinks and fucking walls.' His voice is deep – there's a sing-song rhythm to the way he says his words. 'In a few years they'll ask you back to the same room to strip the same walls, paper them in a new fashion and paint over the cracks in their marriages. And that's what's ahead of me. Walls the fucking length of China because I don't know how to do anything else. Secondary modern for me. No la di da High for me. No O-levels. It's hard to make ends meet for myself, so my walls don't spell out Happy Families. Don't you get any ideas.'

He sounded awful and I wondered if his appeal to you was his awfulness, because Patricia you did used to spend an awful lot of time with Mr Brody, as good-looking as he was. Nothing like Edwin at all.

I think the smoke may make me cough. It's reaching the end of the row of toilets.

'Relax. Who knows what the dreaded cards foretell? You might die of a brain tumour before you are thirty. Things could be worse than marriage.' I'm sure you say this, Patricia, although my memory may have blurred the truth but how prophetic if you had, indeed, said this.

104

Then Brody suddenly says, 'Who's Jayne Thornhill?'

And you say, 'A deathwatch beetle.' How did you think that so quickly if you hadn't thought this before? *Is that what you really think of me?*

I'm thinking that maybe you both know I am here, but then I don't think so because you go on to say, 'Tap, tap, tap. Fat, blubbering Jayne Thornhill with her orange hair. Tap, tap, tap. Her sausage fingers writing her obscene diary – writing the letters of the alphabet in different orders. Which way will she move? If I fasten her with a pin, will her legs bleed? Do insects bleed? Entomology is interesting but I bore easily.'

'I see,' Brody says. Then it sounds as though he is putting his cigarette out and he says, 'It's just that I don't know how much longer your headmistress is going to employ me to strip your artwork from these girls' bogs.'

'I suppose that depends on *your* feet and *my* artwork.'

'My feet?'

'You drag them so well. My artwork is paying your bills.' There is a breathy pause before you say, 'So strip me.'

Then the talking really stops and I can hear a squishing noise. Oh, that's kissing. Then quick breaths. Then it sounds as though there is the scuffle of feet. Are you both fighting? For you, Patricia, are making strange noises. Then the banging of the toilet, I mean *lavatory* door. Next door! I lift my feet up on to the lavatory. Then you make love or whatever you call it. I can hear it: the kissing, a kind of building which goes on and on until I think you're going to burst open this lavatory door and split my head open or split your sides. I can't help but hear. Both of you, making love, or something like that. I realize the graffiti about me is to keep your boyfriend in a job. Maybe you don't hate me so much.

Then I hear your boyfriend say, 'What do my cards read?'

'The wild card turned up. I like playing the joker,' you say and then banging of doors and you go to Biology. I follow. At a distance.

16
Jayne (32)
1985

'I am guessing, according to Daisy's August birthday, that her conception was a few weeks prior to my *lavatory* eavesdrop,' I said as I arranged yellow roses in Patricia's room. 'But your meetings with Brody had been regular that winter.' I could feel her eyes deep-hole boring into my back: an old familiar feeling. 'My mother taught me to cut back roses hard in the spring. She taught me how to prune, to find the bud and cut just above it, at a slant so that the flower grows free.' There was some vague recollection of having told Patricia this at our garden plots some sixteen years earlier.

For now I bought her flowers: daisies and roses. To give the room some fragrance. She would watch me snip the ends of the rose stems and once a thorn stabbed me. A globule of red blood oozed thickly from my right forefinger and I recalled how hers did the same when she terrorised me by publishing the words of my diary. When I turned from the vase, she was actually staring at the clock I had mounted on the opposite wall. She turned away and watched the cherry blossom float in the wind outside the bedroom window. She looked as though she was counting. Patricia would often look as though she was counting … something.

'You see,' I said. 'You have to care for your rose, Patricia.'

As I arranged the flowers, I told Patricia how I cared for my potatoes when I was fifteen. 'I 'chitted' the seed, Patricia. I lay the tubers in shallow trays that January in 1969 and warmed them to let them know that spring was coming. The potatoes' eyes were then opened and then I planted them and waited for them to grow roots.'

'Fuck your potatoes,' she said.

'But my potatoes came too late that spring,' I said to her. 'Maybe that was why I did not win the garden plot prize. I had tried so hard.' I stopped, turned round from the yellow roses and said, 'Shelley planted a small willow – a Kilmarnock. She didn't know its name. She won.'

'Who is Shelley?' she asked.

'The tumour must have affected your memory, Patricia,' I said. 'My memory is clear as to what you were up to in the lavatories that winter of 1968 and early 1969 so I don't know why you have letters from another man who you claim to be Daisy's father.'

'You know, Jayne,' she said, trying to prop herself up on her pillow. 'What you *believe* is your eidetic memory of people and places for the past is unhealthy. You have always had a penchant for making things up. Like 'deathwatch beetle'. How would I, at sixteen, known what a 'deathwatch beetle' was? Your memory is an unreliable thermometer of truth. Have you not thought what a break you might give your brain if you gave it some space from imagination?'

'Well, Patricia, it's not my brain that is sick. Let's get on.' I pulled the old Olivetti typewriter towards me.

I had started to send the typescript to Edwin so that he could fill in the full stops, subtract the flowering commas and here and there add the flourish of a colon. He was thrilled and excited by both the typescript and the renewed contact with me, fully understanding that a muse such as this, 'needs the right environment in which to germinate, bud and blossom. Whatever is happening at Patricia's house,' he had said, when I met him with Violet at a local coffee bar, 'must be productive. This typescript becomes richer and darker by the chapter, but I do implore you to allow me to take Violet home to Milton where she belongs.' He had looked about the rather messy coffee bar and patted Violet's blanket which Daisy had embroidered with our baby's initials.

'Soon,' I had said. 'Not yet. It would be too upsetting for Daisy to lose the baby just at this point.'

Edwin was all understanding and patience.

There was one time, when I had been typing in her bedroom, bouncing up every so often to give Patricia her medication, or to get a drink of water, that I stopped and thought what I might write next, whipping off my spectacles, for my contact lenses had utterly disappeared. She looked away from the speckled wallpaper, looked away from the clunk click of the clock upon the wall and said to me, 'Have your fat, blubbering sausage fingers ceased to type? It is all I hear, day in, day out, that tap, tap, tap. Infernal tap, tap, tap. What are you doing?'

'We're writing my story,' I said. 'All you have to do is listen.' Then I added. 'For once.'

'But who,' she said surprisingly, 'is the psychopath stalking through your story and *why* Jayne, *why* does she stalk?'

The psychopath was, of course, Patricia but I didn't know why she had stalked me all of my life and, in truth, I had stopped because I needed a cup of tea, anxious to see if Daisy had fed Violet. Thick darkness had now coated the bedroom, which already was smelling of decay, even though I was trying very hard with the flowers. I was getting cold. And I was thirsty. I suppose I looked for some reason for Patricia's actions, but I never was able to discover, well, not until later when we began to see through the glass less darkly. The only clue she gave me was when she fell asleep that night. I thought she was going to die there and then but she fell asleep saying, 'Mother sent me flowers every birthday. Father said Christmas Day was Jesus' birthday but she sent me flowers every year on my birthday. Roses mostly. I like flowers …'

'Their moment is brief,' I said.

The clock rapped. She looked at me with a kind of hatred in her eyes even I had not seen before and I felt an old and familiar physical feeling: my spectacles began to mist over. The knowledge of the brevity of Patricia's life focused my thinking and I needed to know more before her eternal silence, although Patricia and 'eternal silence' was an oxymoron to me and has remained so.

'Patricia,' I said. 'Do you remember the clock on the High Street? The hands on the clock never moved.' Neither did she. I carried on. 'We always thought it was half past four, didn't we? But the hands were stuck. We had all those extra minutes and we didn't know. Well,' I said, cleaning my spectacles on my handkerchief, 'we don't have time now. The clocks are all set at exactly the right time. Alas for you, Patricia, time cannot stop. Or be reversed.'

She looked at me without even the energy to cock an

eyebrow.

'Tell me. When did you find out my birth mother was Margaret Crawford? And how did you have my birth certificate?'

I paused. But nothing. Never ask two questions at the same time. My tone was now clipped. 'Did you know the whole time we spent on the 366 bus that my birth mother was giving me my bus ticket every evening? Weren't you ever tempted to shout or sing that out?'

I was actually tempted to shout now but Daisy was at school and Violet was, thankfully, sleeping in the cot. And Violet's erratic sleeping was making me irritable. 'But why in God's name did you do what you did on that bus? Who was Margaret Crawford to you?'

**

A few weeks before Patricia died, in May of 1985, she asked for a Biro. She pulled a large sheaf of paper from her one bedside drawer and an envelope. The paper and envelope were blue. She started to write and I was watching her when she looked up at me and said, 'This is private. I'm putting my affairs in order.'

It's what the district nurse said with a nod of her head. The district nurse was the only authority who was allowed to enter the house. *Time to put your affairs in order.*

'I'm sorry,' I said and closed her bedroom door behind me.

**

When she did eventually start to die, I was anxious for some startling revelation. She avoided sentiment like the plague but these words sprung unsurprisingly from my lips. 'I forgive you, Patricia.'

She managed to scrunch up her eyebrows. 'Why do I need your forgiveness?'

'That summer day last year …' I said, but I wondered if Patricia was listening, could hear, for her eyes wandered to the wall. I looked into the hooded half-closed eyes. 'You wanted to square a circle.'

'Circles,' she muttered.

'If you don't want forgiveness for the way you treated me, then what about asking God for forgiveness for what you did to us on the bus?'

'Who?'

Did she mean *us* or God?

'Patricia, *why, why,* did you do it to me?'

But Patricia had gone, trying to say something, moody bird of passage. And all I could hear in my head as I looked at her was, *'Why, Jayne, why. Why a 'y' Jayne, why is there always a 'y'?'*

Her last words were, 'You never had to live with …'

None of it made any sense. Until later.

17

Post Patricia

I wish I could have just posted her: through a letter box along with that blessed blue envelope. And then of course there was the typescript. Edwin had been so proud: proud of his baby and his wife and her typescript. He understood that the muse worked in the strangest of ways, that for some inexplicable reason, Patricia and her illness, her need for me, contributed to this huge, worthy typescript. For Edwin it was all such synchronicity but for me the typescript, quite frankly, had been a smoke screen. I had been into squaring circles: my circles. But this was obviously why he had typed the dedication. *To Patricia Vickers, my muse, my friend, my mentor – to whom I owe so much –* on the fly leaf cover before submission to a publisher.

I suddenly burst into tears and happened to be looking in the direction of the pram when Edwin put his hand to his mouth and exclaimed, 'Lovely. I am so sorry. How could I have been so thoughtless? You meant to dedicate your book to our little Violet.'

There had been no changing of Violet's name. I had taken enough from Patricia thus far so I relinquished Violet's premature christening. 'No,' I said. 'That was not my intention.' I looked across the Formica topped table at Edwin because we were in that grubby coffee bar. Suddenly I felt awful. I really couldn't have Patricia's name on that flyleaf.

'Daisy. You meant to dedicate the book to Daisy. Of course, Patricia's daughter. How foolish I have been.'

No! Patricia should have no association with the book at all. 'Edwin,' I said.

He looked at me, a question mark falling on the Formica topped table.

'You. My dedication was always meant to be for you, Edwin.'

**

Life for Edwin now took on renewed meaning and he vigorously posted the typescript to all sorts of publishing destinations whilst patiently waiting for the promised day Violet and I would return to Milton. His beautiful six- month-old daughter responded little to his steadfast gaze, but all would be well when the funeral was over and life could return to normal or a 'new normal' as we might say. I had always agreed, from the time Edwin had taken the typescript for proofreading, that Violet and I would be returning to him after the funeral. After the body was carted away, I took all the letters from Daisy's 'father' to Patricia and all of Daisy's unopened birthday cards from her 'father' – I mean what use would it be to give them to her now? – all the old typescripts written in schoolgirl longhand with my diaries and wrapped them in the blue Kashmir scarf. I then placed it all, along with the red and white scarf you bought me on my twelfth birthday, Shelley, in the freestanding wardrobe, where it had been found months beforehand.

The exact day of the funeral, chosen as it was the May

half-term with Daisy's CSEs in mind, I was hoping to bury more than Patricia's body. Events had overtaken me, like undertakers and so forth all of which Edwin and I paid for. Searching Daisy's drawers for something black for her to wear I found it: the iris blue envelope which Patricia had obviously given to Daisy to post (it was addressed quite, quite strangely, I might add) and it was in amongst brassieres. But I didn't have time to think about the blue envelope and what the contents might be because it was then that I saw the doll. In some ways I was pleased that I hadn't totally lost the plot because it was the same doll which had been wrapped and placed in this very drawer replacing, albeit for a short time, my own Violet the day she was born. Why would Daisy do such a thing? I left Daisy's room and went into Patricia's bedroom with the iris blue envelope and the full intention, of course, of opening it.

I was about to do so when I heard footfalls on the stairs and hastily put the iris blue envelope in the pocket of my black dress. Thank goodness my dress had a pocket or this story might be completely different.

'Will you move into Mother's room, Jayne?' It was Daisy. There was a thin shaft of sunlight coming through the narrow sash window and falling on to the white cotton sheets of the empty double bed. I suddenly realized that Daisy had no conception that my place, and Violet's, was with Edwin. I turned to look at this forlorn child with her three trembling lips. Daisy looked singular and isolated in that bleak bedroom. How was I going to break this to her? 'We will have to go home. And, Daisy, you have relatives.' After a fashion, I admit. I didn't like to mention the issue of her father, so I said, 'You have a grandfather.'

The child went to pieces. These days, I believe, they call

it a meltdown and Daisy was often given to these, almost melting away before my very eyes. Edwin was pounding on the stairs and he came to the bedroom door with Violet in his arms. The cat slithered through the door and took up ownership of Patricia's bed. Daisy's reaction, at the time, I assumed was a result of her grief. 'But I've just lost Mother. You can't take Violet away from me. She's all I've got. I've done everything for her. I've managed to get her to take her bottle. No one's managed to do that. You don't realize how attached she is to me. Violet will suffer dreadfully if she isn't with me.' The child exploded into tears, rushed to Edwin, took Violet from him and pulled the baby to her. She began stroking her like a puppy. 'She's my only friend. I have no other friends. Violet loves me. I love Violet. We won't be parted.'

Edwin looked at me. I looked at Edwin. The cat had fallen asleep. What were we to do? I was thinking about the doll I had found in Daisy's drawer and what an odd thing it was for her to do when Edwin placed a protective arm about Daisy's shoulder. 'And you shall not be parted,' he said to the child. 'You will come to live in Milton with Violet, Jayne and me.'

Well, that was a surprise in itself, and such a welcome one for I loved Daisy as I loved myself, but then three subsequent surprises turned up on Patricia's doorstep that funeral morning in May. The first came in the shape of Benji Jacobs. I was initially sheepish, wondering if he had succumbed to those past awful rumours about me but there wasn't a flicker of accusation on his face and he had grown tall and slim and bespectacled in a City kind of a way. I believe he was doing rather well for himself as a nineteen eighties' market trader.

'But I heard you had become a dentist, Benji,' I said.

'No,' he smiled. 'I'm a far cry from canines.'

116

Benji is the kind of man who turns up for all the important ceremonies in life and I'm sure we will go to each other's funerals. We are alike. We both like to please people. His smile says that, even with a beard. He has the kind of face that has a 'yes' written on it: to everything. However, I suddenly panicked on seeing him so soon after Edwin's generous offer and possibly, initially seemed inhospitable. What if he were to take Daisy away to ... Dagenham, I think that was where he was living and say 'no' to Edwin's idea of fostering his 'daughter'? When he told me that he was about to be married and that his flat in Dagenham was very small, I ventured, 'Benji. I know Patricia always said you were Daisy's father,' and then I paused and he looked at me, smiling, thankfully not picking up on the nuance of my statement, 'but she, Daisy, has become so attached to our little Violet and we thought we might foster.' I needn't have worried because there was a 'yes' upon Benji's beard which I said made him look very swish and that Daisy had given me his address to notify him of Patricia's passing.

The second surprise was the vicar. Well, I thought he was the pastor who would be administering the rites but in fact there transpired to be two vicars at Patricia's funeral which I thought over-generous considering some of her qualities or lack of them. Reverend Vickers was indeed a charismatic man, as big and bold as he was a Bartholomew. He had aged somewhat since our school days but still appeared to be the fireball I remembered him to be. When he said, 'She was more devil than angel,' the words seemed strange emitting from a man wearing a dog collar. He told me that he had always insisted that Patricia sing in the church choir and paid for her singing lessons. 'She had the voice of an angel and could have made a good living as a singer,' he said. 'But

Patricia had no application or discipline.'

This was true.

He thanked me profusely for organising the service 'etcetera, etcetera,' and then asked what might be happening to Daisy. This was a second panic situation and I looked around for Daisy but she was nowhere to be seen. As a matter of fact, I had not seen Daisy for a while. I said, 'Why, Reverend, were you thinking of taking Daisy in?' to which he simply replied, 'Good Lord, no.' It was relief all over as I was relieved that Edwin had come to such a decision that we should foster Daisy Jacobs who was tending to Violet with a passion.

The third surprise was the bunch of two dozen red roses. Signed – 'With Love' and no name.

**

We buried Patricia but it wasn't the end of her. I expected to feel some kind of relief on her death but I didn't. I felt only guilt for making her face time. By contrast, Benji looked very relieved, after he asked, 'Is Patsy really dead, Jayne?'

I assured him she was. But I was at once taken back by this seeming term of endearment. 'Patsy'. I had never thought of Patricia as a 'Patsy' in my life and far from it. I simply nodded and said, 'Patricia was always in for longer terms than were expected.'

'You can say that again,' he said.

So I did.

We threw the anonymously sent roses one by one on to her coffin and after this my thoughts turned to refreshments. When I got home, to Patricia's home, I served the vol-au-vents but it wasn't long before everyone left, saying they had to get home to the dog. This included Edwin, because he didn't believe in kennels for our Samson so I kissed my husband 'goodbye' and said I would see him on the morrow. Reverend Vickers thanked me for contacting him and, as he was leaving with a prawn vol-au-vent in his mouth I said, 'I found out your contact details enclosed with my adoption papers,' I said. 'I have no idea why Patricia was in possession of them.'

His cassock had just begun to float up the garden path when he turned, dusted the vol-au-vent crumbs from both his hands, narrowed his eyes at me and said, 'Your name is …?'

'Jayne Thornhill.'

There was a brief pause before he said, 'I have no idea why she should have them.' And away he swirled leaving me in no doubt that he had associated my name with the 'rum do' as my birth mother described the incident on the 366 bus some many years before.

Benji Jacobs was the last guest to leave, which worried me slightly. As he stood at the mantelpiece, beneath the stag's antlers, I wondered if he was having second thoughts about Daisy. He had the anonymous rose sender's card in his hand and was frowning. When he caught me looking, he smiled a Benji smile and said, 'Are you sure about taking Daisy in, Jayne?'

I looked around quickly to see if Daisy was in the hallway, but she was upstairs getting Violet off to sleep. 'I'm sure,' I said, then added, 'we're sure. This was Edwin's idea.'

'Edwin will be a good father,' Benji said.

'Well, Daisy hasn't lacked for them,' I replied.

There then followed this odd moment. I thought he might cry after all that apparent relief but he said something which I have always thought a little odd. He said, 'Rachel told me that you were adopted.'

I was embarrassed. So much had passed since I first met Margaret Crawford the previous summer that I had been rather neglectful in communicating with my birth mother. I barely nodded.

'Who would you say are your real parents?' he asked.

There was no hesitation on my part. 'My parents,' I said.

He gave me a look of misunderstanding.

'My parents,' I said again. 'My mother and father. I mean the people who were there for me. My father taught me how to plant seeds and my mother buttoned my coat.'

Benji Jacobs thanked me and then threw, yes he threw, the florist's card on the mantelpiece. He was about to leave when the major drama of the day exploded. Daisy, who had put Violet to bed started screaming uncontrollably in the upstairs hallway. Benji and I ran up the stairs. He threw his arms around Daisy. 'What is the matter, Daisy?'

'The letter, the letter,' she shouted.

'What letter, Daisy?' Benji said.

Daisy was blubbering away. 'The letter Mother gave me to post. She made me promise. She made me promise to post it and not tell anyone and I promised her. I promised her I would and I've lost it. I lost the letter. I can't find it. It was in my drawer and I was going to post it tomorrow because I haven't had a stamp.'

'Benji, Daisy, let's go downstairs,' I said. 'You will wake Violet.'

'Not if Grandpa is down there,' she screamed.

'He's gone. He's gone, Daisy,' Benji said. 'It's just the three of us and Violet here now. Everyone's gone.'

We went down to the 'front room' as Patricia would call it and I was thinking fast. I sat Daisy down on the dank brown sofa with Benji one side and me the other and the cat at our feet. This house would need furniture clearance. So would the cat. 'Daisy,' I said, my hands on the pockets of my black dress. 'I found the letter the other day.' There was a suitable thinking time pause before I said, 'When I was looking for something black for you to wear. Your mother told me about the letter and how she wanted it posted so I did,' I fibbed.

This and another vol-au-vent seemed to do the trick. I made some cocoa before Benji left and as he was leaving, he said to Daisy, 'I'll see you very soon my darling. Are you sure about this?'

Daisy turned to me and smiled with her three lips. I winked back, the way Patricia used to, signalling inclusivity. 'Violet needs me, Dad,' she said.

As soon as Daisy was in bed I went upstairs to Patricia's bedroom. She was still there, Shelley. So much time had been spent with her in that bedroom. The sky blue coverlet was laid out on the bed and I swear I smelt that mixture of rose water and vanilla. She was there and even more so when I looked at her familiar spiky schoolgirl handwriting on the iris blue envelope. I went downstairs and headed for the iron.

18

Shelley (32)

My Awful Red Letter Day/Sometime in May 1985

Dear Jayne,

And this is my story.

I'll begin mine on this particular May day. The day I received a crisp, white envelope. It sat on the clean, kitchen marble top, propped up by the coffee pot. Danny had gone to the surgery. Early shift before he went into the House. We were living in Stress City with him trying to manage the two careers but being a politician was winning.

The crisp, white envelope was sealed with my tomorrows. It sat on a backdrop of clean, white walls. Strange that a man who had spent all his life surrounded by antiseptic should insist on the same decoration at home. But I loved him. And I wanted to open this crisp, white envelope and phone and tell him there was hope. I loved him because despite all the dashed hopes in these last few years, he had simply smiled and in the words of *Othello's* Lodovico said, 'O, bloody period'. Loving Danny. I loved him for what I thought was his kindness.

I was wishing that I was back in the tea shop on the Parade in Cambridge: *Auntie's* it was called. I wanted to see him spooning baked beans and reading *The Guardian* – because now he firmly reads *The Financial Times*, and half a dozen other newspapers – and I wanted to see his face as I said the two words, 'I'm pregnant'. I had never, have never seen those deep blue eyes so happy. 'We're starting a family,' he said. We both looked out of *Auntie's,* looked across at King's College and it was one of the happiest moments of his life, he said. I wanted to do that all over again, have those moments back, re-play, re-wind the arms of the clock and have it all turn out differently. But clocks cannot be turned back. That's what Miss Harefield-Mott, Miss HM, Miss Headmistress had said and she was right.

And here I was, on this May school half-term and at last the crisp, white envelope pushed its way face down on to my mat. Clinical returns. All those cold instruments inside of me that finally bring clinical returns. I thought about my college tutors who had constantly given me clinical returns on my hard-worked essays that did not come up to blackboard scratch. I thought of the heartfelt relief eleven years previously when the pregnancy test swam positive and when he looked up from spooning the baked beans and smiled with his deep blue eyes. What a relief that had been. Ah, what an escape it was going to be from academia, even if I had never made it to the university as Danny had done. We just let people think I did, being at a teacher training college close by for a short while until I became temporarily pregnant. I never had the nouse for Oxbridge but I went to Cambridge: after a fashion. Well, it felt as though I had been there, swanning our way down under the Bridge of Sighs, twenty and pregnant with hope and Danny's baby.

And now, I sat, for in this not knowing there was still hope. All those cold instruments and this crisp, white envelope would tell me if I, we, still had some grain of hope. Dared we hope? It's the way we used to receive news in those days: on crisp, white paper not online.

I suddenly surprised myself. I leapt at the envelope, tore it open and caught the inside of my forefinger on its sharp edges and bled. But I closed my eyes, for I did not wish to read the writing on the cold, crisp white notepaper.

And when I do, this May day becomes one of the worst. O bloody periods.

**

The day got darker. Danny had called and I couldn't hold back on the news and the tears. I found myself taking a bus into town and staring into the window of Mothercare at all those things that I would now never buy. It was the smell of a baby that I would miss: fresh, powdered, new sweetness. 'Maybe it was those long years of self-starvation that had done it to us,' I had said to Danny on the phone. Who knows what the dreaded cards foretell? Patricia used to say that all the time, didn't she?

'Well, well, well. Congratulations, Shelley.'

I turned round. Who knew and could be so cruel? But as if on cue, there was Mave, full to the brim, almost about to break waters it seemed. I did not want to be here and I did not know what to say.

'You pregnant too?' Mave said, black curls gleaming in the precinct fluorescent lighting. 'It must be catching. I saw Jay Thornhill right in this very spot last November and she was exactly in my present condition.' She rambled on. Maybe imminent birth makes women garrulous. I would never know. 'Your brother got married last summer,' she said

124

as a statement: just to let me know she knew. 'To your best friend Lydia.'

Lydia, who was also pregnant. But I said nothing. We both knew that my brother Paul had abruptly got off at Charing Cross years ago with a copy of *Time Out* under his arm and a big slice of Mave's life.

'Patricia relished telling me that your brother was getting married,' she said, with an eye on a Moses basket in the window.

I flinched at the name. But then wondered how on earth Patricia knew my brother was getting married…

'But your brother never held any interest for me after I dumped him at Charing Cross. Benji Jacobs was very good to Patricia,' she went on.

'Well, we haven't seen Benji since school,' I said, not really knowing why. I had liked Benji. Everyone had.

Then abruptly she said, 'Are you still working in the shoe shop?'

'No. I went back to finish my training as a teacher.'

'Oh, of course,' she said.

I wasn't sure if she meant she knew I had trained as a teacher and had forgotten or that is what she might have expected of me.

'Jay Thornhill was living with Patricia.' Mave must have been able to detect the sheer bewilderment on my face. 'By all accounts they came very close. She's dead now.'

'Who's dead?' I said.

'Patricia. The bitch.'

'Mave. You were always very thick with Patricia.'

'I never was.'

'Bull. Shit,' I said.

'She was a drain on my resources,' she said turning on her

heel into Mothercare like she had a special passport and of course she did. Resources were very important to Mave. Shit, I thought. You went to live with *Patricia?* And then: Patricia is dead. The witch is dead.

When I got home there was an express delivery of white lilies addressed to me. Why did he send white lilies and write, *In Deepest Sympathy, Doctor Daniel?*

19

'For Christ sake's, Shelley, why didn't you say something?'
It was the first time I knew Greg to shut his office door. He
had called me in first thing on Monday morning after that
dreadful May half-term. For me there was about to be a total
eclipse of the sun.

'The student came to me in confidence. How could I
betray that confidence?' I said.

'The girl's in hospital. The father broke her hip.'

Nothing was said for a long time. Greg turned and looked
out of that window which was fairly new to him but I knew
so well. The daffodils had disappeared and so had my
chances of ever becoming a mother. I couldn't help thinking
back to that Mothering Sunday in 1969 and then thoughts
jumped to those lilies Danny had sent just before the weekend
and his face when he had returned home that Friday evening
on seeing them. 'They must have got the cards mixed up,'
was all he said. 'I had a very close patient who died.' He
never sent bereavement flowers to patients' families. I was
confused. And now this. I was staring hard at Greg's back, at
the lines on his dark green, corduroy jacket. Finally he said,
'How long have you known?'

At first, I thought this new head meant something else but
then I realized why I was here. The words stumbled out. 'Jade
came to me three times over the period of a term. I promised
I wouldn't betray her trust in me.' Then I added, 'I couldn't

be sure she wasn't making it up. Jade's a challenging student. I didn't want to cause a fuss and …'

'You should know the rules,' he said, turning to face me. 'You have to let the student know quite clearly, if under the age of eighteen, prior to any discussion related to abuse or legal issues, that you are bound to inform your line manager.'

'But then she would never have confided in me.'

'Perhaps it was a cry for help,' he said.

A cry for help. 'I … I've been taught to …'

He sighed. 'There's a time to speak and a time to be silent,' he said. 'You need to seriously examine what you have been taught in the past. And if ever, ever a student comes to you with any talk of abuse or legal issues, speak to me.'

I got up to go, thinking we could dust this down, forget all about it and move on when he stopped me by saying, 'I'm sorry, Shelley. We can't walk away from this. I have enormous respect for you as a teacher. This work you have started on the Tree Project is invaluable and you instil trust in the most difficult of students, but you must know I'm going to have to inform the Board of Governors.'

I thought only of Danny's political career: he had just started the year before, trying to get established on the back benches and we never seemed to have any money despite his GP's salary. What if I were dismissed? The stigma! I went to open that huge wooden door: the door of the inner sanctum when Greg delivered another blow. 'I have to warn you.'

I turned back to him.

'This is a formal caution. I will need to inform the Chair and discuss at the next governors' meeting. County often swoops down when these kinds of issues are involved.'

A thought ran across my mind but before I could register

it, he said, 'And I'm not covering my back here. You know the rules.' He was of course strained because he was nursing his wife through cancer and in time I forgave him for my receiving a caution. It didn't go further than that but Greg followed all the correct channels. Maybe these days it might be different but in 1985 it stopped there.

After that I threw myself into the Tree Project. There's something I call 'the jigsaw syndrome'. I like a complete picture where all the pieces fit into place. One of the challenges of tracing family trees is that the pieces don't come in a handy box. The pieces need to be sought. Every morsel of information will contribute something to the bigger picture at a later date: you just have to be patient. The pennies will drop into the right place … eventually. And they did, didn't they? Patricia, why she did it, Daisy's father. I like things to fit even if the final picture isn't one we would have constructed for ourselves. It's why I went to sell shoes in the Milton department store in 1974, when I was temporarily pregnant. It was very satisfying: finding the right shoes for the right feet.

But there I was that day in early June 1985, Jayne, standing on the same spot, albeit in different shoes, being reprimanded for the very thing I was instructed to do twenty-five years earlier by an altogether different head. The head who wore Hush Puppies and told me quite clearly to keep my mouth shut. Now I was being cautioned for doing that very thing.

You would call it synchronicity.

A year after my caution your first Young Adult book, which had a weird familiarity, came out in 1986. I remember seeing the title and feeling as though an electric bolt had passed through me: *Girls in a Line* and a strange pseudonym, Tricia Dee, in bold on the spine.

I wondered if I possessed one.

Part 2
1969

20

Shelley (53 going on 16)

I'm sorry I rushed out of the store when you mentioned her name, Jayne. We need to re-visit 1969 for me to give some kind of explanation.

The Tree Project was an excuse. I didn't ask to meet you in Milton just before Christmas 2005 to request patronage. Sorry, Dolly. That's what Miss Simkiss, our simpering Biology and form mistress, would say, isn't it? Sorry, Dolly, I lied again. Although I never really lied, did I? I just never told the truth. Is there a difference? You looked good when we met that December in Milton. You and your publicity head shots were far-flung from the stodgy Blue Stocking Jayne Thornhill I remembered. It was good of you to travel so far especially when Daisy was about to give birth. Of course I didn't know who Daisy was then and what she transpired to be to me.

This particular lunchtime, just before Christmas, just before I emailed your website and met you in the Milton department store, I did a gander down that awful year: 1969. You see, I had needed to find the missing pieces of the jigsaw puzzle. Danny had suddenly decided that autumn to throw in his political trowel and move to the country. Although Danny was never very likely to take up gardening as a hobby. He never liked digging over old ground. 'We will both retire,' he had said and been very specific about the area he wanted us to locate to. Of course I immediately gave in my notice to leave at the end of the autumn term, hoping I could carry on with the Tree Project by remote control. Although I didn't seem to be in control of anything. So it was up to me to declutter and pack up the past. Looking back I probably chose to go up to the loft that light-headed lunchtime because of what Greg had unearthed in me an hour or so beforehand. I had been giddy from that day's lunchtime retirement champagne or from the seeming suddenness of relinquishing a job I loved. The landline was ringing. I guessed it was Greg calling because of what had happened between us. I didn't know why he wasn't ringing my mobile which was right beside me. I felt guilty. Guilty about Greg and about what happened an hour or so before, guilty about even being up in the loft and raking over the past. Danny had told me to dump the diaries and memorabilia. 'Let sleeping dogs lie,' he had said. When I mentioned the need to clear out the loft, he said *leave that suitcase*. The one to which he holds the key.

Danny had remained beautiful despite the years: still the deep blue-eyed boy with dark eyebrows which sprang into motion, especially when he lit a cigarette. He carried on smoking, but not in public, of course. It seemed safe up there, tiptoeing over the floorboards. There was the old, locked suitcase belonging to Danny and old photograph albums. There were photos of me and my brother Paul, clasped in sepia: me three or four, Paul about six, in a fireman's helmet, sticking out his tongue. It's a green moment for my eyes are puffed out with raging envy as Paul's fingers are firmly grasped with superior dexterity to the steering wheel of the toy car which belonged to me. Always others doing the driving. My thumb caressed our flaxen heads: I wished I could have just sat in the sunlight and looked at photos of my blonde children. My children would have had streaks of Scandinavian.

I was supposed to be bringing our lives down from the loft but I had gashed my ankle; slopped blood on the lemon-fitted carpet trying to bring down some books. So I sat. My diaries were scattered around me: I never gave up archiving the past. I sat in my torchlight picking out certain years like sticky, white nits. 1985: that ugly year when the medical results came through, when Danny had strangely bought me the white lilies before our half-term holiday to Cannes. 1976: the year of our marriage. A spider trickled across my wrist and then across the red and mottled 1969 diary. What was I doing up there? Was I trying to find the girl I once was, the girl in her slim adolescence? Where was she? The red mottled 1969 diary fell open. This was the proverbial can of worms …

**

Tuesday 4th February 1969

I know they play strip poker in the toilets with the painter/decorators during breaks and lunchtimes – when they're not doing 'the other things'. I heard them talking about straight flushes and raising more than their bets when I was on playground duty today and the 'Wet Paint – Do Not Enter' sign had gone up again. Brody – he's the boss man – was saying that school ties didn't count and Patricia said that they counted where she came from. Then Brody's two assistants were shouting 'off, off, off' and the first years doing leapfrog by the toilets' brick wall stopped and stared.

I told them to go into school – the bell would be soon ringing, but it wouldn't because I could hear Beefy Bell Ringer Brenda Baker shouting at one of Brody's assistants, 'Oh, sick, Dave. That feels like a mongrel's lick.'

I heard Brody saying that Dave was a noisy player and Steve said Brody had poker-player eyes. Don't know what that meant.

Dave, the cheeky one, then said, 'I'm trying to concentrate on my hand,' and there were sniggers from inside the toilets because I can imagine what his hand was doing. 'A bra for a flush,' Dave said and then the boys started shouting, 'off, off, off' again and Brenda was saying her ear drum was blocked.

Patricia never appeared for Biology after today's strip poker session. Neither did Jayne. In fact Jayne bunks off most sports lessons and I've no idea where she goes to, only sometimes I've seen her out at our garden plots burying things.

Shit. Paul is going to drive me to school now that he's passed his driving test and borrowing Mum's car because Dad says she won't take driving lessons so Paul might as well drive it. When am I going to see Danny Diego again if my brother is giving me lifts to and from school? I live for the top of the 366 bus after school.

**

I live for the top of the 366 bus after school. Prophetic words. Trams now.

I ignored the graffiti on those lavatory walls. Rachel told me once, no, twice in one day – first in the Geography room and then later in the Biology lab – that I had mental glaucoma and I looked the word up in the dictionary: couldn't read the

136

writing on the walls. But I did *see* what Patricia Vickers and her cronies had daubed on the walls of the lavatory, with lipstick, with nail varnish, with excrement. The words were always focussed on you. I just chose to turn my head away. I saw you grow though. After it happened in 1969, you grew. Oh, I know your thighs bulged, your stomach slopped, your jowls burgeoned but it was as if you refused to disappear. Not like me. I just wanted hell to open up and swallow me whole – I certainly had a problem swallowing anything at all after it happened. But you, they made you feel invisible and then all too visible at different times. You grew in more ways than one. Your amber head was bent over romantic novels after it all happened. Did the romantic novels replace the garden allotments and those freezing lavatories in terms of your escape route?

**

The Loft

There was no heating in the loft. I was cold all over, shivering from the effects of the champagne, the lack of food and the memory of those moments. I had to keep an eye out for the time on my mobile phone. It was coming up to three o'clock. I could never be sure what time Danny would get home from the House, if at all, but I shouldn't have been up there going over all this. Should have dumped the lot in one go. I remembered Miss Simkiss's '*Dust it down. Forget all about it. Make a secret of your secret.*' Make a secret of your secret. But just maybe the fifteen-year-old Shelley wanted to say something to me. That fifteen-year-old always *wanted* to say something. She just found speaking up so very hard, Jayne.

So, so, sorry, Dolly.

Spider, you are scuttling across my words and down and up my spine. I should have been thinking about Christmas cards and changes of address but the floorboards were speaking as I dragged my bloody ankle towards me.

**

Friday 7th February 1969

Lost my shoe. Jayne said she tried to be ill today but her mum wouldn't let her be off from school. She will get another detention on Monday for forgetting her swimming costume and she asked me to tell Miss Simkiss that Patricia had nicked her diary!!!

I know things are bad for Jayne but she's a stick insect. I can't shake her off. In lessons she turns around and mouths the words, 'I must speak with you.' I told her in the Geography room that I didn't know it was Patricia who had taken her diary, that I needed proof before I would grass on her. I think it was Mave. Patricia always gets others to do her nicking. I did see Mave fidgeting with Jayne's watch in the changing rooms before Maths and then I heard that Jayne was ten minutes late for her C stream Pythagoras lesson and got a bollocking and detention. Now I notice Jayne is forever checking her watch and then checking the school clocks because Mave must have switched the hands back making Jayne late. It's a wonder Jayne has time to do anything she spends so much of it in detention.

When Jayne left the Geography room, Rachel said, 'Shelley, you do have mental glaucoma, you know.'

I've just looked it up in the dictionary. It means blind in

138

the head, I think.

Rachel also told me in the Geography room that Benji is really annoying her as he borrowed 'some stuff' and won't return it. I asked her what 'some stuff' was and she looked cagey. 'My papers. I told you I lost my papers. I've asked everyone if they've seen my papers and no one has. Everyone's got glaucoma,' she said. She then went to cut back her tarragon to keep the plant tidy.

After lunch, when we came back into classroom, someone – and it looked like Patricia's writing – but I can't be sure – had written parts of Jayne's diary on the board. About how she was adopted and how she hated her adopted mother and how she wished she could find her real mother. And then how Jayne wants to be married to Danny Diego and the names of their children would be Rebecca and Joshua. So pathetic!! I was rather hoping I would have Danny's children and had been experimenting with Christian names which went with his surname. I didn't want to read anything more on that blackboard so I opened my 'Jackie' magazine and that was when Rachel said again, 'You have voluntary mental glaucoma, Shelley.' I think that means I want to be blind in the head.

Jayne started crying and saying about the words on the blackboard, 'I didn't write it, I didn't write it,' and when she went to rub her eyes they got covered in ink blotches because her fingers are always stained with blue ink, because Jayne doesn't know how to fill her fountain pen properly. Her diary says she wants to be 'an authoress' but she can't even fill a fountain pen properly. How can you ever be an authoress if you can't fill a fountain pen? Miss Simkiss came in to take register and everyone was sniggering (because someone had put more dirty bits about Danny on the board too). Miss

Simkiss looked at the board and said, 'Truth is a jewel which should not be painted over. Who said that?' Rachel made a note and then Miss Simkiss said, 'Rub it out, Shelley. Rub it out.' Maybe Miss Simkiss has mental glaucoma.

Got B+ for my Toad in the Hole today. Wearing my plimsolls in school.

**

Truth is a jewel which should not be painted over …

Nine o'clock. Beefy Brenda Baker rings the hand bell. Brenda isn't quite as beefy as you, Jayne, but both she and Patricia are tall and hefty in the upper body. Brenda sees her bell as power and she frequently says, *Oh, shut your gob.* She just as frequently opens hers. She has a Veronica Lake fringe which flops over the right side of her face, so we speak only to the left eye.

Girls whisper in clutches. Whispers rise. There's jittery Miss Simkiss wearing what Rachel calls her ubiquitous white lab coat and the cherished long fingernails which claw the register, tut tutting as she retrieves her red chiffon scarf from Charlie's neck. 'Who put my scarf on the skeleton?' She looks over her horn-rimmed spectacles, a pre-requisite for post-war trained teachers. We repeat, 'Good morning,' after her and Patricia rips open a bag of peanuts, spilling them. Miss Simkiss pretends not to notice. 'Form Notices. Toad in the Hole in Domestic Science this Friday. Please do not forget your ingredients: sausages, flour and eggs.'

The girls rummage in bags and tread peanuts into the Biology lab floor. Miss Simkiss continues with her unheard monologue, 'Please avoid using the school lavatories whilst Mr Brody and his workmen are engaged and Jayne …'

Miss Simkiss's voice dips on your name. She pauses. Quiet. More quiet. You could hear a peanut drop. 'Jayne, *why* did you not have your swimming costume in PE on Friday?'

Quiet again. Miss Simkiss examines you over her horn-rimmed spectacles. We examine your reaction. You examine the peanuts on the Biology lab floor and keep check, check, checking your watch. I want to say, 'They don't play the same game twice,' but I don't. We have played this scene out though many times before with gloating satisfaction. Your National Health spectacles will very shortly steam up and blind you giving you physical glaucoma. Miss Simkiss breaks her self-induced silence. 'As usual, do you have nothing to say for yourself, Jayne?' And then Miss Simkiss waits, pushes up her horn-rimmed spectacles and folds her white, lab-coated arms. Picking on a sticky, white nit like Jayne Thornhill is one way of bringing the attention to herself because Domestic Science ingredients are important: I've seen Miss Love (who is far from it), the buxom Domestic Science teacher berating Miss Simkiss in the corridor for forgotten ingredients.

'I forgot, Miss.' You lisp on the 's' and never use Miss Simkiss's surname. You never offer excuses now because Miss Simkiss always says, 'Excuses, excuses, you can't ride on excuses, Jayne Thornhill.'

'Forgot? Forgot?' Miss Simkiss is saying, 'Astonishing. Astonishing, Jayne Thornhill. We soon forget what we have not thought deeply about.'

You see, you can't win: you can't give an excuse and you must not forget and now Miss Simkiss is off on her personal mission to truth. 'Who said that?'

'Proust, Miss Simkiss.'

'Yes, yes, well done, Rachel Sherman. *Remembrance of*

Things Past. Straight line for Oxford. I'll process you a commendation, Rachel, and you a detention Jayne Thornhill for forgetting everything you shouldn't. Rachel Sherman and Shelley Witherington, you are my head and Jayne Thornhill, you are my tail,' she says pointing one way door for a head and one way window for a tail suspending you, Jayne, somewhere above the playground. Rachel looks at me with dark eyes and eyelashes that need no spit on the mascara block and sighs with remorse. Rachel has said that Miss Simkiss is divisive, elitist and wins us no friends which is true because Patricia yawns and gives one of those inclusive winks to Mave and Brenda. Sometimes Miss Simkiss makes us form a line as to where she places us academically. Rachel's the brightest of us all. But Miss Simkiss never ever places Rachel first in the line which I don't think is fair. Rachel's not keen on Miss Simkiss. And I don't think Miss Simkiss is that keen on Rachel as she says Rachel is too big for her boots. Rachel started off the new school year in September by berating (that's Rachel's word) Miss Simkiss for giving us plot allotments in the autumn. Rachel wanted to plant soft herbs – marjoram – in the spring but Miss Simkiss said O-levels would be on us all by then and we'd just have to make do. Rachel said Miss Simkiss liked things tidy but messes things up.

'Look at the state of my Biology lab. Patricia, pick up those peanuts you have just spilled.' Miss Simkiss does not make eye contact with Patricia. Only Rachel does that. Rachel's mind is highly developed but her body has a lot of catching up to do. Her family discuss politics and Yassir Arafat at the tea table, whereas all we do is listen to Paul complain about A-level workloads and how Mum's car is running. Rachel isn't allowed out on Friday nights.

I think I hear Patricia whisper under her breath that she is not a Monkee and beefy Brenda Baker with the Veronica Lake fringe and Mavis O'Leary with black curls which bounce stoop quickly to sweep up the peanuts. Patricia is definitely the organ grinder.

'Ingredients for Toad in the Hole next Friday,' Miss Simkiss says to her Nulon hand cream 'and leave my Biology lab tidy.'

You crumple on Miss Simkiss's exit because now, you know, it will begin. *'J – A – Y – N – E.'* Spelling out your name with letters and shouting the letter Y. *'Why a 'y' Jayne, why always a 'y' Jayne? Why is there always a 'y' in your name, Jayne?'* The whole class rushes out of the Biology lab in snorts of laughter, even Mave O'Leary who pretends to be nice at times. Rachel quotes Shakespeare, as she does, 'Lilies that fester smell far worse than weeds' and that Mave will frequently *volte-face* to suit her own ends. I asked Rachel what that meant and she said a complete turnaround: often to cover one's own back. Where does Rachel get all this information? Mave is probably Patricia's most underhand agent. Miss Simkiss had better watch her red chiffon scarf or Mave will permanently remove it.

My mother bought you a scarf, Jayne, on your twelfth birthday: the birthday party that nobody turned up to but Rachel, Tamsin Goody Goody Two Shoes Prew and me. The birthday party your mum made a really special effort for, with a Victoria sponge chocolate cake because she had just told you that you were adopted that week, because twelve was a good age to know. Your mother bashed tambourines and sang hymns in the street and we wondered if this was why you were so strange or if it was because you were told you were adopted at the age of twelve. Anyway, a week later

Mave had the scarf my mother bought for you and Rachel accused her of theft because we recognised the beautiful red and white silk. But you said, 'No. Mave liked it and so I gave it to her.'

I never liked you much after that.

And then some time after that you arrived in school in new, black patent shoes and got told off because, as Rachel said, patent is 'verboten'. You had new pencil cases and new pens that you gave away. Your mother had attempted to put your hair in romantic ringlets and everybody laughed but when they wanted your new hair slides you gave them away too. It was months later that I heard my dad talking about your dad and saying this was all the result of something called 'compensation'. My dad knew the firm of builders your dad worked for before your dad was killed. I heard my dad saying that your dad was a good builder, a good man and 'good living'. The family never touched a drop. Left the C of E and joined the Sally Army years before.

But right now you linger so that you can receive some verbal support from Rachel and me. I do want to tell you that it's not worth thinking too deeply about swimming costumes. You say, '*Why* when you're form prefect, Shelley, don't you tell Miss Simkiss what Patricia is doing at lunchtimes?' You lisp away.

I can see why your *whys* get on the girls' nerves and why they are always saying *why, why, why* back to you. You stand with heaving and fretful bosoms, a lower lip quivering and your stringy amber hair, which brushed, never looks as though it has been. What is it about that hair? I want to tell you that I try but I don't like to be seen talking to you too much because then it will just make my job of being form prefect that much harder. As Brenda rings the hand bell for

144

assembly, I'm feeling jittery about standing alone in the lab with you, with you and my best friend Rachel. I do say, 'Do you want me to tell Miss Simkiss about what they do to you after PE or how they let the stick insects out of the tanks?'

There's this pause where you check your feet, then check your watch and Rachel says, 'Jayne, Patricia Vickers is a twisted psychopath who wants to stalk through everyone's story. She's a parasite, so don't keep playing welcome host to her.'

Of course I know what you mean, Jayne, because I know what they do at lunchtimes but they lock the doors and it's hard to prove. And I don't mean the strip poker in the lavatories. We sense a noise at the door but perhaps it's just Charlie's bones tinkling in the wind from an open window. But I don't know what Rachel means by psychopaths or 'playing welcome host', so I know you don't, Jayne. You bite your lower lip like you do and speak in the hushed whisper because the walls always have big ears and you say, 'No. About the other things, when they lock the doors and ...'

Rachel places her nose in the air and sniffs. You and I, Jayne, can smell it too. It's rosewater. But Rachel says the sweet and sickly smell of vanilla is mixed in the hues somewhere. It's Patricia's domineering scent, probably applied to disguise a recent aroma of Players No.6. We turn and she is there bulking out at the Biology lab door; even Charlie's bones jitter. It's rare to see Patricia on her own. She moves in packs. She stands outside doors and waits and listens. I've caught her doing it. She speaks. 'What will you do next week, when you have to remember your swimming costume, Jayne?' Patricia simply asks the question and waits, hovering momentarily like some dangerous wasp. Did she hear what Rachel said about parasites, for her eyes skirt

Rachel who bubbles beneath her striped school tie and says to Patricia, suddenly, 'Boo. Be gone.'

Patricia smiles and Patricia is gone. But not before screwing up her eyes and saying to you, 'Got the time of day, Jayne?'

And as you check your watch, Rachel says, still bubbling at the knot of her school tie, 'One of the problems with Patricia is that she is never *seen* to be doing anything malicious.'

I'm about to ask Rachel what 'malicious' means when I see your knees begin to shake, Jayne. You bite your lip. You know, Jayne, what lies ahead. They nick your swimming costume, they rip away your towel and they make you stand naked in the PE changing rooms. Then we can't help inspecting your sloppy stomach which masks the tufts beneath. Brenda Baker says she wants to search your hair for sticky, white nits and then you know you will lose marmalade tufts from your scalp. Mave O'Leary never goes for the scalp as she is protecting nurtured fingernails. Sickofantic, Rachel calls them.

You turn on your heel and beneath your heels, as you walk out of the Biology lab door, those white ankle socks slip uncomfortably. You will now dread the swimming lesson one week ahead.

**

Monday 10th February 1969

Tricky Vicky (Patricia Vickers) set up this really clever game today. Rachel and me walked into the Biology lab and Jayne Thornhill was sitting in the middle of a circle of girls next to

146

a Bunsen burner. Jayne was asking questions like: 'Will I have two children?' to which all the girls laughed and shouted together 'No!' Then Jayne asked, 'Will I have one?' To which all the girls shouted, 'Yes!' and then they laughed. Jayne asked, 'Will my husband be ugly?' and then they sniggered and said, 'Sort of ...' ha ha, snorting down their noses. Then Jayne asked, 'Will childbirth be painful for me?' and they all screamed, 'Yes!' Jayne couldn't work out how they all knew this story about her and how they could all answer together 'yes' or 'no' and especially when she asked another question, 'Will I be happy when I marry?' and they all went 'Well, we're not sure. Maybe!!' I watched Tricky Vicky Patricia Vickers and she didn't join in. She just sat on a stool by the stick insects and watched before she then said, 'Why don't you ask if Danny Diego loves you, Jayne?' Jayne said she didn't want to ask but Patricia said, 'Go on, Jayne. We know the story.' So Jayne said, 'Does Danny Diego love me?' And everyone screamed, 'Yes! Yes! Yes!'

I hated this game. Jayne cried before she went off to detention because she knows Danny doesn't love her and the girls were just taking the mick. It wasn't till we were on the way home and Rachel said, 'I've found it.' I said, 'You mean you found your papers?' She said, 'No. If Jayne asked a question ending in a consonant then everyone shouted 'No' together. If she asked a question ending in a vowel they shouted, 'Yes'. If her question ended in a semi-vowel which is a 'y' then they said they weren't sure.'

How can Rachel be so clever and why, why, why is Jayne Thornhill SO stupid.

PS Got my period.

**

The Loft

Periods. How much I had wanted them in 1969 and how little had I wanted them once I left school. I bathed my ankle with an old piece of rag. I would go to the doctor with this ankle except I had one coming home at some point. Hopefully not for a few hours. My mobile phone flashed up three-forty pm. Still time but so much blood. I wasn't going to read on until I saw the next entry was the frogs …

21

Miss Simkiss has been promising the sex lives of the amazing, adaptable frogs for weeks. We have been waiting to observe her hot flush when she embarks upon this particular part of the syllabus. I am watching Rachel's bowed neck taking notes, whilst I methodically take a needle of a compass to the Biology lab work bench. Rachel's black ponytail bunches at the nape of her neck, wisps of curls gather at the apex of her spine. I can recreate the hairs on her neck. Rachel is fixed on her notes for Rachel is going to be a gynaecologist. Not a teacher or a typist or a secretary but a gynaecologist and she's going to Oxford to read Medicine like Danny Diego and maybe she will marry Benji who will be a dentist. Benji Jacobs loves Rachel's perfect teeth. Rachel's parents love Benji Jacobs. Only Rachel's not sure about marriage because she will see the world, walk the wall of China, strip naked at Greenham Common, censor Mary Whitehouse and lay flowers at Aberfan. Benji Jacobs has other plans for Rachel.

I am now halfway through digging deeply into the letter 'L'. Because I DO LOVE ...

Benji, unlike Rachel, has the kind of mouth and smile which wants to please people. Rachel is not bothered about pleasing but she smiles. And Benji looks after his teeth so he has an even-toothed smile which matches his fair temperament. Benji is fair in all senses of the word: too fair and light-eyed for a Jewish boy. I'm gritting my own teeth as I dig into the surface of the wood, looking upward at the red chiffon scarf, so that Miss Simkiss does not notice I am finding the 'V' particularly hard going.

Benji nags Danny and me when we buy red liquorice and sherbet to gnaw at, on top of the 366 bus. 'Sticky problems,' Benji says. 'That constant sherbet sucking will create a sticky film of bacteria and that plaque will produce acids,' Benji says, who is going to study Dentistry at King's, London – he has it all lined up – 'which will attack tooth enamel and when the tooth enamel breaks down, a cavity will form and you could be toothless by the time you're fifty.'

That seems far off. Danny says Benji could get pissed on a wine gum if he ever ate one and one of Danny's ambitions is to get Benji drunk on more than a wine gum. Rachel is trying to concentrate but she is not happy. There I am, scraping away at Danny's 'D' with the compass needle. Miss Simkiss is telling us, 'to visit a pond on a spring night and hear the courtship chorus of croaks, twitters, chirps and trills.' This is unlikely.

The girls' eyes drift from Miss Simkiss's white lab coat and red chiffon scarf to the windows of the Biology lab, where, on this seasonably freezing February morning, Brody's two assistants are painting window frames. They are also screaming out buttercups to 'Build Me Up Buttercup, Baby' on full volume from their transistor radio and Rachel twitches with irritation because we have O-levels in a few months. She doesn't need to cover The Tooth because Benji has given her his notes from two years ago.

Miss Simkiss is telling us that frogs are formidable musicians. The painters scream out the lyrics. 'And,' Miss Simkiss says, 'it is generally the male frogs who serenade.

Frogs make their calls with the help of one or two pouches of skin called vocal sacs. Sound is produced when air rushes over the vocal cords on its way from the lungs to the vocal sacs.' Miss Simkiss demonstrates air rushing over the vocal cords with hands and white overall arms which swish. 'Some frogs call so loudly that they can be heard miles away,' she says.

We are fixed to the broad shoulders, the glisten of the taut skin on their forearms, a throb beating through our limbs and other places. I have almost abandoned the two 'N's I am about to engrave: always capitals.

'And with any luck the females are listening,' Miss Simkiss drones on and applies some more Nulon hand cream which Rachel says she does to protect her frog-dissecting hands. All but Rachel listen to buttercups being built up rather than the frogs' sex cycle, for Dave is dark and curly with cheeky freckles and Steve is tall and willowy and moody and they bristle with male hormones and tasty testosterone. I don't actually think Rachel has started her periods yet. Jayne tries to tell the PE mistress she has one three weeks out of four, on a Friday, to get out of swimming. Jayne says it so many times, one week she had to swim even when she did have the curse. Which is one of the reasons she disappears in sports lessons now. Unfortunately Miss Simkiss has Jayne tracked for swimming.

DANNY DIEGO – which are the forever engraved capitals I am aiming for – is my brother Paul's friend and we've been going out for thirteen weeks and four days. Ever since I played Bianca in the boys' school production of *Othello* and Danny played Cassio and I had to give him Desdemona's white handkerchief. We all wet ourselves at the end of the play when Desdemona is murdered through jealousy and throws herself backward, tragically dangling her head and long hair at the end of the bed. Lodovico had to say, 'O bloody period'. Officially Bianca wasn't supposed to be on stage at the end but there had been problems with chatting in the wings – so even dead people got resurrected and the whole cast congregated around Desdemona's death bed and her dangling head in the finale. Danny told me he played Cassio so that he could put it on his UCCA form and application to read Medicine at Cambridge and I am thinking this as I am well into carving his surname on the Biology lab slab of my heart.

Dad told my brother Paul he should have done the same and Paul asked how playing Cassio was going to help Danny Diego cultivate a bedside manner and I smiled and thought about the possibilities of having sex with Danny Diego. Danny has said that adolescent boys, 'have sex, I mean *think* about sex', he said, so many times a minute but I can't remember how many times he's said. I think about 'it' frequently and wonder how many more times a minute adolescent boys can think about 'it' than I do.

Mum said it was a shame there were no black boys in the sixth form to play Othello the Moor and Dad said, 'Wait a few years and they'll be down here and living next door and you won't be so happy with the slump in your house value.' Dad thinks about the value of house properties a lot. He's thinking of quitting the Law and taking up the property business full-time. I've almost finished registering my love for Danny Diego forever.

Miss Simkiss is now covering frogs' ears and Rachel is bent upon her notebook. I add some 'X's. Mave is applying a top coat. There has been some serious nail painting going on. Brenda of the Bell Ringing and Film Star Veronica Lake

Fame is sticking her tongue out at Dave to let us know she has a special place.

'Frogs' ears called tympana are very small and difficult to see but frogs' ears are tuned to hear the calls of their own species. The similarity of their vocal calls helps the females identify and locate the male of the species.'

I can hardly hear what she is saying, the transistor radio is so loud. '*Be dum be dum be dum ...*' Miss Simkiss has to raise her voice. 'No small feat in a noisy pond packed with all kinds of frogs and toads singing their heart out.'

The transistor radio sings out about not calling when you say you will.

Danny has not called all week.

Miss Simkiss eventually gets on to what we have been waiting for all week: the culmination. The culmination of this clamour is known as amplexus: when the male climbs on the female's back.

Perhaps Danny has not called because I told him on Boxing Day that, 'I want to wait'. I feel as though I am spending my life waiting. My mother says it's best to wait. 'Wait,' she says. 'Make them wait because it will be better for everyone in the long run.' What's 'it' and who's 'everyone' and what 'long run'? I'm already sixteen sitting with my September birthday so it would all be legal, wouldn't it, Danny says. Three kisses – finished.

We have been waiting for Miss Simkiss to reach the culmination, of which she has faithfully promised, not because we don't know about frogs having it away but because we like to watch our form teacher blush. All the teachers are going through the change.

**

153

I am.

After it all happened in spring 1969, I didn't feel like culminating anything at all. In fact, I went right off everything. Mum tried to get me to eat, but I just wanted to disappear. My periods stopped abruptly but I didn't regret their absence. I welcomed my ovulation cycle disappearing. I wanted everything to disappear. It was hard when they made me head girl. Mum was delighted. I wasn't. She said, 'Anyone would give their eye teeth to be standing in your shoes.'

But my shoes never seemed to fit.

What is memorable about this Biology lesson is not the sex life of frogs, or the Buttercup accompaniment by Dave and Steve. It is the fact that I have noted in my diary, not that frogs' ears are called tympana, but that neither Patricia nor Jayne are present. And towards the end of the lesson, when we reach the culmination, Patricia enters on a cloud of rosewater and vanilla. Like Miss Simkiss, Patricia looks slightly flushed, albeit for similar reasons, I'm sure: the former by 'culmination' theory and proxy and the latter by doing the practical. On proximity, Patricia smells a little different … aftershave. She gives Mave and Brenda one of her special winks and looks out through the Biology lab windows. So do I.

From the Biology lab one can get a very good view of the patches of land which have been assigned to our care this fifth year and the senior toilets. You frequently escape to both venues, Jayne. I know. I'm a prefect. I'm sent to sniff out

154

inconsistencies. What we can see is Brody telling his employees: Steve and Dave, to keep their noise down and move on. Brody is older than his two employees. He's probably in his early twenties. He's everything his name suggests: broad and brave and attractive in an animalistic, craggy kind of way. When he lifts one eyebrow and gives a small grin, he knows it pleases girls, makes them feel special. He also knows he is now being watched by thirty fifteen-year-olds. He looks into the Biology lab and exchanges a quick, sideways glance with Patricia who winks at him once again.

Then you enter the Biology lab, Jayne.

Immediately Miss Simkiss, who has pretended not to see Patricia enter the lab, pounces upon you. 'Where have you been, Jayne? Why have you not been in my lesson?'

'I've been to the toilet.' You bite your lip, then check your watch which has now become a nervous habit. It's as if you're telling the world that you are diligent about time. As soon as you say this though, I know at once that you know you shouldn't have said that because I see you lift your eyebrows to the lab ceiling as though you wished you could take those words back. Patricia looks at you, Jayne, and I feel both breaths quicken. Patricia will not take her eyes from you. I bet you wished you could have taken those words back, Jayne, because whatever happened, Patricia certainly made you pay torture after that. What happened in the senior bogs that Biology lesson?

'*Lavatory,* Jayne, *lavatory*,' Miss Simkiss says. 'Eggs and tadpoles next week.'

As she packs away her exercise books, I see Rachel brush away a tear. I look at her with a question mark and she mouths, 'My papers.'

**

The Loft

I wished we could return to the previous September when we started that fifth form academic year: new slide rules, erasers and when the hockey touch lines had been freshly painted. All those Daddy Long Legs climbing the walls after the wet summer. My thoughts turned back to the beginning of that year because, even though I didn't realize it on this snowy, lofty lunchtime in 2005, that discussion we had as a family just before Paul turned eighteen was ultimately important. The torchlight searched out that 1968 black-and-white checked diary.

22

Sometime the previous September 1968 I think, and around my 16th birthday …

It was September: the beginning of that academic school year and it was Dad who told me to plant the tree. I remember when Dad suggested it as the following day Paul was about to become eighteen but we weren't celebrating in a big way as eighteenths were just edging in about that time. 'They're making us grow things on a plot of land behind the toilets,' I said.

Paul said, 'What do you mean, they're making you 'grow things?' Speak in proper sentences.' He was jiggling his fingers like he always did when he was waiting for food or lying.

'I was trying to say,' I said, 'that they want us to have fresh air …'

'Who wants you to have fresh air?' Paul said, seeming dismayed by the shepherd's pie that Friday evening. I had made the pie in Domestic Science during the day.

'The school,' I said. 'Everyone has a small plot of land and I'm always at the end because I'm a W and we have to grow things. But I have to go on playground duty in the breaks as I'm form prefect and I'm playing Bianca in the boys' school play, so when will I get time to grow things?'

The other girls had already started planting that autumn. Rachel was both diligent and beautiful as she knelt at her patch of herbs. 'Rachel said that herbs not only provide flavour to food,' I told my family, 'but they can have medicinal purposes and they are healing agents. The Neantherthals used herbs for ailments sixty-thousand years ago and Rachel also said that the Swedish word 'druug' means dried plant. You can get morphine from the poppy.'

'You want to make sure she's not growing cannabis,' Paul said. 'What have you put in this shepherd's pie?'

'Shush,' my mother said.

'What's the fat girl growing?' he asked.

'Purple-sprouting broccoli,' I said and he snorted with laughter.

Quite strangely, I saw Patricia kneeling beside you and you both talking. I had always thought this was odd, that in the still, autumnal air you both knelt side by side, whispering, and I saw you pointing, as if offering up advice. Everyone was planting whilst I was being given handkerchiefs in the boys' school production of *Othello* and losing them because that's all that Bianca did in the play.

'Benji Jacobs is going out with your friend Rachel, isn't he?' Paul says but doesn't ask. He carries on. 'Benji Jacobs would get pissed on a wine gum.'

'Benji doesn't eat sweets,' I said. 'He's going to be a dentist.'

Paul looked across the table at me and in a stage whisper said, 'God, you are naïve.' Then in a louder voice he said, 'Well, Danny and I plan to get Benji pissed on a lot more.'

Dad sighed deeply and pushed his chair back from the table and said, 'Paul. Please.'

Paul then said, 'Well please, Dad, what about me getting the second car for my eighteenth birthday?' and Mum said, 'No. When you're twenty-one. It's my car.'

'You can't drive,' Paul said.

'Neither can you, yet,' Mum said.

'But you never will,' Paul said.

There was one of those long, awkward silences where people breathe very deeply and Dad was doing a lot of deep breathing on this meal and he said, 'Plant a tree.'

'Can I?' I said.

Dad said, 'It will be there forever, but you'll need to dig deep and plant well. A weeping willow or a silver birch?'

'If you didn't give so many donations to the girls' school, we could afford three cars,' Paul said.

Dad lifted one of his dark, heavy eyebrows but continued to look at me when he said softly, 'Education, education, education.'

Education was important, I knew.

'There's a weeping willow in front of the school by the entrance. It's in front of Miss Harefield-Mott's office. I like it,' I said. 'But our allotments are not big enough for that. Is there a smaller willow I can plant?'

'What do you think, Dad?' Paul said getting back to his topic of conversation. 'Can I have the car for my eighteenth?'

Dad sighed again and looked at Mum. 'Gwen,' he said. 'Paul will be taking his driving test next week. You always make some excuse to avoid your driving lessons. It makes sense to give Paul the car for his eighteenth tomorrow. But no drinking and driving, Paul.'

As far as Paul was concerned that was a given. He shouted, 'Yes! Yes! Yes!' and then said the shepherd's pie tasted of sick. Mum burst into tears. I don't know why. It was me who had cooked it. And then finally Dad said, 'It's Neanderthal, Shelley. Neanderthal,' sighing again with a spot of despair.

**

The Loft

I was about as stupid as those Daddy Long Legs, Jayne. The landline was ringing again. Perhaps I should have gone down and told Greg to stop phoning because Danny would be in soon and he hated Greg phoning me about work issues. Danny always said enough of our marriage was taken up with political phone calls which made most of the money so I should keep Tree Project and student issues firmly in college situ. Maybe I should have gone and got some black bin bags and just dumped the lot that afternoon but I checked my mobile phone. Now four-thirty. I had been up in this loft for two hours. I picked up the red mottled 1969 diary again. I couldn't help myself.

**

Tuesday 11th February 1969

I was on playground duty in this freezing weather when I heard Miss Harefield-Mott asking Mr Brody, 'How long do you think it is going to take you and your young men to complete this job?' She was in her big muffle coat standing outside the lavatories.

They've been around the school since before Christmas. Mr Brody blew through his teeth and said, 'It's hard to say.

There's still the stripping, and re-plastering to do, you see.
You gotta let the re-plastering dry before you re-paint it – or
whatever you want to do with it. And we've been filling in the
cracks where it's been re-plastered once it's dried 'cos of the
shrinkage.'

Then Dave, the funny one with the dark, curly hair and
eyebrows which are low over his lids, said, 'Oh yeah, you've
gotta be very careful of the shrinkage. That could be very
nasty.' Then Brody – they call him Brody – said, 'You've
asked us to do all the woodwork and that's gotta be rubbed
down and filled up.' And Dave said, 'Yeah – lots of rubbing
down and filling up.'

'If you want the woodwork to look good and I assume you
do, ma'am?' Brody said.

'Indeed,' Miss Harefield-Mott said.

'Then all your cracks have gotta be filled up and rubbed
down nicely. You can't just tosh a coat over it and hope it's
going to look good 'cos it won't,' Brody said.

Then Miss Harefield-Mott said she was having a slight
problem with the back alley, the changing room and the
showers. Dave and Steve sniggered very rudely and one of
them said something about rubbish being left up the back
alley. Brody said was it the same problem as the girls' bogs
and then Dave farted. You should have seen Miss Harefield-
Mott's face. 'Lavatories,' she said. 'Lavatories.' She asked
Brody to 'erase all the graffiti from the walls in the toilets
and the back alley, the gym changing room and the showers
because it's hard to identify culprits' and then he said,
'We've spent weeks washing off what those girls put on those
walls.' And Dave said, 'Language I've never fucking heard
before!'

Miss Harefield-Mott looked as though she'd just eaten

161

shark shit and when Brody said he'd got to submit a new quote, ''Cos it's got to be sealed or it'll bleed through,' she twitched uncontrollably, her nose moving up and down in beat with the corners of her mouth. And then Miss Harefield-Mott talked about how we were a poor school and, 'Will you do your bit for education and could your young men be a bit more discreet as this is a High School and not a brothel?' As Miss Harefield-Mott left one end of the toilets, I quickly scarpered out of the other end and I heard the boys laughing and then Brenda, Mave and Patricia burst out of the lavatory doors and Steve shouted, 'Skeletons in the cupboard. We're doing our bit for education.'

So is Dad. He's always making donations to the school.

Remember ingredients for jam tarts on Valentine's Day!!!!!!xxxxxxx. Read 'Jackie' in Music today and checked my willow. It's not doing much.

**

When you walk in for afternoon registration, I know you have escaped the lunchtime 'activities' because your hands are covered in soil and you've been tending your vegetables. Your white ankle socks are stained with mud. You see the chalked writing on the blackboard and run to your schoolbag. It's gone – you realize that your diary has gone and that everyone is looking at you. You look around, especially at Mave to see if you can find it and retrieve it, but everyone is smiling at the blackboard. Then your hands, a smear of soil and blue ink, because we've watched you try to fill your fountain pen in French this morning, go to your big, round eyes and you end up looking like some caged and foreign bird.

162

One of your big weaknesses is that you cry.

It doesn't matter if the words on the board are yours or not. The game has begun and it begins with Brenda Baker who tells everyone to *shut their gob* and then she retrieves your blue leather-bound diary from her school bag. Pushing her lop of fringe back from her right eye, she reads in a mockingly sing-song voice and adds a lisp in too, which unfortunately for Jayne, Brenda does only too well,

'You find them everywhere
The crowd of slags
Who stand in the corner
And smoke their fags.
As soon as you enter
You know them by sight
They screw you for a while
Because you're supposed to be tight.
Leather jackets, cropped hair
And black rings round their eyes
Go ahead, chew your gum
And flirt with the boys.
But stop for a moment
Come out of your crowd
The music's stopped playing
Do you feel proud
Of what you are now?
Now you can't hide under
Make-up and smoke and music and crowds
Now you're like us.

Oh yes, sorry light up another fag
You see I forgot you are only a slag.'

Big mistake this.

Then Patricia says calmly, 'Jayne, is that what you think
of us?' She looks around at the rest of her group, smiles and
gives a wink like, 'This is going to be fun.'

Actually, I'm thinking your poem is rather good but it is
not going to politically please the likes of Brenda Baker,
Mave O'Leary or Patricia Vickers who never were virgins in
the first place. Neither those satellite girls like Sharon
Newman nor Linda Leech, who have lost their virginity
literally in very public ways. Tamsin Prew doesn't mind at
all and later Rachel says she's impressed with the quality of
this writing but it needed a break in the stanza after the word
'boys'.

But this, of course, is only the beginning. You know this
as your hot tears mist over the lenses of your National Health
spectacles. With a sharp weapon like your diary (and how
foolish could you be to bring it into school, Jayne?), there
will be much worse to follow. And that way lies your torture.

**

Patricia threw a bottle of blue ink at Miss Minster: the weak-
jawed Miss Minster who twitched with only one side of her
face whilst Miss Harefield-Mott did it with both. Miss
Minster turned her back to move to the piano, didn't she? On
Miss Minster's return to school in a clean new dress, her
bottom lip had quivered in an effort to maintain some dignity.
Your sad, ink-stained eyes had reminded me of Miss

Minster's blue-blotched and hunched paisley-patterned back the next time they chanted words from your diary. For now it was not only Patricia, Brenda and Mave who are enjoying your diary, because after your 'Crowd of Slags' poem they have Sharon Newman and Linda Leech on their side and all five girls whine your next poem. They are leaning over Brenda Baker's shoulders and sniggering and whining and shouting these words.

'To laugh, to dream, to think or cry
To float away and somewhere die.
I'm not at school, I'm not at home
I'm in a world which is all my own.

The girls around just talk and talk
But I'm on a boat and the seagulls squawk.
Or else I'm somewhere where no one can find me
Thinking happily, sadly, of Danny maybe.

To return again, to learn again
I hear in the distance someone calling my name.
Amidst my thoughts amidst my tears
I love someone who doesn't know I exist.'

Rachel doesn't think this poem is quite so good and I don't like Danny being involved. After all, he's *my* boyfriend. And there are big laughs when his name is mentioned. Patricia remains silent but we feel that she is orchestrating because Rachel says later when we're checking the hockey team list, 'She's orchestrating because she caught your eye in the penultimate stanza.' I don't know what these two last words mean and I'm too tired of it all to ask Rachel and then off we go to Music.

Miss Minster had only been trying to teach us 'Dear Lord and Father of Mankind, Forgive Our Foolish Ways'. But it was blood, of course, that Patricia had been after.

**

The Loft

The blood on my ankle is now congealing. How many more pages before I reach the darkest part?

23

Wednesday 12th February 1969

Patricia did something really awful today to Jayne. It's so disgusting I can't bring myself to write about it. It's to do with the pages of Jayne's diary.

'You're such a baby, Jayne. Why a 'y' Jayne, why is there always a 'y' in your name, baby Jayne? Baby Jayne. Baby Jayne.' Then Patricia and her ites sing 'Baby Jayne'. Then Patricia did something really disgusting. I can't bear to even write about it but this is what happened. Patricia said that the information in Jayne's diary would rock the top of the 366 bus. Slug, she keeps calling Jayne 'slug'. This was when we were waiting for Miss Simkiss to turn up for Biology.

'Oh, no, Patricia. Please don't read it out on the bus. Not in front of Danny, Patricia, please.' Jayne cried yet again!!!

Then Patricia starts reading from the diary. 'Perhaps one of the things I have a lot of is HOPE.' *Patricia emphasises the word 'hope'.* 'HOPE' *Patricia says each time,* 'HOPE. I *hope* things are going to change for the better soon. I *hope* I'm going to get a boyfriend. Maybe Danny!!! I *hope* I will see him at the bus stop. I *hope* he will one day like me. I *hope* he is going to one day ask me out. Without *hope*, I can't live.'

Then Patricia says, 'That's a whole crap full of HOPE, Jayne. The thing I cannot understand, slug, is why you bring this bird's crap into school. Why can you not learn? Why, why, why, Jayne?'

Jayne asked Patricia why she was doing it to her.

'Why, why, why? Why always a why, Jayne? Why always a why?'

Jayne said she would do anything. 'Anything for you, Patricia. Anything. If you give me my diary back. Please.' Lisping away.

Then Patricia starts reading or singing from Jayne's diary, 'Danny, you are everything I have ever wanted in a boy and I long to feel your tongue in my ear.

'Shall I carry on, slug?' Patricia says. 'Dear Danny, I think you are the only person I can really talk to. I know I have not actually spoken to you but I can tell in your walnut-whip eyes ...'

And then everyone laughs at 'walnut-whip eyes' with Brenda Baker saying, 'Oh, my God this is such a gas and shut your gob whilst we listen to this, Linda Leech. Carry on Patricia ...'

Patricia winks at her sickofants and goes on, 'that you are the kind of person who really cares and would really listen to me if I were to talk to you. Last night, I could see on the top of the 366 bus that you thought that slag Patricia Vickers was really stupid ...'

And then everyone apart from Rachel and me, because we think Patricia really is stupid, goes, 'Oh ...' in a big kind of a loop.

'The way she sings everything she wants to say. She really gets on your nerves, trying to get your attention, whilst I just sit and write my diary – all about you. Why do you always sit next to Shelley Witherington on the bus going home? Let me wrap you in my warm and tender love – Danny Diego – from Jayne Thornhill.'

Then everyone is looking at me because of my Danny and Jayne is crying and wiping her spectacles on her school skirt, saying she will do anything for Patricia if she doesn't read her diary in front of Danny and then Patricia starts singing, 'I would do anything for you dear, anything.' And Jayne is asking Patricia not to broadcast this and Patricia is saying that she is the BBC and then Patricia stops singing and says, 'Beg.'

'What?' Jayne says.

'Beg,' Patricia says.

And Jayne asks, 'How?' and Patricia says, 'On your knees, slug.'

And Jayne does.

And it's then that Patricia brings out the baby's dummy.

Why does Patricia do this to Jayne?

PS. PAUL HAS SOLD HIS CAR DAD GAVE HIM FOR HIS EIGHTEENTH BIRTHDAY LAST SEPTEMBER!!! THIS MEANS I CAN TRAVEL HOME ON THE BUS AND DANNY CAN STAY ON AN EXTRA STOP AND WALK ME HOME EVERY NIGHT AS USUAL.!!! YES! YES! YES!

**

Thursday 13ᵗʰ February 1969

'Suck on it and I will give you one of your pages. If I have any more pages left by the time Danny boy is on top of the bus, I will not be able to resist reading your compositions.'

Jayne was desperate. She's desperate to get back the pages so that Danny will never know. So she did it. She sucked on Patricia's pink dummy rather than have her writing read to Danny on top of the 366 bus.

Jayne is begging Patricia to let her suck the dummy so she can get her pages back. She looks so stupid and pathetic. Every time Jayne sucks on the dummy, all the girls laugh and then Patricia tears out a page and returns it to her 'baby slug' but not before passing it around ...

'I'm just beginning to taste life and it is tasting bitter because we all have our own problems and they are problems we cannot share with our parents. I do not know when I stopped being a child and perhaps I'll never realize when I become an adult. I just know I'm in the 'in-between' stage. This time is so very hard and it depends which way I take it now that will determine my whole future. I cannot cry hard now because my tears are written down on the paper. Tears are only sad thoughts being let out and I am letting my sad thoughts out on paper. I write everything down so when I am older and have children of my own, I do not forget how to think as an adolescent and how adolescents feel.

I feel like I want to cry
Or die
Or just do something
Besides nothing
I want to dream
And float away
On a cloud
That carries me nowhere.
Depressed
My head on the bed
Pale blue sky
Turns a darker shade,
Slowly.
Alone
Face cupped in hands
Hearing buses and cars
Birds singing
Monotonously
Thinking
Of everything
Nothing or anything
Heavy feeling inside of me,
Depressing.'

I told Miss Simkiss today that I wanted to resign as being form prefect as I no longer wanted to be an elected representative of authority. Miss Simkiss's eyes fluttered across to Charlie and then to the stick insects. She took out her Nulon hand cream and said, 'I'm sorry, Dolly but I believed you had your heart set on being head gel in two years' time when you reach Upper Sixth. Being form prefect can only stand you in good stead for the future. You're being groomed.'

I didn't know that.

Then Miss Simkiss says, 'Being head gel can be very nice to say when you are filling in forms.'

I told her to let Rachel have a chance at being form prefect. I did it last term and Miss Simkiss said that was pointless because Rachel Sherman could never be head gel as she was Jewish and couldn't attend our religious assemblies so only C of E gels could be head gel. I said that Patricia let the stick insects out of their tank and she said, 'Tell-tale.' Her lips pouted when she said it. I told her it was the truth and somehow I had a feeling that an aphorism was coming on. 'Smith said, "What is more mortifying than to feel you've missed the plum for want of courage to shake the tree?"'

She said that being form prefect and head gel were rather nice plums and I said that being head gel could be helpful but I also tried to tell Miss Simkiss how they strip Jayne naked and that's why she forgets her swimming costume so what was the point in giving her a detention every Monday. Miss Simkiss told me that only I could know my plums and asked me why I was wearing plimsolls.

**

Miss Simkiss asked me once if I smoked. I looked at her wide-eyed, but it was the stench of Danny's Players No. 6 on the sleeves of my blazer. He chain-smoked that spring and summer. 'Oxbridge entrance,' he said. 'My dad's on my back.' He never quit smoking, despite inside medical information or the need to abstain during all those half-finished conversations with patients.

You were desperate, Jayne: desperate to retrieve your pages so that Danny would never know. When Patricia broadcast the contents of your diary, on top of the 366 bus later that week, because she'd got fed up with the dummy routine, I watched your unnecessary terror.

She opens the blue leather-bound diary, which no doubt Mave has secured for her, and cuts her finger on the sharp gold leaves. A globule of deep red blood oozes from her forefinger. Rachel is sitting behind me with her pudding basin hat on back to front and I hear her say to Benji, 'That's Divine Retribution. It's a marvel Patricia bleeds at all.'

I think everyone hears because Benji tells her to 'shush'. Patricia pretends not to hear as sometimes she does with Rachel because Rachel is forearmed with verbal wit. I see you, Jayne, look at the bleeding finger, check your watch and then look at Danny as Patricia sings the contents of your love for my future husband whilst leaving a trail of blood across the pages of your life.

But yours was an unnecessary terror for he never heard her, Jayne. Your words and Patricia's were deaf to his ears. Danny has only ever been concerned with the postage stamp on which he lives. You need never have worried. He was thinking about how to chuck me.

24

Friday 14th February 1969

I think Danny is trying to chuck me. When I got on top of the 366 bus tonight I was hoping he might give me a rose, or a box of Milk Tray, or a Valentine's card, or a silly cuddly toy, or a Bromley's lemon soap, or a peck on the cheek but he just lit up (a Players No. 6) and said, 'My dad's on my back.'

I wasn't in a very good mood because the pastry on my jam tarts had sunk. Miss Love said, 'This is not like you, Shelley. Not like you to be distracted.'

But I was in distruction. I couldn't concentrate on my pastry.

Rachel said I may have lost Danny and my shoe but she's lost her papers. Rachel says concentrating for her exams is becoming difficult and one of the most difficult things is not being able to grieve because you can't be sure they've gone for good. She looked sad and tired. She looked as though she knew they had gone for good but that she didn't want to give up hope. I thought it was a funny way to think about papers.

Patricia was trying to get Danny's attention, singing out stuff from Jayne's diary but Danny spent most of the time home talking to Benji who bores everyone with teeth. Benji was saying that the only way to identify someone from their

174

*remains is their teeth because teeth are unique. He's now
thinking about becoming a forensic scientist. He made a ring
for Rachel in Woodwork today out of a bit of metal. I thought
it was sweet. But Rachel didn't say much about the ring. She
was very quiet and she kept watching Patricia and I heard
her asking Benji again for 'my papers'. Benji was talking to
Danny about maybe switching from Dentistry to Forensic
Science and Danny kept saying his dad was on his back about
Oxbridge exams at the end of the year and how he should be
studying and not going out. I think he wants to chuck me.*

*Patricia cut herself on Jayne's diary which I think serves
her right. Rachel said much the same thing although
sometimes it's hard to understand what Rachel is going on
about. Jayne started crying and the bus conductress gave her
a yellowed handkerchief. Patricia threw the diary to the front
of the bus and the bus conductress, the one with the hair
coming out of the mole on her chin, she picked it up and said
to Patricia, 'No more swinging on the platform of my bus or
I'll report you. It's an open platform with no doors and it's
dangerous.' The bus conductress picked up the diary and
gave it to Jayne. But when the bus conductress went down the
stairs, Mave wrenched it away from Jayne and I think she
dug her long claws into Jayne which made Jayne squeal like
a piglet – well I'm not very sure how piglets squeal but she
did – and then Jayne started crying yet again. They aren't
bored with the diary game yet.*

It's dangerous.

**

Danny stayed on the extra stop as usual to walk me home
from the bus stop that night. He said, and I find it difficult to

tell you this, Jayne, 'She gives me the creeps. She never stops staring at me.'

'Patricia?' I say.

He looks at me quickly. 'Jayne fucking Thornhill.'

He isn't walking backwards tonight. Usually, he walks backwards so he can continue talking to me as we walk along the pavement. I marvelled at the way he could walk backwards, he's always been so physically 'balanced', and how such a beautiful boy could want to walk backwards to talk to me. But this Valentine's night, my Danny is edgy. I am trying to tell him about plums and swimming costumes but he just asks me why I am wearing my plimsolls. When I say, 'Patricia Vickers must have stolen my right shoe,' he says angrily, 'Why did Patricia Vickers steal your right shoe?' Like this is really important. Like he is my mother. 'Oh, I don't know why Patricia Vickers does anything,' I say, hoping to steer the conversation away from chucking me because how am I going to face the rest of the class being chucked by Danny Diego when he has become the favourite wallpaper on our blackboard all week? And I am form prefect. And Rachel will still be going out with Benji which will make going to youth club difficult. 'But everyone is losing things. Tamsin Prew who never loses anything has lost her entire gym gear including *her hockey stick*.'

'Jolly ones,' he says.

This looks like being our first quarrel but I sense more. 'What's the matter, Danny?' I finally ask after a long pause during which he has even refused our customary red liquorice.

'What do you mean?'

'You're jumpy tonight.'

'A-levels. Oxbridge entrance.' He kicks at his school bag

again and again and the punching noise gets on my nerves. 'My dad's on my back.'

I sigh. 'Where else would he be?'

I bite on to my sticks of red liquorice, which we sometimes dip in sherbet because Danny said it was an aphrodisiac, although as my mother would refer to sex without using the three-lettered word, 'nothing had happened'.

'Can I have a fag or will you dob me in, little Miss Polly Prefect?' he says lighting up.

'Okay, what's got up your nose?' I am about to be brave.

'My dad's on my back.'

'So you said.'

'My dad's freaking out. Shelley, I …'

'I'm sorry. You've been studying really hard.' A knob of liquorice is stuck in my oesophagus.

'This isn't easy …' he says, sounding a dash dramatic.

'I know studying isn't easy. Maybe I could come over and help you with some notes.'

'No. That wasn't what I meant. Shelley …'

'We could give one another more time apart to study and …' I am becoming desperate. I mean I know I wasn't one for reading the writing on the wall but Benji *has* given Rachel a ring, albeit handmade, on Valentine's Day and here am I with not even a cuddly toy. This is getting serious.

'Yes, that's what I meant. Shelley …'

'What do you mean?'

'I mean …' he's dragging on another Players No. 6.

'We could maybe see each other Saturdays,' I say, 'or on the way home from school and then after the exams we could …'

'No. That's not what I meant.' His face hardens. There is

this dire silence: a silence where we both know what he means and I stop eating the liquorice it was so dire.

'Danny. Are you trying to tell me something?' I finally say.

'We're not having much fun these days.'

I think he'd heard that line on *Coronation Street* or something. 'So?'

'We could be friends ...'

Oh, God. 'I thought you loved me.'

'I'll always love you as a friend.'

'So you're chucking me.'

'Looks like it.'

'Is there someone else?'

'No. Of course not,' he says. 'You should see the pages of chemistry I need to cover before the summer.'

'Of course.'

'Will you be all right?'

'Of course.'

'See you around.'

I cried for days.

25

Tuesday 18th February 1969

Patricia never comes to Biology. She does it elsewhere. Miss Simkiss tried to tell us about the results of amplexus today but I was in abstraction. I got the notes from Rachel at lunchtime who said that she had a flaming row with Benji on Friday too and she knows Patricia heard because they get off at the same stop. Rachel said she has been tempted to chuck Benji because he won't give her back her papers which she lent to him to read. 'It's odd,' she said, 'because there's no way either Mave or Patricia could get their hands on papers I've given to Benji.' Anyway, when I looked at Rachel's notes, I saw that the results of amplexus is a mass of frogspawn – 2000 eggs and inside the eggs is a tiny black dot which is the embryo of the tadpole. The tadpole takes only two weeks to hatch and that's the result of having it away. I said to Rachel, 'You could just get pregnant and take a holiday.' Then I added, 'I think Danny chucked me because I wouldn't have it away with him.'

And she said, 'I think my periods have started.'

'Oh,' I said and gave her a big smile.

**

For years after this and during my self-starvation, my periods came as a surprise. Tuesday 18th February continues …

**

Miss Simkiss told Rachel to take Benji's ring off her left hand. Jayne keeps searching her bag to make sure that none of the pages Patricia has returned to her have been removed. You have to keep an eye on Mave.

I tried to tell Miss Simkiss that Patricia Vickers was bullying Jayne Thornhill. Rachel came with me. Miss Simkiss said, 'Who?'

I repeated Patricia's name and she said, 'Oh, Shelley, I see no proof of that.' She repeated truth is a jewel and all that. And then Rachel said, 'I know George Santayana said that, Miss Simkiss, because I looked it up, but he also said that in order to remember the truth one had to change it a little bit and I'm afraid I can't subscribe to both notions at the same time. In fact I have the feeling that these aphorisms are often written or said with a tongue in cheek, so to speak, and so maybe we shouldn't use them to fit every circumstance.'

I know she said this because I made her say it again, dictate every word and I wrote it in my diary during Miss Minster's Music lesson. In fact I did wonder if Rachel had previously rehearsed this and came with me to see Miss Simkiss with that sole intention.

Miss Simkiss's claws went to her floating red scarf and she stuttered and said, 'Oh do you, Rachel Sherman? Do you? Well, sorry, Dolly. Sometimes you can be too clever for your own boots!'

'What on earth does that mean?' Rachel said.

'It means what it means,' Miss Simkiss said.

I told Miss Simkiss that Jayne's diary had been stolen and her eyes widened and she said, 'Where?'

I said I thought Mavis O'Leary had taken it at the bus stop when we were waiting for the 366 bus one night last week. Miss Simkiss sighed heavily and then said, 'Oh, Shelley, would you bring a diary into school? It seems like inviting terror to me. And why are you still wearing plimsolls?'

My heart's in nothing at all.

**

Rachel told you, Jayne, to learn your theorems off by heart. 'You get full marks for just putting the theorem on paper,' Rachel says to you. 'Just learn the theorem of why the square root of 2 is irrational.'

But you, of course ask, '*Why* is it irrational?'

Rachel tries to explain about the 'proof of contradictions'. 'If you want to show that A is true, assume that it's not. One will then come to a contradiction. Thus A must be true since there are no contradictions in mathematics.'

You frown in your maths' 'C' stream confusion. '*Why* are there no contradictions in mathematics?'

Rachel sighs and whispers to me that it's a bit like expecting Riley her dog to understand Einstein's Theory of Relativity. Miss Simkiss walks through the Biology lab door and Rachel says, 'Here comes proof that silly Dolly contradictions walk and wear Nulon hand cream.'

There are three things which stand out in my mind, Jayne, those few weeks before Mother's Day.

Number One: you are now wearing Elbeo tights you and your mother have purchased from me in the hosiery department the previous Saturday. I was red-eyed as I had cried all through the night on account of being chucked the previous day and I was exhausted from listening to soul songs on Radio Caroline under the bedcovers. Your mother kept thanking me for my friendship with you. I had tried to imagine her in a black, beribboned Salvation Army hat and banging a tambourine. It wasn't hard: her shoes were sensible lace-ups.

Number Two: Miss Simkiss saying that lots of tadpoles get eaten by predators and watching beyond the Biology lab towards the girls' toilets and seeing Brody almost smash Patricia's head against the brick wall that Tuesday afternoon. At the time I tried to work out why he would do such a thing. Did you know that out of two thousand baby frogs born only five make it to adulthood?

Number Three: watching Rachel stand up for you on the top of the 366 bus that Tuesday night before half-term after the talk of irrational contradictions.

26

'Your willy. Does she say your willy?' Brenda's standing at the top of the 366 landing. I can see small squares of bubble gum protruding from her waistline, where she keeps a hidden cache for assemblies and Brenda can see nothing much at all because the Veronica Lake fringe makes her blind to the world. The front brim of her pudding basin school hat is turned up to possibly give her some kind of view.

'No. *Wispy*, she says *wispy* hair,' Patricia says reading from the now torn blue leather diary with the gold-edged pages, sitting in the back seat. 'Oh my God … Look at this bit … *I would love your tongue in my ear and …'* Patricia never wears a hat at all and I'm supposed to report her.

Brenda is saying, 'This is such a gas,' and Mave is saying, 'Bird's crap,' because it is her favourite saying of the month – she's 'borrowed' the phrase from Patricia.

'*And your palm against the inside of my …'* Patricia is unusually excited and squawky and saying what great bedtime reading this is for arousing Jayne. '*My dear Danny – I would love to marry you and go to bed with you – to feel your warm body close to mine and to wrap you in my tender love, and feel you inside me.*' She snorts and the girls all say, 'Oh, my God.' But I am not sure these are really Jayne's words because Patricia does not seem to be reading from the

183

diary but by now, nobody cares. Whatever Patricia reads is taken as Jayne's Gospel.

'*You have the loveliest Adam's apple and …*'

'Shut up, Patricia,' I say and surprise myself because I know she's just making it up now.

'No, you shut your gob,' Brenda Baker says.

'Give me the diary, Patricia,' Rachel says.

I'm watching Danny lighting up in the bus shelter below. I want Patricia to stop before he comes up the stairs. If he does come upstairs. But Benji's with him and Benji will come upstairs to see Rachel so Danny will come up. But tonight he won't sit with me and it will out. That I've been chucked.

'Lovely literary style, Jayne. B plus. Listen to this: *School medicals at the end of term and I will have to get weighed*,' Patricia reads and winks a wink to the rest of the girls.

Mave shrieks about Jayne breaking the scales.

'I said, give me the diary, Patricia,' Rachel says.

'Why? Because your best friend is the form prefect? Or because she is Danny's girlfriend?'

'I'm not Danny's girlfriend anymore.' I surprise myself again by speaking.

There's a silence but I notice that Patricia does not seem surprised. Everyone but Patricia and Rachel are surprised. Brenda Baker even mouths, 'Oh, my God', like it's as big news as Kennedy's assassination but I do feel as though my guts have been smashed.

Patricia carries on reading from the diary. 'Listen to this: *Danny, darling, why do you bother with Shelley Witherington? You have already said you are not serious about her. She is a stuck up cow who won't tell about what Patricia is doing lunchtimes …*'

That hurts me. Did you really think that? Maybe you did. Or maybe it's Patricia who thinks that and is making it up. Why isn't Patricia surprised that I am no longer Danny's girlfriend?

'The author of these words is now dubious,' Rachel says aloud.

'How can you enjoy doing this to Jayne?' I say.

'Oh, oh, oh,' Patricia says in short bursts of mock surprise. 'Rachel's shadow speaks.' And this hurts me as Patricia looks up from the diary and straight at Rachel, not even turning to see Benji and then Danny come up the stairs. I stare at my plimsolls. Rachel moves from our seat and takes a step towards Patricia in the back seat. Patricia is always in the back seat or the back corner seat in the classroom.

'Don't get involved, Rachel.' Benji tugs at Rachel's blazer and tries to steer her to my seat from which she has just risen.

Then in Rachel goes. It's like she's been storing it for years. 'Don't get involved? Don't get involved, Benji? I'll damned well get involved. Life's full of people who keep their mouths shut and don't get involved. People who go quietly by. People who remain silent and let others carry the can so that they can carry off the fruits. Shelley – you want proof that Patricia Vickers is a scheming, manipulative bitch, then she's staring you in the face.'

'Rachel, you're beautiful when you're angry but you don't know what you're getting into.' Benji looks petrified whilst Danny carries on smoking his Players No. 6 and looks down at the bus shelter.

'Oh, shut up, Benji. I'm sick of this. Patricia – give Jayne back her diary or I'll …'

'Twisted psychopath. Is that what you call me, Rachel

Sherman? I am the twisted psychopath stalking through your story.' Patricia has obviously held on to that one for a good ten days and not let go. Rachel has said this about Patricia in the Biology lab ages ago.

'You are – to do what you do at lunchtimes,' Rachel says.

'You shut your gob about that, Rachel Sherman,' Brenda Baker says.

'No, you shut yours, Brenda Baker. Patricia Vickers, you are evil,' Rachel suddenly says and I am wondering if this is the result of her starting her periods. I have never seen Rachel this shitty or brave when she says, 'You deal in evil. You're empty. Not only is your head empty but your body is too.'

'Rachel. Don't,' Benji calls.

Patricia stares at Rachel. Neither Patricia nor Rachel were concerned about pleasing people. Patricia has leaned back in her corner seat, protected by Brenda Baker to her right and Mave's bobbing black curls to the front.

'You can't feel for anyone, because you feel nothing at all.' Rachel is standing holding the handrail. 'You're only concerned about your own self and your own ends. You are self-serving. You have no soul.'

Patricia looks at Rachel. Rachel looks at Patricia. Patricia is about to lurch. But then she does something extraordinary. Instead of plunging into Rachel, she rises, kicks Brenda Baker out of the way, swoops past Rachel and falls on to you, Jayne, taking shreds of hair, pulling your marmalade hair out in tufts, wisps. You scream. Patricia is twanging at the elastic on your pudding basin school hat which has slipped around your neck. Rachel dives in and tries to help. But I'm frozen. Should I get involved?

I shout, 'Danny, do something.'

You scream. Piercing screams that I only heard once again

in my life, later that week. Benji pulls Rachel off, saying, 'Don't get involved, Rachel. You don't understand.'

The bus starts up. The bus conductress with the mole on her chin comes up the stairs to take fares. And we all sit back in our seats as if nothing has happened. Rachel sits next to me, panting.

When Patricia gets off the bus, Danny rises next from his seat. Patricia has gone down the stairs now and, I can't believe you said this, Jayne, but you stopped him before he went down the stairs and you said, 'I'm really sorry for the things I wrote about you, Danny. Forgive me?'

Danny is taken aback. He shakes his head. 'Jayne, you don't need to apologise to me. What's in your diary is of no concern to me. I have bigger problems and I'm not what you think. Look, have fun.' He gets off the bus without looking at me. They all get off the bus and I move to the back seat and watch them all disperse in different directions because I live one extra lonely stop on. Fun is the last thing you will be having and I don't think you ever got that diary back.

**

The Loft

I had been down to the kitchen now and got the black bin bags with the full intention of dumping all the diaries and taking them to the skip the next day. It was almost six. It was dark and I hadn't given a thought to food. The hands of my kitchen clock needed to move on and ridding myself of these words was the only way I was going to do it. I considered taking a heater up to the loft but Danny always warned against electrocution.

27

At half-term, the snow takes us by surprise: thick, velvety kind of snow which calls on blow heaters for the bedrooms. There are fireplaces in each room, but we only light the ones in the hallway, dining room and living room. Dad doesn't want to spoil 'the feel' with central heating. It's the kind of snow which stops buses from running and birds from singing and garden plot allotments from growing, so all you can hear is the crackled trickle of the Move's 'Blackberry Way' from Paul's transistor. On these days I can almost hear my brother's brain through the bedroom wall. He's got A-levels on it. On most evenings I hear Dad's voice: furious with Paul for selling the second car which really belonged to Mum but because she wouldn't learn to drive was given to my brother for his eighteenth birthday the previous September.

The gardeners are clearing the snow from the gate to the front porch. They rake over the surface of the silence until Mrs Standing starts vacuuming. Mum orders a taxi for her on days like this because Mrs Standing's too old to drive in these conditions. Mum's shouting at Paul, 'If you hadn't sold the blessed car, you could have collected Mrs Standing.'

'Oh, learn to drive yourself,' he says. There's the vacuum, 'Blackberry Way' and the drag of shovels on the driveway whilst the principal parts of 'expello, expellare' are far from my mind.

I can only think of Danny and how I don't want to just be his friend.

**

Monday 24th February 1969

The curtains are not drawn but it feels as though they are. It seems so dark. It's as if what they do brings on a heavy cloud. Then they get out the pieces of paper with the alphabet on and they put them in a circle and then they put the glass in the middle and then they all put their fingers on the glass and the glass spells out names of people who say they are spirits and died by a motorbike accident like Andrew Barnet – aged 16 and suicides and stuff and it's really scary. They ask the spirits if they can see into the future and some say they can and some say they can't. There are so many people in the Biology lab – children who have died young or in accidents and Linda Leech takes down their names and ages and it's getting crowded. I think Patricia is pushing the glass.

No one now goes to their garden plots at lunchtime except Rachel and Jayne. Rachel found my shoe down the side of the radiator in the Biology lab but she has not found her papers. The snow has cleared. Rachel says her herbs have suffered but 'she's doctoring'. My willow is much the same.

Memo: *Scotch eggs in Domestic Science this Friday. Someone put a beauty sash across Charlie which read, 'Queen of Gravesend'. Ha, ha, ha!!!*

**

Something spooky happened today. I recalled the date – Thursday 27th February. But then that had been only the beginning and it was all over by Mother's Day.

**

Thursday 27th February 1969: *Something spooky happened today …*

'Let me out of here. Oh no, Shelley. Let me out of here.' Jayne's tugging at the Biology lab door but Mave says, 'It's locked.'

Mave's locked it and nicked the key. I can tell. Mave has Miss Simkiss's red chiffon scarf around her neck. Patricia puts her hand on the glass: they're in a huge hug around one of the Biology benches. 'My mum tried to contact my nan this way,' Brenda Baker says.

'Did she?' they all chime together and look up at the big bell monitor.

'Nah,' Brenda says.

'Right. Who is the slug?' Patricia says and so it begins.

The glass crawls slowly, always slowly at first, as though either the glass or the girls need to draw energy. 'Jay …' they all sing-song, drawing out the vowel and then all eyes down for the scraping to the next letter which is … 'T,' they whisper. Of course. You close your eyes, Jayne. Your knees shake.

Rachel and I are by the Biology lab door, unable to escape: flightless birds sitting on high wires surveying the scene, trying to remain aloof, detached. You look as though you will wet yourself. How much can anyone take?

Then 'the glass' spells out '*D – I – E* '.

'How will she die?'

Your throat emits a tiny sound. How many times have you died within these school scenes? The glass moves again, this time making a scraping sound on the wooden bench. Always silence during scraping. Mave and Miss Simkiss's red scarf stand out from the circle. The girls spell out the letters, '*N – O – T – H – E – R.* Not her. Not her,' they repeat, one after the other.

'Not Jayne to die. Who then?' Patricia asks, eyebrows furrowed. Does she move that glass? She seems surprised that the glass has said that Jayne Thornhill is not to die. I wonder why she holds such power. Even sensible Tamsin Prew is drawn into this dark and dangerous game. We're supposed to be at lunch, supposed to be on our knees at our gardens. Does no one miss us? Does time stand still? I look at the clock above Charlie. I have to be on playground duty soon. Even Rachel is scared to confront them. They are always so highly charged at these times, heads bent on the circle, fingers taut on the glass. Jayne, Rachel and I never touch the glass, but I have been tempted, to test out the weight of Patricia's pressure.

Again the glass moves. '*M – U – R – D – E – R.* Murder, murder, murder.' The word sends ripples of delight down the spine of the group which hugs the hypnotic circle. I watch the glass spell out the word 'murder' as it leads fingers across the cracks on the Biology bench. The cracks also spell out our graffitied words: names of past and present loves, engraved for eternity. At times, the glass bumps clumsily on the boys' names engraved on wood: Dave, Steve, Chris, Cliff. Dug out in love.

'Who will murder? Who?' Patricia asks the glass.

The girls begin to get more frenetic in their reading of the alphabet. ' 'J.T. Jayne Thornhill.'

You begin to cry and Rachel reaches up and places a protective hand around your shoulder.

'Stop it, Patricia,' I say feebly, knowing I am powerless to influence the movement of this glass. I am not convinced in spirits. I am certainly not convinced by them. Rachel has not denied their existence but she says, 'If they exist at all, they are meddlesome in their ubiquity.'

Rachel has reached up to your shoulders, Jayne, and pushed you gently onto a lab stool. You remove your spectacles and are burying your head in Rachel's non-existent bosoms which are about the right height for you to do so. Rachel leaves you and moves close to the circle. She's standing directly behind Patricia. 'Just pack up and give us the key, Mavis so we can get out of here,' Rachel says.

Patricia turns round and swipes Rachel across the face.

The girls are concentrated on the circle and so this act of violence is ignored although both Rachel and I know that a line has been crossed: like chalked hockey lines where certain players cannot go. Rachel looks at me with incredulity and places a hand on her left cheek.

'Who is the father of my baby?' Patricia screams at the glass. 'I said, who is the father of my baby?'

One or two girls look at each other with the same kind of incredulity that I have just seen on Rachel's face but the glass is now spinning and scraping across the bench: a life, ironically on its own. The girls spell out D – I – E – 'Die, die, die,' the girls chant. The glass goes crazy spelling out P – V – D – I – E.

'Why are you saying that I die? Stop it,' she shouts. Patricia is usually so composed but, it seems, spirits are things over which she has no power. The glass is whipping

192

around the bench from letter to letter, across the backdrop of a red chiffon scarf and with the speed of electricity, and the girls are shouting, 'Patricia – Die – Patricia – Die …'

Then the girls shriek, 'G – O. Go, go, go. Go where?' they ask.

'Stop it. Stop it, you fucking spirits. Fuck off,' Patricia says removing her forefinger from the glass. The glass still moves. Without the pressure of Patricia's hand, the glass still moves. The glass is still moving. I can hear banging on the Biology lab door. 'I said fuck off you spirits,' Patricia says, back-stepping from the circle. 'You are supposed to be my fucking friends. Don't you tell me to die! I want to know who the father of my baby is – so you fucking tell me now.'

'Mr Brody, Mr Brody.' I can hear Miss Simkiss's voice from outside the door. 'Fetch Mr Brody.' There is a rapping at the Biology lab door. 'Shelley, what is going on in there?'

'We don't have a key, Miss Simkiss. Patricia has the key.'

'Tell me. Tell me who the father is.' I think Patricia may be crying. I'm not sure. But she is shrieking at the glass. The girls remove their fingers from the glass and step back from the circle. We are all watching Patricia, amazed. You, Jayne seem almost relieved, now you have been removed as the focus of attention.

'Tell me who the father of my baby is,' Patricia shrieks.

'Fetch Mr Brody,' I hear Miss Simkiss say away from the locked Biology lab door and then, 'We've sent down to the painters for tools to open the door.' Miss Simkiss's voice sounds urgent. 'Open up now. Open up.' I can sense the terror in Miss Simkiss's voice. Brenda Baker has not turned up for bell duty and the hands of the clock are well past registration. This will come down on Miss Simkiss's back.

But Patricia goes on. 'You fucking liars – you fucking

liars – the lot of you,' Patricia shouts. 'You are supposed to be on my side and you are fucking telling me I'm going to die. You're dead. The lot of you. You are just a bunch of dead spirits and you know fucking nothing – you fucking idiots.'

The girls turn to look at Patricia. They are all well back from the glass and I swear this happens, I swear, I saw it with my own eyes. Almost simultaneously this happens: the girls turn to look at Patricia, the door is broken open and Brody stands with Miss Simkiss and the glass, of its own volition it seems, shoots from the bench and smashes to the ground, splintering into thousands of tiny fragments.

It all happens so quickly. Did the glass do that on its own?

Patricia sees Brody, sees the smashed glass and she screams. She just screams; piercing screams which travel through my body and set my teeth on edge. Mave removes Miss Simkiss's red scarf and puts it behind her back. Patricia is still screaming. And as the Red Sea must have parted, so does the cluster at the Biology door, as Miss Harefield-Mott enters and takes her place beside Charlie.

We curtsy.

Miss Harefield-Mott looks at Patricia. We all look at Miss Harefield-Mott looking at Patricia. Patricia's screams die down as if Miss Harefield-Mott's presence has silencing power. Oh, it does, for now all we can hear is Patricia's breath: an exhausted heaving and now sighing and now subsiding. Patricia does not look at Miss Harefield-Mott but at the tiny fragments of glass on the Biology lab floor. Rachel scours the room as if checking that the energy from the glass has not been displaced. Miss Harefield-Mott gives a royal and monumental twitch and says, 'Hush. Hush.' She stands there in her Hush Puppies and says, 'Hush.'

Hush. Hush.

And the Biology lab hushes. There is now a quiet crowd in the corridor outside and Miss Harefield-Mott lifts her eyebrow to Miss Simkiss indicating to close the door.

Hush.

Miss Harefield-Mott has the power to silence all mischief.

**

The Loft

The next entry came upon me suddenly. Had I chosen to forget the date? My legs and arms were freezing. How long had I been up here? I couldn't bear to read it, couldn't bear to go over all that ground again and I was hungry. I hadn't eaten anything since breakfast, drinking only champagne at lunchtime. I looked at my mobile phone. It was now six twenty-five pm. I wished I could go back to that day and make it all so different. No. I couldn't read it. As I made my way down the ladder and reached the top of the stairs the landline started to ring yet again. Greg was almost stalking me. I took the stairs slowly and the phone kept ringing. I lifted the handset. I said nothing. The receiver said nothing. I waited. Then I said, 'Greg. It shouldn't have happened. Don't phone me again.'

No. It shouldn't have happened. I went into our porcelain kitchen and took some cheese from the fridge, ripping a slice of bread in two and ate. As I did so, I scraped my ankle wound on the open dishwasher door. Danny had always warned me about leaving the dishwasher open because of the thin skin on my ageing, lower legs. I took a bottle of red wine with a screw top, a glass and a tea cloth to tend my bloody ankle. Then I made my way back up the stairs and ladder. I knew what the first line of that entry was.

28

Friday 28th February 1969

There has never been any day in my life which has been as worse as this. I hope there will never ever be any day, ever again, in my life as worse as this. This is what happened and as I write now, sitting in my bed – it is midnight – I cannot see the words. Already these words are smudged with ink and tears coming out of my eyes and I am still waiting for the news. This morning I had to go and see Miss Harefield-Mott instead of going to school assembly. This is how it happened. This is how it happened and nobody will believe me. So I am going to write it down just as I have it in my head.

Before we got to school, it was one of the mornings Rachel was early so she walked back from the village and met me at my stop. We are waiting for the 366 bus and we are talking about our ingredients for Domestic Science – eggs and sausage meat. We go upstairs and get the back seat before everyone else gets on and I say, 'Rachel, when Danny gets on, will you shift and let him sit next to me? I need to talk to him.' And Rachel pulls a face and says, 'What if Benji doesn't catch this bus?' And I say, 'Oh, please, Rachel. Just this once.' And she smiles and says her period is over and okay. Well, Danny gets on and Patricia and Mave and Brenda Baker and Jayne Thornhill. So Rachel gets up from the back

197

seat and beckons for Danny to sit next to me on the back seat. The bus is filling up now and because of this moving around, Rachel is only left with a seat next to Patricia who is narked because she likes to spread out.

At first it's a bit quiet with Danny but that isn't why I'm crying right now writing this. Benji is not on the bus. It's Friday and he swims for the school. Anyway, I talk to Danny about how my mum has given up driving lessons and how Paul has sold his car he has been given for his eighteenth and how mad my dad is. We talk about school medicals at the end of the week. I feel like we are friends.

All the time Patricia is singing the words from some Monkees' song which really gets on our nerves, especially as she is sending it up as she hates the Monkees. Jayne is at the front of the bus and she turns round and widens her eyes and gives a silly grin.

As we are coming up to the bus terminus, Danny gives me a kiss on the cheek and I'm like – oh, ducky and I say, 'Danny, do you want to try again?' because I have heard this on 'Crossroads'. I notice Jayne gets up and waddles up the gangway, with half a dozen eggs in her hand for Domestic Science. She wants to be first to get down to the platform of the bus so she can have a swing as we swerve round the corner into the stop even though the bus conductress has said that she will report us if we keep doing it. I get up to go down the stairs and Danny gives me another kiss on the cheek so maybe he has decided he still loves me. He lets me go before him. Then Patricia gets up and butts in before me to get down the stairs. Patricia is immediately after Jayne and follows her down the stairs. I am after Patricia and I leave Danny upstairs.

When I get to the bottom of the stairs it is really crowded on the open platform, so I cannot stand on the platform. I can see Mave and Brenda to the right of the platform but I can't remember them going down the stairs. Maybe they went down the stairs before Jayne. The platform is full, so I stand on the bottom step of the stairs. There are first formers – standing – queuing to get off in the downstairs area and they are all laughing and heaving forward. Brenda and Mave are to the right of the platform. But there are no girls behind me pushing me forward and Patricia Vickers is directly in front of me on the left hand side of the platform.

In front of Patricia is Jayne Thornhill at the edge of the open platform. She has her fist tight clenched on the bus rail to take a swing as the bus swerves round the corner into the terminus. There are other first formers on the right side of the bus rail but the swing is not as good as being on the left hand side. Jayne is so big at the front of the left hand side of the platform that there is only room for Patricia to stand behind her. And me on the first step of the stairs.

Now the bus conductress with the mole and the hair on her nose (I found out today her name is Miss Crawford) is standing next to me where the bus conductress always stands and just before we get to the corner where the bus swings – all the girls are squealing and giggling – Miss Crawford is shouting, 'Sit down. All girls sit down and get away from the platform.'

Everyone is pushing and crushing and heaving but I am untouched because I am on the first step of the stairs. Danny is sitting on the step above me and he puts his hands on my hips and moves them up and down and I'm enjoying this and thinking that maybe we are back together again. Then it happens and I know it happens. Patricia Vickers who is directly in front of me and on the left side of the bus platform turns round to face me and then she leans heavily with all her weight on Jayne as the bus swerves round the corner into the terminus. I know that Patricia does this because I am right behind her and I was not thrown forward on to Patricia. I see Patricia hold on to the handrail with both hands and turn to me and with her back she leans really heavily on Jayne with all her might and then I see her PUSH. Whoosh.

Jayne is swinging – one arm out and feels the push. Jayne looks quickly behind her and shouts out, 'Stop it, Patricia.' But Patricia looks at me and PUSHES again just like she pushes on the glass. She pushes with her back, so she is facing me and I can see her doing it. And I scream, 'Patricia …' but I don't do anything. I don't stop her pushing and then there is someone else screaming. I don't know who else is screaming and then there is a huge thud.

The bus comes to a halt at the terminus stop. All I can see at first are Jayne's eggs for Domestic Science – smashed across the kerb and I think how Miss Love will blame Jayne for not bringing in her ingredients. There seems to be a silence. Everyone seems to be looking. I'm looking for Jayne and it's okay because Jayne is standing on the kerbside but she is not wearing her spectacles. But then I look down at Jayne's feet and I see the blood. It is coming from a school hat and I know that school hat. It is Rachel's school hat. Rachel. Her pudding basin school hat is not on her head. I cannot see her head properly. I can only see blood. Everywhere. I think I see Jayne's spectacles somewhere on the roadside beside what I know to be Mr Brody's white van. Then I see Mr Brody. He is kneeling besides Rachel. His van is parked just by the bus shelter. He is shouting for an ambulance and touching Rachel's arm and telling the girls to 'Move away, move away.' And he dashes to his van and brings back a white overall and I think he is trying to – I think it's called 'staunch' the blood. But there is blood coming from Rachel's head.

And Jayne's feet are standing by Rachel and Jayne's holding a school scarf in her right hand and she starts to cry and says, 'I tried to catch her scarf. I tried to catch her by her scarf.'

**

The Loft

I shone the torch on my bare leg. The gash looked deep. Dabbing the tea towel on the wound with one hand I poured myself another glass of red wine with the other. I could be drunk by the time Danny got home but I would go down the ladder soon and freshen up so he would never know. What would he do if he knew what I had been doing? For there was worse to come and my face was wet with tears.

29

The girls who were on the 366 bus this morning have been told to stand in a line outside Miss Harefield-Mott's office: in alphabetical order and in silence. There's a black gap in front of you, Jayne Thornhill. Where there should be an 'S': for 'Sherman'. The first formers have entered and left the headmistress's office in quick succession: red for 'engaged', amber for 'enter', green for 'free'. I'm thinking about traffic lights. And now only three girls are left in the cold vestibule. Patricia is digging into Jayne's bull-shaped blazer but I'm too weak with worry to say anything at all. You turn, Jayne. Your eyes are fixed on the polished parquet and then you look up at Patricia. 'Shelley saw what happened,' you whisper.

Patricia says nothing.

'Shelley's a witness. You pushed me, Patricia,' you say.

Patricia flinches briefly as if she had been whipped lightly with the nip of a nettle. It is a moment – a tiny moment of small defiance from you, Jayne, and then it evaporates. The last first former comes out of Miss Harefield-Mott's office and almost immediately a senior member of staff ... which member of staff was it? ... calls your full name and you enter on an amber light leaving Patricia and me ... alone: alone in the cold vestibule, which smells of polish and antiseptic from the nearby medical room. The senior member of staff, possibly she is the head of mathematics: the grey-haired teacher who always wears the same brown and green woollen suit, comes out of Miss Harefield-Mott's office and I watch the red light ping. Engaged. The senior member of staff tells us that we can sit down and then she re-enters the inner sanctum, closing the heavy oak door behind her. Alone again. We sit. The sixth form prefect comes to ring the brass bell to herald end of registration. Brenda Baker has been excused. Being a 'B' for Baker, Brenda has now long gone home, as has Mavis O'Leary. Just.

We sit.

Thirty minutes later the same sixth form prefect comes to ring the same brass bell to signal the end of the first lesson of the day. I study the prefect's sensible laced-up leather shoes. I look down and study Patricia's shoes which are not sensible. They are brown, summer sandals with blue flowers. I am trying to work out what flowers sit on Patricia's sandals. Are they cornflowers? In the distance the chatter of beginnings echoes along corridors. Schoolgirls can be seen through the glass-fronted vestibule door, appearing on the hall balcony, making their way to the Science laboratories. The time climbs on. A first former comes through to the vestibule and asks Matron for a plaster. I feel like crying because I'm wishing I could give Rachel a plaster. I don't cry. Instead I concentrate on the sight reading test stuck to the medical room wall. The door has been left open. I try to make out the last line of letters. My eyesight is good. I know what I see. I do not have glaucoma.

Still no Jayne.

The senior member of staff comes out of the office and leaves through the vestibule door. More minutes pass. Suddenly Miss Simkiss comes speeding through the school hall and opens the vestibule door. She gives us a cursory, almost irritated glance, knocks on the mighty oak door and is allowed in on the amber. The sixth form prefect comes to ring the bell for end of second lesson. The prefect looks at her watch and frowns at both Patricia and me as though we are already both guilty of a crime. Patricia is, but me? Seconds after the bell has been rung there is the next inevitable burst of blabber. Minutes pass before there is quiet: quiet all but for the first former requiring the plaster. I can hear crying and consolation. I wonder if the first former was on the 366 bus this morning. Maybe the first former's mum works and she cannot go home like the others. Patricia yawns. I look at Patricia. I have not looked at Patricia until now. 'You go saying anything about what you *think*, what you *think* happened you silly, spoilt and stuck-up cow, then I promise – I will make you pay, Shelley Witherington, I will make you pay. Believe you me.' *Believe you me,* she says and repeats those words, 'I will make you pay some time, some day.'

She did.

I have never forgotten those words in that cold vestibule on that cold February morning, spoken to the scent of antiseptic. I wonder if Patricia has spent the first lessons of the day forming, rehearsing these words in her head or whether she has waited until time told her that Jayne Thornhill could not be making a straightforward statement. I do not look at her but notice the sun glinting on her tiny gold-plated pierced studs. 'You cannot silence me like you silence the others,' I say to her.

And she says, 'No. You are quite capable of silencing yourself.'

I am not understanding what she is saying. I understood in later life. Patricia built walls, wrote on them and she saw through them. The high-heeled secretary is now knocking on the oak door. It is then that I see Patricia's eyes flicker with concern. Up until this point, neither of us could have known that the police were being involved. But a uniformed policewoman comes out of Miss Harefield-Mott's inner sanctum office and is escorting you, Jayne, and she says, 'Your headmistress says to lie down in the medical room and rest until your mother gets here.' You say nothing but you widen your eyes at me, stick insect-like at me, appealing for support. But this is not stick insects. I hear a noise. It sounds like the movement of an insect. But then I realize this is the sound of quick, sharp, breaths. It's Patricia. She looks terrified.

'Police,' I say to Patricia.

'Fuck the police,' Patricia says, and I think the policewoman who is re-entering the hallway hears this. 'They are calling in parents.'

The policewoman looks at both of us, takes a seat opposite us and folds her arms. We are criminals.

'Are they calling in parents?' Patricia asks the policewoman.

'Only to take you home.'

'But I do *not* want to go home.' Patricia looks as though she might cry. Some people never cry. I've never seen Patricia cry.

'It's best,' the policewoman says.

'But my father is a very busy man.' Patricia whines these words, as if putting her father above all concerns.

'Your mother then.'

'But my mother …' Patricia's voice trails down to her grubby sandals and the policewoman gives her an unobtrusive, sympathetic smile. The amber light has come on and the policewoman indicates that Patricia should enter.

Patricia jaunts into the inner sanctum and I have this ludicrous thought that for once she is wearing her pudding basin school hat. As if this tiny token of compliance could exonerate her from her crime.

The policewoman says, 'It won't be long before you are able to give your statement. The headmistress is seeing to this in alphabetical order, so you are next in line.' As if I didn't know.

I watch the red light and listen to tears from inside the big oak door. The muffled tears go on. I watch as Patricia exits with the policewoman and is shown into the medical room and told to rest. I think how stupid it is to ask Patricia and Jayne to rest in the same room. That's an irrational contradiction, Rachel would say. I watch as the first former with the plaster and a third former with obvious period pains are expelled from the medical room. I watch as Miss Simkiss leaves Miss Harefield-Mott's office. Miss Simkiss looks up at the clock and rushes out of the vestibule door, presumably to a biology lesson. I hear Patricia crying from the medical room, 'Please do not call my father, please not my father, *please* not my father.'

When the policewoman shows me through the oak door at approximately eleven-thirty am Miss Harefield-Mott is sitting behind a desk the size of the hockey changing room. The windows are wide and large and the room has plenty of light. A policeman sits on a high-backed chair, drinking a cup of coffee. Miss Harefield-Mott sips at her coffee before looking over the rim of the cup and her spectacles and says, 'Shelley.'

I feel thirsty.

She waits. Then I remember to curtsy and she nods her head for me to sit down. 'This is Sergeant Maskell, Shelley.'

There is a pause whilst I look at Sergeant Maskell and he looks at me: with gravity. He has a moustache like a besom. Miss Harefield-Mott also looks grave, sitting upright in her own high-backed chair. She says, 'Can you tell us,' and she pauses as if to emphasise her next phrase, 'in your own words,' and another pause, 'what happened this morning as the 366 bus came into the terminus when you were on your way to school?' Her words are clear and measured and she twitches now, with her whole face.

'I was standing at the bottom ... I was standing *on* the bottom step of the stairs.' I swallow.

Sergeant Maskell has started to take notes.

'Yes. Go on,' Miss Harefield-Mott says, slowly, deliberately, quietly.

'It was very crowded. There were girls pushing and shoving and ...' and I'm thirsty, 'and the bus conductress had warned us about standing up before the bus stops.'

Whenever I pause, Miss Harefield-Mott says, 'Yes.' Always slowly, deliberately, gently.

'And 'I'm the Urban Spaceman' was playing on someone's transistor radio.'

She raises an eyebrow in disapproval. 'Yes.'

'Patricia Vickers,' I say and Miss Harefield-Mott and Sergeant Maskell look up at me, 'Patricia Vickers,' I repeat, 'was right in front of me on the platform and Jayne Thornhill,' I cough now but carry on, 'was hanging on the bus rail at the front of the platform.'

There is a stillness as I look beyond the policeman, I think I have forgotten his name by now, my head is fuzzy, and I see the toilets and beyond that, our gardens, our patches of land. Rachel told me this morning that she was going to check if any of her oregano had pushed through. 'I never knew

Rachel was there …'

'Use your handkerchief, Shelley.' I do as I am told; my nose is running. The policeman flicks a page over in his notebook and then licks his Biro. I don't know why he does this.

'Take your time, Shelley,' Miss Harefield-Mott says. 'Was it then that you saw little Rachelle Sherman fall from the platform of the bus?' I want to correct my headmistress but I don't. The emphasis is on the wrong syllable and Miss HM's 'ch' is soft. The emphasis of Rachel's name is on the first syllable not the second. This seems important.

'I never knew Rachel was in front of Jayne Thornhill.' I didn't. I didn't see Rachel get off the bus, I had forgotten … I had been so busy talking to Danny … 'Jayne Thornhill is … a big girl … and you can't see much when Jayne is in the way.' Then I said, 'It was my fault, you see.'

Miss Harefield-Mott takes her spectacles off quickly, as if this gives her more clarity. '*Your* fault?'

'I had asked Rachel to leave me alone so that I could talk with my friend.' There's a nasty rough bump in my throat.

'Talk to your friend about what?' she says quickly.

I don't know what this had to do with anything but I'm feeling awkward. 'My brother selling his car,' I said because I didn't want to say that I wanted to know if my boyfriend still loved me and would still go out with me. Miss Harefield-Mott did not approve of love. There's another stillness when Miss Harefield-Mott puts her spectacles back on and looks down at some papers and then back up at me.

'Go on,' she says.

'That meant that Rachel was the first to get up to get off the bus.' Then I added, 'I think,' because I couldn't really be sure. I had been chatting to Danny. 'By the time I got to the bottom of the steps, Patricia was in front of me and pushing to get to the front of the platform and it wasn't until I saw Rachel ... it wasn't until I saw Rachel ... she had been carrying the eggs for Domestic Science ... We are, we *were* going to make scotch eggs today ...' I blew my nose on my white handkerchief. Why had I asked Rachel to move from the back seat? If only ... I could only think of the eggs and the blood and when I first saw her ...

'Yes, but it was an,' Miss Harefield-Mott pauses for a sliver of a second before she says, '*accident*, Shelley. It wasn't your fault.'

'No. It wasn't an accident,' I hear myself saying.

'An *accident*, Shelley,' she repeats.

'No. Patricia pushed Jayne.'

I can hear the chink of Miss Harefield-Mott's bone white teacup on its saucer and I can hear her distaste for what I have just said. The wind on the windowpanes is whipping up slightly when the policeman says, 'This is a serious allegation. Would you like to ...'

Miss Harefield-Mott ignores the sergeant who brushes at his moustache in embarrassment. 'Can you be absolutely sure, beyond any shred of doubt? This is a very serious allegation. Think again, Shelley.' And here her clipped voice is hushed and gentle, 'The bus was very crowded. Could it not have been that you, yourself, were pushed from behind?'

'There was no one behind me, Miss.'

'But who was the friend with whom you were discussing the sale of your brother's car?' She says this quickly: the way I have seen my father in court come in quickly when questioning a defendant. I feel that way now.

'Er ... Oh yes ... that was ... that was my friend – Danny Diego.'

Miss Harefield-Mott whips her spectacles off and raises her eyebrows. 'I see,' she says. She says these two words as if she *does* see. As if, in some way, this is the answer to everything. But then of course, I remember. Danny *was* behind me. He was sitting on the step behind me. 'Yes. My friend was behind me.'

'And he was leaning on you?'

'Yes,' I said, because Danny was leaning on my hips and I had liked it but he wasn't pushing me forward. The 'Yes' slipped out because he was leaning. But he was only leaning on my hips and I couldn't say that.

'Forward motion of bodies on the bus, Sergeant Maskell,' Miss Harefield-Mott said as if the jigsaw puzzle was now complete but I am thinking Danny of course must have seen Patricia turn and with all her weight push Jayne. Who was questioning Danny?

'Miss Simkiss told us that you had reported Patricia Vickers bullying Jayne,' and she replaces her spectacles on her nose to check the name on her papers and says, 'Thornhill.'

'Yes,' I say. 'In the showers and they stole her diary.'

'They?'

'I can't be *sure* it was Patricia Vickers who stole Jayne's diary.' I feel I need to say this. My father has always told me that one needed proof. Courts are not interested in *hearsay*. Hearsay is something my father has never been interested in.

'Well, this is what it *seems* you told Miss Simkiss. And now you can't be sure.' There is a nasty edge to Miss Harefield-Mott's voice now. I have not heard her ever speak to me in this way before. 'You told us at the beginning of this interview that no one was behind you on the bus stairs. And now it transpires that a,' and there is another fraction of pause

210

before she says, with that nasty taste in her mouth 'male friend was behind you. Can you be absolutely *sure* Patricia Vickers pushed Jayne?'

'Transpire? We didn't transpire …'

'You see … you see, Miss,' I realize the sergeant is speaking to me, 'an allegation like this is very serious indeed. We're talking statements, pressing charges and court appearances here.'

I know all that. I know all that. I want to tell him my father is a barrister but he goes on. 'All the same if this is what you …'

'And we have spoken to Miss Simkiss and she says there is no proof whatsoever that Jayne was being bullied by Patricia Vickers.' Miss Harefield-Mott takes control once again. 'And even if that were the case, which seems unlikely, I have no reason to disbelieve my staff.' She takes a deep breath and I am confused. 'Now, *I* am sure Patricia Vickers did not see Rachel in front of Jayne. This notion of intentional pushing is nonsense. Now,' she repeats, '*no girl* should have been standing on the platform when the bus was moving, so *all* girls on the 366 bus this morning will be processed a detention.' And then she looks at the sergeant and says, 'I hope your men are interviewing the bus conductress who has allowed this to happen because in *my* view this woman should never work in this capacity again but that is by the by.' She looks back at me and off the spectacles come once again. These spectacles come on and off her nose in rapid succession. 'I take a very poor view of you meeting boyfriends before school begins, Shelley and never do something so foolish again. Two wrongs make nothing at all.'

Then she gives her involuntary twitch.

211

I feel awful, just awful at having asked Danny to come and sit with me and asking Rachel to move. I blow my nose again when the sergeant says, 'Do you want to make a statement, Miss? It's possible to …'

In Miss Harefield-Mott jumps again. 'No.' Her 'no' is thrashed upon the desk like some tennis racket. 'Shelley is a very bright, tidy girl with a very promising future ahead of her, unsullied by court action.'

Court action? *Court* action? I never thought it would come to this. My father …

'With all due respect, ma'am, I …' The policeman speaks to Miss Harefield-Mott like *she* is *his* headmistress too.

'And it is my job to protect my pupils,' she goes on. 'The girl has already said that there was pressure on her from behind. This is an unfortunate accident. Forward motion on the platform of the bus. Shelley, go and lie down in the medical room until your mother gets here.'

This is my order to rise. The audience is now over. I walk towards the large oak door but I then turn. I must ask. 'Miss Harefield-Mott?'

They both look towards me.

'My friend – Rachel. How is she?'

'She is unconscious but in first-rate hands. We will let you know if there has been any change in her condition. Run along. This has been a chapter of accidents.'

I curtsy, close the big oak door behind me and see in the hallway a huge man with long flowing robes. He looks like God. Then I realize he is a man of the clergy. My heart goes like the Buttercup song – *de dum de dum de dum de dum*. Has he come with news of Rachel?

But then I remember Rachel is Jewish.

30

'Rachel's gonna be fine, Danny. They say the first forty-eight hours is crucial.' Benji is speaking to Danny at the bus terminus.

It's Monday 3rd March and Rachel hasn't woken up yet. I haven't had a chance to speak with Danny. I have been crying in my bedroom all weekend, playing the Beach Boys' 'In My Room', over and over again. But no one has complained. Not even Paul, who has been really sympathetic and stopped being angry.

'I've spoken to her mum.' Benji looks at me. 'She responded to her mum last night.'

Then there is this pause. There's Benji, Danny, Patricia and me. Jayne is sick. I don't like to say too much in front of Patricia. There may be a court case although Dad says it won't come to that. He says it's just a silly misunderstanding. But it doesn't seem that way to me when Benji says, 'They won't let me in to see her. I'm not family. But she's gonna be okay, Danny.' He says this as if reassuring Danny but Danny doesn't look as though he needs reassurance. 'I mean she's got so much to get on with. Her O-levels.' Benji bites his lip as if to stop himself crying.

'Maybe they'll defer her for a year, Benji. She's gonna need time,' Danny says, which I think is really sensible but not something I want to think about right now. I just want Rachel back on the 366 bus and tidying tarragon. Dad wanted to drive me to and from school. Mum has been upset that she's unable to drive me. Paul is getting it in the neck because he has sold the car. Dad had to leave court on Friday to come and collect me but tonight he has Chambers' Meeting. So here I am at this awful bloody bus terminus.

'Oh, yeah. The doctorate can wait, eh?' Benji tries to laugh.

Then Danny does something really nice. He puts his arm about Benji. And this is when Benji gets really upset and says, 'It wouldn't have happened if I had been on the bus on Friday morning. Because she would have been alongside me.' I think Benji is crying. I can't be sure. 'She wouldn't have been at the front of the bus. Why was she at the front of the platform anyway? You were behind her on the platform, weren't you, Danny? You saw her fall, didn't you?'

There's a short pause and then Danny looks across to Patricia and me. Patricia has been unusually silent during all this. 'Yes. I saw everything, Benji. I saw it all,' Danny says and I really need to speak to him. I am so relieved to hear him say this. I have wanted to talk to him over the weekend but my dad has said I should not speak to anyone. Not speak to anyone about this unless I have a solicitor. Dad could see that scared me but he said if I didn't say anything then it 'wouldn't come to that'. Just say nothing. So I didn't say anything for now. I let Danny and Benji do the talking.

'I feel sorry for you, Danny,' Benji says. 'To have to have seen it.' Then he looks at me and Patricia. 'And you two as well,' he adds. 'I wonder if she is still wearing my ring.'

'They might remove jewellery,' Danny says. This is the medic in him.

'You're talking as though she's dead,' Benji says.

Danny gives a half-nervous smile. 'That would be real serious,' he says gently and I think I could swear he looked sideways at Patricia. Danny's on my side, I'm thinking. He's on my side. He's going to stand witness. He's going to stand up to Patricia. I can see it in his dark, determined blue eyes. I know Danny's determination.

'She took to wearing my ring about her neck 'cos they don't allow jewellery in school. But it was only a piece of metal from a tin can. I made it in Woodwork. She said it was the thought. She'll be okay, eh, Danny?'

I am wishing the 366 bus would come. Usually it's here waiting after school but the bus conductress wasn't on this morning's Monday bus. There was a different bus conductor and so maybe everything was going to be different from now on.

'Benji, maybe it might be worth thinking about the possibility ...' Danny says.

'Of what?'

'I would not worry about Rachel, Benji.' It was Patricia speaking. She had said nothing throughout this. Without her two sidekicks, Mave and Brenda, who have been picked up by their parents tonight, she seems different.

'But I love her, Patricia.'

'You said that to me once. Christmas Eve.'

Danny and I exchange a surprised look but then Danny takes a quick two drags on his Players No. 6, like he does when he's quivering with nerves.

'Oh, yeah. But we didn't mean it, did we?' Benji says. 'We were just having some fun.'

'Fun?' Patricia stares at Benji hard and repeats louder, 'Fun?'

Benji says, sniffing. 'Someone gave me too many wine gums. You know I get pissed on a wine gum.' He tried to laugh but no one was laughing especially Patricia who was just staring at Benji as he was about to dig a deeper grave by saying, 'You're the kind of girl who likes a bit of slap and tickle, aren't you, Patricia? That was never serious like me and Rachel.'

'Not serious?' Patricia says looking from Benji to Danny. 'It wasn't *serious*?'

Danny throws his Players No. 6 to the pavement making a grinding noise as he puts it out with his shoe whilst Benji adds quickly, 'You never told Rachel, did you?'

'I am surprised to hear you had plans for the future,' Patricia says. 'The truth is she was always talking about chucking you.'

The 366 bus pulls into the terminus.

**

Tell the truth? Yes, I had tried to tell what I thought to be the truth. Danny had been my only chance and when he stays on an extra stop that Monday evening, I am thinking it is going to be all right. Especially when he says, 'Shelley, I think I've made a mistake.'

'A mistake?'

He looks tortured. I sigh with relief. He has seen what I had seen. Together we are going to face the authorities with the truth about Patricia Vickers. I feel lighter but when he says what I have been hoping he would say for weeks, it means little to me because he goes, 'I should never have chucked you. Can you ever forgive me?'

Forgive him? Of course I could always forgive Danny

anything. 'Forgive you?'

'Can it be like it was?' he says.

I didn't realize then why Danny was doing his own *volte-face* as Rachel would say. But I know now. How darkly we looked through the glass then and what sense the past makes now. I nod quickly. I'd even go back to buying red liquorice and sherbet but there is the unavoidable weight of Rachel in my heart. Maybe Rachel would just get better quickly and it would all be okay. Maybe she would do her own *volte-face*. 'Have you spoken to the police?' I say.

'The police?' he says, looking really worried. 'No, but my headmaster called me into his study on Friday lunchtime and asked me about it all,' he says. 'Did you say something to the school?' He says these words quickly.

'Yes. I said you were behind me on the stairs and saw everything.'

Danny puts his head to the side, screws up those dark blue eyes as if I am making an assumption. I have because he says, 'I told Benji that to make him feel better. But I didn't see anything at all, Shell.'

'Really?' I say.

He came in and played some records and put his hands on my hips and other places again.

**

Miss Simkiss had been my only chance. Miss Simkiss would put it right. Miss Simkiss who had said, 'Truth is a jewel which should not be painted over. George Santayana.' Well, Rachel had said George Santayana. Rachel had also said that George Santayana said you had to change the truth a little in order to remember it. I didn't really know what that meant

217

and I am wishing I could ask Rachel right now. So I am carrying my jewel to the staff room that Tuesday breaktime and I knock on the door. My intention is to ask Miss Simkiss if I could make a statement of truth.

'Miss Simkiss, I would like to make a statement of truth.'

Miss Simkiss's head pokes protectively around the staff room door. Like she's protecting the staff's real lives. One hand is behind her back like all teachers who open staff room doors but the smoke rises above their heads. 'A statement?'

'For the police.'

Miss Simkiss flinches at the volume of my voice and looks upward as if she is consulting a mental noticeboard. 'I have a free period after registration. What do you have after break?'

'It's Tuesday. Double Music.'

'Oh, good. You will hardly miss anything. We'll meet in the Biology lab. I will clear this with Miss Minster.' She gives a small smile. 'Chin up, Dolly. We will get this sorted out.'

So when I meet Miss Simkiss that Tuesday afternoon, leaving my classmates to practise their new hymn, there is a spring in my step and my chin is up, for something is to be done and Miss Simkiss is going to sort it out. Miss Simkiss closes the Biology lab door behind her and tut tuts as she retrieves her red chiffon scarf from around Charlie's neck. 'That's where it got to.' She swings round and says, 'Now, what's all this twiddle twoddle about the police?'

I'm not liking the sound of *this twiddle twoddle*. I clear my throat. In the distance I can hear the solo voice of a classmate practising the current hymn. 'The policeman asked me on Friday if I wanted to make a statement but I didn't understand at the time.'

Miss Simkiss says nothing but continues to look at me. I feel as though I must continue. 'You see, Patricia pushed Jayne on the bus yesterday morning.'

Miss Simkiss looks at me, as if expecting more information.

'And Jayne feels I ought to make a statement.'

'*Jayne* feels?' Miss Simkiss raises an eyebrow.

There you are you see; I mentioned your name.

'And what do *you* feel?'

I look down at my leather lace-ups for Rachel has found my right shoe behind the radiator. I think I can hear Tamsin Prew's taut and measured voice accompanying Miss Minster's plodding piano music. 'Patricia pushed Jayne.'

Miss Simkiss then says something which I find unbelievable. Miss Simkiss folds her white overalled arms which smell of a different brand of tobacco from Danny's, and her lips turn downward. 'Shelley, I have to say, when I saw Patricia in Miss Harefield-Mott's office on Friday, she was most upset.' She waits for some reaction. I respond by raising my eyebrows scornfully. Miss Simkiss goes on. 'Precisely, Shelley. I can sense your reaction to Patricia's distress.'

Patricia's distress? I have seen Patricia angry, but never distressed, although admittedly, her cries from Miss Harefield-Mott's inner sanctum office the previous Friday morning had sounded like distress. I think I can hear Miss Minster chastising a pupil for not knowing her words and the music begins again. Plod, plod, plod.

'Patricia is most upset by the way you and Jayne have been treating her. In fact, when I was called into Miss Harefield-Mott's office yesterday, Patricia did not seem surprised by the fact that Jayne had made this very serious

219

allegation against her. And she went on to say that she expected you to support Jayne's allegation because you both regularly conspire against her.' Miss Simkiss says this all in one go, not allowing me to speak.

'But Rachel and I tried to tell you the truth ...'

'Shelley, don't bring Rachel into this. That is not fair.'

'But you said that truth is a jewel ...'

She cuts in, 'Oh, really, Shelley. Does it *really* matter? Now just take a rubber and erase this silliness.'

I look at the blackboard. It is covered in white chalk and the names of French cheeses. I remember how Miss Simkiss had asked me to erase the girls' chalked daub copied from Jayne's diary and how Rachel has said something about there being an aphorism to suit every occasion and why she was therefore suspicious of them.

'Let us say then,' Miss Simkiss says, 'that Miss Harefield-Mott and the police were prepared for your,' she pauses momentarily, 'story.' Miss Simkiss does not allow for interruption. 'Now, Shelley. Jayne is prone to fantasy. Everyone knows that she is not quite the ticket.' Ticket, ticket, ticket. She says this word with flourish. 'We know that by the rubbish she has written in her diary ...'

Miss Simkiss must have read the writing on the blackboard wall as I had been rubbing it out and saying to the class at the very same time, 'Truth is a jewel which should not be painted over.'

'But you, Shelley. You are credited in this school with more discretion than Jayne Thornhill.'

'But you said truth is a jewel which should not be painted over.'

'George Santayana said it,' she bites back quickly as if it isn't her fault. 'But he also said that you have to change the truth a little in order to remember it. Maybe you have changed the truth too much. Mmmm?'

Me changing the truth? I'm confused. This is what Rachel told Miss Simkiss last week and now Miss Simkiss was changing it all around, turning the school tables but I don't understand why. Miss Simkiss is doing a *volte-face* all of her own. It's suddenly too much: the nasty edge in the voice, the smashed eggs on the roadside, the police, being awake all night waiting for some kind of news, even Danny's *volte-face*. I cry. I feel Miss Simkiss's hands upon my shoulders. I hear her soft 'Dolly' voice saying, 'Make a secret of your secret, Shelley. After all, secrets just sit and suppose. Dust it down. Put it away. Forget *all* about it. Maybe you saw what you wanted to see. Mmmm?'

I take out my handkerchief and blow my nose. Miss Simkiss's hands are upon my shoulders and in the distance, I can hear what I think is the voice of an angel. It sounds like the voice of an angel but there is something macabre in its resonant beauty. I begin to feel sick.

Breathe through the heats of our desire,
Thy coolness and thy balm;
Let sense be dumb, let flesh retire;
Speak through the earthquake, wind and fire,
O still small voice of calm,
O still small voice of calm.'

The solo voice is reaching through the walls and down the corridor; a singing voice I know well but in a different context: the top of the 366 bus. A voice I could never forget. The voice is clear and sweet and with seeming heart and charity. Patricia's voice. Contralto. And at that moment, I am wondering where God is hiding when Dave with paint pail and brush, opens the door abruptly.

Miss Simkiss jitters. 'Yes?' she asks him.

'I've a bit of touching up to do,' he says.

'Well, be quick about it,' she says.

And Dave winks at me as the girls troop in from Music and I find my stool next to Rachel's empty one.

'You've been crying,' Mave says astutely. Mave, the magpie would snatch at anything that glistened and has picked up a story in the Chemistry lab that morning. She simply says, 'Patricia's for it tomorrow.'

I raise my bleary eyes from the white handkerchief and frown in misunderstanding.

'I know,' Jayne says. 'Because Shelley was behind me on the steps and so was Danny. They're going to make a statement that Patricia pushed me.'

'I didn't mean that,' Mave says. 'I mean school medicals tomorrow.'

Dave looks up from the radiator as if he is listening. He is touching up with white paint and Patricia comes through the Biology lab door.

'Oh, Patricia,' Miss Simkiss says. 'You do have your appointment for school medical tomorrow?'

'Do *not* give a fuck,' she says.

Miss Simkiss pretends not to hear again. 'Have you quite finished your touching up?' she says to Dave.

'Quite,' he says and takes his pail and his leave, but Dave isn't smiling. He motions to Patricia to come with him and she turns to go.

'Where are you going, Patricia?' Miss Simkiss asks.

'To the bog.'

'Oh,' she says and launches into the tidal wave of

222

cauliflowers that can be expected at this time of year, for we have finished with frogs and are moving on to winter crops: potatoes and tubers. 'A few winter crops are waiting for winter to bring on their adolescence. Many crops,' Miss Simkiss says, 'need the thermal trigger of cold weather to bring about their sexual awakening and prepare them for procreation.'

Patricia is in the playground heading towards the 'bogs'. Why were the school medicals tomorrow so important? I looked back to Miss Simkiss. Where is Rachel and has Miss Simkiss ever had sex?

31

'You may or may not be aware,' Miss Harefield-Mott says as I press my moist palms down on the seat of the hard-backed chair, 'that Patricia Vickers was removed from this school last Wednesday lunchtime.' The headmistress gives a small smile of satisfaction.

I had not known. This is only Monday morning. Patricia wasn't at school for the two days following medicals on Wednesday and her absence always brought relief. I had put Patricia's absence down to delayed reaction of guilt. But my mind was on Rachel and there had been no news for two weeks. Yesterday I gave my mother a box of Black Magic and a bunch of daffodils. I kept asking my mother to phone Mrs Sherman. But my mother said quietly, 'Not today, Shelley. Not today.' My mother didn't want to interfere. So this was really good news. Patricia had been expelled. They believed Jayne and me.

Miss Harefield-Mott leans back in her chair and sighs deeply. 'Shelley. I received a telephone call early this morning. I am so sorry to have to tell you that little Rachelle Sherman died late last night. She never recovered during these two weeks from the coma and she would have known nothing.'

Known nothing. Nothing. She would have known nothing. I feel nothing. Nothing. I hear only the thudding tick of the clock above Miss Harefield-Mott's hockey room sized desk. I am feeling nothing and expect to feel something. My mouth forms an 'O' shape. As if 'Oh,' Rachel has died. There are pins and needles in my toes and now my knees. Look at all those criss-cross patterns on the carpet beneath my feet. I feel something. Rachel would be feeling nothing. Knowing nothing. Rachel can now know nothing … feel nothing.

'Rachel?' I say.

'And I want to make it absolutely crystal clear that Patricia Vickers's removal from this school is totally unrelated to this accident,' Miss Harefield-Mott says, picking up a pen as if to give her statement authority.

'Accident?' I say.

'Patricia Vickers has been removed from this school on the grounds of health.' She gives this word 'health' much weight. 'Shelley.' She changes the tone of her voice as she says my name. She is softer, gentler. 'Miss Simkiss said that you were considering making a statement alleging that Patricia pushed Jayne Thornhill, thus causing little Rachelle's death.'

'Well … I … Yesterday …?' My voice trails off towards the high, glossy windowsills. I am watching the nodding daffodils bending towards each other – whispering to each other. There's the rhythmic click of the clock, the sounds of schoolgirls from the playground: sounds of life … onward.

'Yes, it happened yesterday.'

'Mothers' Day?'

Miss Harefield-Mott looks down at the huge, leather diary in front of her on the desk. She has obviously not made the connection for she shakes her head, makes some show of consulting the date whilst I look out towards the daffodils and weeping willow. A schoolgirl shriek splits my head apart.

'Well, that is neither here nor there,' she says. 'Shelley.

Miss Simkiss said you were considering making a statement alleging that Patricia pushed Jayne Thornhill, thus causing little Rachelle's death.'

She has already said this.

Death. The tree and the daffodils and even my numbed feet and knees are very much alive. Feeling nothing might be better. I look beyond the weeping willow and the daffodils and the toilets. I think of Rachel's beautiful little patch of ground which she has tended to, which should have produced medicinal herbs that could not heal her now. I have visited her neglected patch of ground in the last two weeks and her herbs have died because she has not been there to doctor them: help them grow, keep them tidy. But Rachel was waiting for winter to bring on her adolescence; hoping, she said, that her hard, evergreen herbs would push through: budding, kissing, growing and nourishing. Rachel had just started her periods: all that blood. I've heard that the moving curtain of branches from a golden weeping willow can be a comfort.

'But you know, Shelley, this could be unpleasant for so many people: Mr and Mrs Sherman, Patricia and Reverend Vickers ...'

Dazed, I look away from the gardens and at Miss Harefield-Mott who says quickly, 'Who I might add, do an awful lot for the school. Unpleasant for Miss Simkiss and of course yourself, Shelley. Patricia's father would want to defend the case and oh ... it's a very messy business indeed.'

I turn to stare into the glaring March sunlight. I hear the words. Who was Reverend Vickers? And I hear the tick of the clock slicing at my moments making them hard-edged. I feel Miss Harefield-Mott turn towards the high window too. Miss Harefield-Mott speaks slowly, gently, in a holy half whisper, as she continues to join me viewing the outside gardens. 'Very untidy. Shelley, Reverend Vickers is a member of the board of governors ... and your road ahead could be rough.' When she says 'rough' her voice is high-pitched, regretful.

Reverend Vickers is a member of the board of governors.

'Consider this, Shelley. Consider your future if this is your road to be taken. No matter what the outcome of such an enquiry, there is always going to be a stain on your name. There will always be a stigma attached to the name of Shelley Witherington.' The words 'stain' and 'stigma' have the stinging edge of rim on a tin of condensed milk. I feel criminal.

'Even if you and Jayne are found to be telling the truth,' and then she says quickly, 'or what you both consider to *be* the truth' and now she slows down, 'there will always be the doubting Thomas who will suggest that you and Jayne are telling fibs.'

Fibs. Fibs. Her voice shoots off into the high-pitched note on 'fibs'. *Truth is a jewel which should not be painted over.* I am trying to remember what Rachel has said to Miss Simkiss about aphorisms for this seems very important as I stare at the daffodils and think of Rachel's once sweet-smelling but now barren patch of ground. What will happen to all Rachel's notes on Frogspawn? Will they identify her by her lovely teeth? Will her teeth have been smashed when she fell? And oh, I realize that Rachel will soon be at the undertaker's. The undertaker's on the High Street. The undertaker's with the stopped clock. The clock that always reads half past four. I always thought it was half past four when we reached the High Street until Rachel pointed out the hands were stuck and we had more time. I wish Time had stuck now. I wish we could go back to half past four on Thursday 27th February: the evening before it all happened. That was the day of the séance, wasn't it? When the glass spelt out DIE, DIE, DIE and M – U – R – D – E – R. I hadn't believed in all that stuff then, but maybe I do now. Miss Harefield-Mott is speaking in those Hush Puppy tones which match her shoes: it's a tone for special occasions which need special words. I can barely hear her now above the tick of the clock.

'I wish I could turn the clock back,' I whisper.

'The arms of the clock cannot be turned back, Shelley. What's done is done and cannot be undone. And I urge you, Shelley, to consider your future.'

I look at my headmistress. Why is she talking about my future? Rachel has no future. Why am I entitled to a future? Why have I been shown the green light? What am I doing here?

'You're a bright girl, Shelley, you are my cream, and when *I* consider your future, I am excited for you.'

'My future?'

'Look out on to those playing fields, Shelley,' she says softly, very softly and we look out of the window, beyond the weeping willow with its slender, yellow shoots falling to the ground and the daffodils and the mucky toilets and the abandoned patches of ground and we view the vistas: those playing fields and she says, 'They are level when one begins one's school career, but as time unfolds, for some, like you, achievement and reward tilt the playing field upward.'

There's an echoing silence, filled only by the clock ticking away at moments Rachel now no longer has. And sometimes it seems that these special, silent moments have echoed down my life, down my years, echoed down my future, for my headmistress so fittingly goes on to explain, 'After all, your parents, like you, have given much to this school and you would be throwing an awful lot away if you pursue this silly claim.' She places her gold-nib fountain pen back into its top with a flourish, 'In fact, it seems, Shelley, that you have caught the Druid's egg, my dear.'

'The Druid's Egg? What is that?' I can barely hear myself speak.

'Caught by default, but once in your possession, success, reward and status will be yours forever.'

And here it is. Catch. Catch the egg. Here is the nub. It comes now. She says. 'It is in my power to promise you that.'

University places, references, ticks in the right places, cups! I didn't know the full ramifications then. I didn't know then that this was a negotiation.

'Because I know there is so much good ahead waiting for you to just go and name it as your own.' Miss Harefield-Mott becomes earnest now. 'So catch the egg, Shelley, put *your* name on it, keep it safe and run, run up the hockey pitch for your future.'

Run? Rachel wasn't going to run anywhere.

'Girls should not step out of line.' Then there is another lengthy silence as though Miss Harefield-Mott is allowing the weight and gravitas of this situation to sink into my brain before she says quickly and efficiently, 'I have made it quite clear to Jayne Thornhill that no one will entertain her fabrications. Easter will take care of all this and next term will be a new chapter.'

There is a silence. A silence in which we both viewed the vistas ahead: the changing seats, the calendar days, the turns and foreign ways, the possible glory spread out before us. We were an unlikely pair, before these minutes, to have sat surveying the future together on a spring day. A future. It was something Rachel did not possess. But I had an egg: caught by a word I didn't understand: 'default'. Was I at fault? Had I stepped out of line?

For Miss Harefield-Mott, the negotiation is complete. 'Unless there's anything else, Shelley, perhaps you would like to rest up in the medical room until your mother arrives. I think it best if you spend the rest of the day in the comfort of your own home.'

Then she places her file in the drawer and I think she put the incident there too. She looks at me and says, 'Better to smile and forget than to remember and be sad.' She smiles and adds 'Christina Rossetti.'

The adjustment of her gown makes it clear I should leave. I stand up, curtsy. As I move towards the closed door, I hear her say softly, 'Shelley.'

I turn.

'I can count on your silence?'

Before I shut the door behind me, I nod.

**

Oh, God. Danny's key is in the front door lock. It's almost ten o'clock. I've finished the bottle. My eyes must be as red as the wine. My lips are sealed though. I wouldn't breathe a word of what I had written or read.

32

Jayne (16)

April 2nd 1969/Two Twenty-Two pm

Dear Shelley,

This is why I felt so isolated. No one, no one was prepared to back my story.

I was now back in the bog – *lavatory*. It was April 2nd. I remember the date clearly. It was the last day of term and although by now Patricia had left school, I was nursing some of my wounds in the lavatory and wanting to leave after O-levels. But Mum said, 'You'll be 'a first' in the family, Jayne. A first to get to university and study English.' I loved my mum desperately but she wasn't very well and I didn't like to tell her why I didn't always want to go to school.

'I'm sick today, Mum. Don't send me in.'

'Oh, Jayne, I'm worried you'll drop back on your studies. I never got the chance of a High School education. Make the most of it. I'm so proud of you, darling.' Then she would put on her plastic gloves to do the washing up and never ask me to give her a helping hand. 'You get on with your homework. You're better off using your time on your studies than on household chores.' And she said she would get me a maths tutor because she dreamt of gleaming spires on my future educational path. But on days like today, the last day of term, there would be no need to forge a 'mum's excuse note' which I had done in the past with such success because tomorrow was the beginning of the Easter holidays. I would spend the whole day in the lavatories if I had to.

The previous morning I had been with the police. And then when I returned to afternoon school, I gave Miss Simkiss a proper mother's excuse note and she said, speaking to her red fingernails because they were more important than me, 'Excuses, excuses, you can't ride on excuses, Jayne Thornhill.' This proved to me that Miss Simkiss spoke for the sake of the sound of her words without any connection to the context of the situation, just as Rachel had always said. But it was probably only in retrospect that I understood, like we do. So I gave up on excuses with the exception of my forged mother's excuse notes because I could never win. But yesterday I had been to see the police. It was the excuse of my school career. It made no difference to Miss Simkiss.

The lavatory on this last day of the spring term was an unpleasant place to be and it made me feel sick at the best of times and this wasn't.

'Daft cow. Well-stacked for a fifteen-year-old.' Oh my, I think that's Dave talking but I have no clear idea of the meaning of the word 'stacked' in this context and the transistor radio is racketing out Neil Diamond's 'Red, Red Wine'.

'She's hardly a skeleton.' That's Steve. Now I do understand. They are talking about me.

'Plenty in the cupboard though.' I think that's cheeky, chirpy Dave again. 'She said she wasn't sixteen until this month so I asked her if she had a bun in the oven. I said, "Well, you can't go on the pill until you're sixteen," and she said she was on the calendar. I said to her, "I hope you can bloody count" and she said, "I'm doing CSE Maths." I said, "Oh, well that explains everything."'

No, they are not talking about me, so who then?

'Well,' I hear Steve say, 'it certainly explains why the boss nearly smashed her head in against a brick wall last week.'

It did explain everything. Others had seen Brody attacking Patricia a few weeks before when Miss Simkiss was teaching Frog Amplexus.

'You won't find the answer at the bottom of a bottle, you know.' And that was Steve talking. I had got so used to telling who was doing the talking and imagining by their sounds what people were doing in the spaces between.

'I said you won't find the answer at the bottom of a bottle, Boss,' Steve says.

'You tell me why we're forced to face our nightmares.' I'd never heard fear in Brody's voice before. But he's frightened. His voice quivers. I feel like I'm having to face my worst nightmares too. Their voices change now. It sounds as though they are drinking something.

'Do you think she'll go through with it?' Steve says.

I'm interested. Go through with what?

'She's a liar.'

'She's a kid.'

'Jailbaiter.'

'She'll never stand up in court.'

'Boss ... I ...'

'She's touched. And I should have seen this coming,' Brody says. 'The police have called and asked me to go in and make a statement. I thought she was sixteen.'

I hear a smacking sound as though he is punching something with his fist. But he's not punching Steve. I have never spoken to Mr Brody before; I've heard him speaking (and singing) many times from this side of the lavatory door. His voice has been coloured in many shades but now the shade is one of fear. His consonants are slushy. 'I've been clean for two years but this will finish me. Even I won't stand a fuck's chance inside if she can lay this one on me. She's crying rape, Steve. She's fifteen and she's crying rape.'

It sounds almost as if Mr Brody might be crying a little as there is a small knob in his voice.

'Boss … listen …'

'Do you know what that means when they bang you up? I've seen what they do to child rapists.'

Rapists? Bang up? Mr Brody had been in prison? Oh my. Was that the meaning of ex-con? Oh, how much vocabulary I learnt in those lavatories.

'Consent. She consented all right. Here. Behind a locked bog door. But why should anyone believe me?'

Ah … Mr Brody and Patricia behind a bog door. Mr Brody didn't make Patricia kiss him behind the bog door. I would have believed him. *I* would. *I* was there: here. In the lavatory next door. But I didn't understand then what Mr Brody was talking about. I would have liked to have helped him but I could hardly burst through the lavatory door with the truth.

'Boss,' I hear Steve say like it was difficult for him to do so, 'Dave says Brenda's going to support her.'

Then there is a space. One of those spaces when I feel people might see my feet or hear my breath. There are more sounds of drinking and heavy sighs before Mr Brody says, 'I don't want to stare at any more walls.'

I didn't understand this. Did he not want to carry on painting? I hear the sound of swinging doors. I wait a long while until I think it's 'all clear' and then I open the lavatory door. But Mr Brody is sitting on the floor with his back to the wall and he has a bottle in his hand. He looks up really concerned and says, 'How long have you been in that bog? We're supposed to clear out when you girls come in.'

I reckon he maybe thinks I have heard his conversation which of course I have but I say, 'I've only just come in.'

'We're painting in here,' he says looking relieved. 'You should be in lesson.'

'What are you doing?' I ask. I don't mean to challenge. It's just that he looks so … dejected.

'Getting plastered.' He laughs but this time it's not his full-bodied laugh. Edwin would always refer to some red wines as full-bodied, rich, fruity, throaty and this was Mr Brody's voice and laughter, but right now his laughter is thin and acidic.

'I came to be sick,' I say.

'I might join you,' he says.

'Are you all right?' I ask him. He looks as though he might faint and then I wouldn't know what to do. Call the school nurse? It would be a tricky situation but he says, 'Tickety boo', which I suppose means he's all right and he asks me if I am all right as he takes another drink from his bottle.

'My friend died.'

'I'm sorry. Had she been ill for a while?'

'No. She fell, well, they *say* she fell off the bus that came into the terminus. Rachel. Rachel Sherman.' I say her name as though it might resurrect her. Rachel should have been at her school medical. That was an odd thought. 'She used to help me with my maths homework,' I say. 'She was … kind. She was in front of me in the alphabet. I always stood behind

235

her.' This was important.

'What's your name?' he asks.

'Jayne. Jayne Thornhill.' I look up at the walls that once again he has resumed whitewashing. 'Jayne with a 'y',' I whisper.

Then he does something quite odd. He lifts his forefinger and says, 'I see.' It's scary for a moment as he approaches me. I'm shivering because he's so close I can smell the spirits on his breath but he just makes gentle strokes on my forehead and says, 'Some people have 'victim' written across their foreheads. Bullies see the lettering very clearly. All you need to do is wipe the word away and believe in yourself. It's as easy as that. It's called looking after yourself.' He throws his brush on the floor, squats down leaning back and takes another swig from his bottle. There is an imprint of the white paint on the back of his tee-shirt.

'How do you know that?' My forehead is still tickling from the imprint he has made there.

'You need to know how to look after yourself when you do time.' He leans across to his transistor radio. Peter Sarstedt's 'Where Do You Go To, My Lovely?' is playing softly.

'Do time?' I ask.

'Banged up,' he says.

'You mean *prison*,' I say.

He nods and for the first time I see what maybe Patricia sees in Mr Brody. Up until now I have only ever really heard him or smelt him. But he is attractive and sexy with the allure of the long distance lorry driver. Before my father's accident on the building site I had met some long distance lorry drivers and they were always very bulky like Mr Brody. I was watching him, almost forgetting we were having a

236

conversation so I asked him, 'What for?'

'What?' he says, having forgotten where we had left off.

'What did you get banged up for?' I ask, my glasses steaming up from embarrassing condensation.

'Oh, I've read the writing on the walls,' he says. 'The lies. I've been employed to whitewash the graffiti about you from the bog, the showers, the changing room. I know the letters of your name well, Jayne. I've whitewashed the 'y' many times.'

He isn't answering the question I am asking.

'Truth is a jewel which should not be painted over,' I say.

I think it would be forward to take a seat beside him on the floor and although I am one acquainted with sitting on lavatory seats, the lavatory floor looks a little too dirty for my liking.

'Who said that?' he asks.

'Miss Simkiss.'

'Oh, well then. *In vino veritas,* I say.' He drinks even more. His eyes are red. His eyelids begin to droop. I think he's tired.

'That's Latin,' I say. 'What does it mean?'

'You speak the truth when you're pissed up.'

'Did you study Latin?'

'No. They made me take Technical Drawing instead.'

There is a space of time when neither of us says anything at all. 'They're saying Rachel fell off the platform because of the pressure from behind. That's what the police said.'

'Police?' He looks up quickly.

'When I went to make a statement.'

'You made a statement?' He seems interested, really interested for the first time in our conversation.

'The police said that 'the pressure' from behind was me.

237

Me. But it wasn't. I tried to grab her scarf to save her but I couldn't because someone deliberately pushed me. Someone wanted to kill Rachel.' This comes out in a gush. I have told the police, told my mother but this is different. This was telling someone else. 'And I know the truth. But at the moment it's just my word against hers. That's what the police said. There was no proof. They said I needed another witness. But I do have another witness because someone was behind the person who was deliberately pushing me.'

'Oh, well then. That's all right,' he says, seeming, I feel, to lose interest in the conversation after all.

'No. The person behind the person who pushed me ...' I can see Mr Brody is looking confused, 'the person who could be my witness, her name is Shelley and she is the form prefect. But she told me yesterday that she's not going to make a statement.'

'Why?'

'She says there's no proof but the proof was right in front of her eyes.' I begin to sniff.

'Who pushed you from behind?'

'Patricia Vickers.'

He stops drinking. He stares at the bottle and then up at me. 'I was there,' he said.

'I'm sorry?'

'I was there.'

I did remember a man bending over Rachel but that was all. I hadn't *seen* too much of Mr Brody, only *heard* him really.

'Have the police asked you to come in and make a statement?' I ask. Mr Brody could help me if he saw what happened.

Then he says very slowly, 'I do believe they have.' He

smiles. 'I do believe they have.' Then he whispers, 'I may just have had my bacon saved.'

'Your bacon?'

'I didn't see anything,' he says quickly. 'Look. Sorry,' he says. We seem to both be very apologetic. 'Believe it or not, I know how you feel. Maybe you don't understand how I know how you feel, but I do. I would help you if I could. You need to use the bog. I'll come back for my things.'

When he leaves, I swear his transistor radio's playing the Tremeloes, 'Silence is Golden'. I just have a feeling that Mr Brody, like everyone else for some reason is going to remain silent. Out of the corner of my eye I see his whisky bottle. He has left his whisky. The bottle is three quarters empty. I pick it up, unscrew the top and carefully wipe the mouth of the bottle. Then I swig at it in the same way that I have seen Mr Brody do so. The whisky scorches my throat, is bitter on my tongue but I take another swig and then another. I begin to feel more relaxed than I have ever done. And I must admit, this was the beginning of a trend for a few years: the swigging of spirits. Until 1976, when Edwin would limit us to a bottle of Liebfraumilch on a Friday with fish and the occasional celebratory full-bodied red on high days.

Mr Brody has also left his paint and paintbrushes. 'Truth is a jewel which should not be painted over.' I'm stumbling forth and picking up one of the brushes. I find myself painting, the Tremeloes helping in the background. I paint in large strokes. I feel so relaxed, calmer than I have done in almost years as I write *PATRICIA VICKERS KILLED RACHEL SHERMAN – THE TRUTH* in capital letters.

Miss Harefield-Mott always said that she would deal with anyone found scribbling on walls with a very heavy hand. But, like Brody, *my* bacon was of course saved and in this

239

way. I will explain. When my artwork is finished I look at my watch. I have one half-hour to go before Brenda Baker rings her final hand bell of the day and of the term. I fall into a sleep in the end lavatory, woken only by the sounds of Mr Brody and his two employees. My artwork amuses them and pleases them no end for I hear Mr Brody say, 'I've got her.'

Steve says, 'How do you mean, Boss?'

'The kid that wrote this, the kid that's being accused of accidentally falling on to the little one at the front of the bus. She has no witnesses to support the fact that the bitch pushed her from behind.'

He called Patricia a bitch.

'But with this information, the bitch won't be crying rape anymore. I'll have her dangling from her suspenders for the rest of her life with this one.' His laugh this time is definitely red and full-bodied.

'What do you want to do, Boss?' I hear Steve say.

'Get whitewashing. I want to be the only one with this information. She won't have any legs to stand on underage rape now.'

Of course, I could have stood witness for Mr Brody if he had told the truth. I could have testified that Patricia consented and that was how she got pregnant but I didn't realize that until years afterwards. But all the same, he had committed a crime: Patricia had been under sixteen when they got up to their doings in the toilets. I mean *lavatories*. When they finish and clear away their equipment, they go, never to return after that.

Just as they are leaving, I hear Brody say to Steve, 'I've had my bacon saved, Steve.'

I didn't understand then, but I do now. And no, I was never caught scribbling on the walls, but as I leave the senior toilets I very unfortunately bump into Miss Harefield-Mott and fall over as I curtsy. Bad timing. I shall never forget the relish in her eyes. It was as if I almost heard her say, 'Got her'. 'Out of line, Jayne Thornhill. You are out of line and – intoxicated. Intoxicated when you *should* have been at your school medical … No good will come of you.'

I was suspended for a good part of my O-level year and my examinations suffered considerably. Truth had been painted over and no, I would never get a school reference for university.

33

Jayne (18)

Towards the End of Our School Career, 1971/Five Thirty-Three pm

I am netting a floating memory: the memory of a senior member of staff, dressed in a green and brown woollen suit, whatever the weather. This senior member of staff is head of mathematics. It is a tired, hot end-of-term evening and you are gliding down an unusually quiet corridor, Shelley, after a late prefects' meeting, about a year after 'the incident'. It's almost as though your feet do not touch the ground as you are now so light. Almost as though you want to disappear into the school scenery because I have watched everything about you thin, even your hair. The head of mathematics looks about, as if to check there is utmost privacy but I have a way of lurking in cloakrooms as well as lavatories. The head of mathematics congratulates you on receiving the mathematics' prize. You give an obligatory smile; you are used to these informal well-wishing asides. Then the senior member of staff says, 'Remind me of your grade, Shelley?' Yes, it was a half-question. The brown and green woollen suit was not being callous. At your response, 'Seventy-two per cent,' the woman's lips form an imperfect round red letter O, as her scarlet lipstick does not meet the ends of her mouth. I know. Seventy-two per cent: pretty average. Oh.

Reaching for my blazer in the cloakroom and thinking for a moment of injustice, I then let the O rise and drift away over the coat pegs.

Part 3

2005

34
Still Jayne (52)
September 2005

Dear Shelley,

If Daisy hadn't found out who her father was that September, I would never have seen you again. Everybody would have been none the wiser and you and Danny wouldn't have been planning to retire and move. I can guarantee you that. This will explain why a number of withheld calls had come through to your landline before we met up in Milton. When I called your sister-in-law Lydia, I asked for your landline number. We didn't want your mobile number. It was Danny we were after.

I had been away to Paris for the weekend, meeting up with a film production company to discuss my pimple popping plot, and had taken the opportunity to collect a painting from an artist in Montmartre. Violet would be twenty-one in the November and she and Edwin had loved this artist's watercolours. Edwin had long gone: 'passed' they call it now – but I knew he would have approved of this present for Violet. The watercolour I had collected was of a cottage in a wood. A cottage I hoped Violet would be able to live in alone but I wasn't sure. It wasn't likely that I would have grandchildren: only by proxy, although you never know. I parked the BMW on the bricked forecourt of the mews. The early autumn roses in the courtyard were dripping their blood red petals on to the mowed lawn: it had been given a haircut by the gardeners who turned up for ten minutes each week. I raised my eyes to the open mouths of the Gothic-faced waterfalls flanking the door which was flung open by Violet. She threw her arms around me shouting, 'Mummy's home, Daisy. Daisy, Mummy's home.' I looked up above the front door but I couldn't see Daisy seated at her bedroom window. I had expected her to be at her sewing machine, making curtains for the nursery which Violet was filling with bunny rabbits. Daisy is a dressmaker by trade. She had to be in. We never left Violet alone in the mews.

I placed my suitcase in the hallway, took off my Jimmy Choos and, holding Violet's hand, we went up to my bedroom. Daisy was seated on my double bed, the blue Kashmir scarf draped across her lap and for a fleeting moment (forget the gap in the teeth, the lighter shade of strawberry blonde hair, and the greenish tinge to the eyes where Patricia's had been watery blue) she looked a carbon copy of her mother. I fixed my eyes upon the large brown envelope, then skirted to my cupboard. 'Why have you done this?' I said as calmly as I could muster. Patricia's abused cat was long gone but several cats, it seemed, had jumped out of bags.

'The doctor needed my personal health records whilst you were in Paris. I found them tied up in a Kashmir scarf,' she said. 'Didn't you expect me to remember the Kashmir scarf? She died in that Kashmir scarf.'

Daisy's birth certificate lay flat-faced towards me on my crisp white Egyptian sheets. That blessed birth certificate. I had managed to keep that hidden from Daisy for years, not wanting Danny or you part of our lives for a number of reasons. But there it lay, a thorn in my arthritic side. 'Daisy …' I went to move towards her, but as I did so I felt a searing pain in my right foot. Thinking it was a result of my hip, I looked down. One of Daisy's needles had been upright in the carpet and the ball of my foot had landed upon it. I took this as a sign of what might lie in store for us on the pathway ahead. But I also checked the carpet as Violet was right behind me.

'My father …' Daisy hesitated, swallowed hard. 'My *real* father,' she said, and then looked up to the ceiling trying to restrain a tear, 'never put his address on these letters.'

'Daisy, I know what it is like to discover that your parentage isn't what you thought it …'

She shook her head. 'How could you do this to me? You knew all along … all these years and you let Daddy and myself …'

I was about to correct Daisy's grammar as Patricia might have done but refrained. This wasn't the time and place.

'I mean the person I *thought* was my daddy …' Daisy looked at me with accusation. 'Daddy will be so upset.'

How could I tell her I thought Benji knew he wasn't her father? And how could I tell her it was because I had so wanted to keep her with me? Once I had discovered … I should have destroyed that blue envelope and its contents except maybe I kept it for its 'Danny' blackmail value in case I ever needed it. Just as I had kind of blackmailed Patricia once I read Danny's letters to Patricia.

'I want his address. This man who is my *real* father must still have my mother's letters to him. He's going to give them to me.' Daisy could be as single-minded as her mother and, sitting astride my double bed that day with the Kashmir scarf in one hand and the brown envelope in the other, demanding her birth father's address, she looked so like Patricia. It was awful.

'I don't know your birth father's address, Daisy.' I was going to say I of course knew how to find it. The blue envelope which was safely tucked away in my Polo Ralph Lauren would vouchsafe … But Daisy cut across my thinking 'You were Mother's *friend*. She told me you were her *friend*.'

'Well,' I said. 'What your mother ever said could never be considered Gospel.'

'And you used Mother's words. That bloody book you wrote called *Girls in a Line* belonged to Mother.'

I had to pull myself together. Daisy was on to something. 'Why do you think that?'

'Look,' she shouted and tore open the brown envelope. I know your handwriting. This isn't your handwriting. All these bits are in your book. Or was it Mother's book?'

Her voice had the same throaty timbre Patricia had when she was screaming at that moving glass in the Biology lab asking who her baby's father was. This was Daisy's hormones. Hormones. (Daisy's outbursts had always been excused as a result of quivering hormones throughout her life with us.) But she *was* going on six months pregnant. Of course like mother, like daughter, Daisy hadn't revealed who *her* baby's father was either. So many fathers, including Edwin, I might add, whom Daisy had christened Daddy Two. For Daisy there was a whole host of paternal possibilities but the blue envelope had revealed all. Then she threw all the A4 sheets of my dratted novel *Girls in a Line* across my bedroom. Oh my, and she was shouting, 'Give me my real father's address. Don't lie to me, Jayne. Give it to me,' as I was looking at the handwriting and thinking it didn't match that on the infamous blue envelope and contents. Why hadn't I noticed that before?

It was then that Violet started to cry. She had been behind me and strong emotions could upset her. So much was happening in these moments. I turned to comfort Violet and I was about to turn back to Daisy and say I didn't have her birth father's address but I knew a man who did, when Daisy shouted, 'Who the fuck are you to me anyway?'

Like her birth certificate it slipped out like a mollusc. 'Well, I'm your aunt,' I said.

35

Shelley (53)
Some Days Before Christmas, 2005

Dear Jayne,

Lydia had contacted me in September. She said that you
had phoned her and asked for my landline number. I hoped
that you would get in touch but I heard nothing which I
thought was strange. So I thought emailing you through your
website about the Tree Project might be a good excuse,
knowing that re-establishing contact with me was in your
mind. Well, I had thought it was contact with *me* that you
wanted. I realize now it was Danny.

It was the last day of my last winter term at Milton
College, just after I emailed you and asked if we could meet
somewhere. Intoxicated by the retirement champagne and the
fragrance of lilies I had been given, I knocked on Greg's
door. I was flushed with the prospect of seeing you. 'Rose
Good,' I said. 'I think I could get Rose Good to come and
talk. I'm meeting her in a few days' time. In Milton. She's
coming to Milton to meet me. I've asked to meet her. I know
her, you see.' I went on to say to Greg, 'Rose Good was
adopted. I was at school with her and I'm seeing her in a few
days to ask her if she would come, be a patron of the Tree
Project.'

His brow furrowed. 'You've just retired in the last half-hour. You're leaving for the midlands after Christmas.'

'But I was always going to have continued contact with the Tree Project.' I felt I was losing what I had for so long cultivated and watched grow.

'Who is Rose Good?' Greg knew you as the writer. What he was really asking was who you were to me. It was when I tried to say your real name, when I tried to say 'Jayne Thornhill', that I broke down. Even when Greg had told me about raising Jude Levington's issue with County and the Chair all those years ago, I had remained dry-eyed. Even when I had received the reprimand, had to take extra training to keep my job, telling Danny it was simply 'a development course', I held my head high. Chin up and all that. I had understood then something of the humiliation you must have felt during those days when I turned my back and read my *Jackie* comic. It must have been the overpowering scent of those lilies that brought the tears on; that and the early retirement champagne. So I told Greg the story.

You never told Edwin?

If there had been an inner sanctum, I felt as though Greg might have kissed me. There is a secrecy and intimacy in inner sanctums which open-plan and open doors will not permit. Greg would have crossed my line if there had been walls and locked doors. Our hands brushed. We had been making love without touching for years. My husband had sat on back benches for so long that Greg was the man I felt I had lived with. It had been distant lovemaking with both men. I felt guilty, confused, and went home and started clearing the loft. Perhaps I read the diaries to prepare for our coming meeting. Anyhow, I believed it was Greg who had been trying to contact me on the landline for the past week. When

I picked up, I had thought it was Greg on the end of the line. I told him to stop calling me. And I believed he had hung up without a word. Now I know it wasn't Greg. It was Daisy.

**

The Day I Re-United With You

I walked out on you in the Milton department store. Sorry again, Dolly, as Miss Simkiss would say. I was never good at confrontation. I realized it wasn't right to ask you to be patron of the Tree Project. I was totally confused when you mentioned Patricia. I had met Mave quite soon after Patricia died and she said you had been friends with Tricky Vicky. I never understood how you could do that. What was I supposed to have said and done? Should I have said we should forgive Patricia or should I have done what I did? Apologised to you for the first time in my life. After all, I had been tripping up on your apologies to me for most of mine. I'm sorry, I'm so sorry again that I walked out on you but every time I looked at you, I couldn't help seeing Patricia Vickers and the 366 bus came flooding back like blood. You had lost weight, your red hair was now a gleaming soft amber, your forehead smooth; you were poised. Where was Jayne Thornhill? I could only see Patricia for despite all of Patricia's spite she was a physically attractive girl. Leaders usually are.

I felt myself being moved downward in a wave on the escalator which squealed beneath me. Out into the December lunch hour a blizzard of snow began to fall. The shop windows were filled with the clichéd slash of Christmas. There was even a warm, brown smell of chestnuts. Soon I would be home. I would clear out the loft and burn the lot.

There would be no loft in our new bungalow because Danny said we were going to convert it for extra bedrooms for some reason but anyway, nothing would be hidden. Danny and I could leave Patricia and 'the incident' behind us. She was dead. It was over. It was time to 'dust it all down and forget *all* about it'. Forget Patricia. Forget Greg. Forget you. Try, even, to forget Rachel. There were going to be no school ties.

Fighting for space in the pedestrian traffic as I crossed the road and past the jeweller's, I resolved to throw away all those old unearned prizes: the cups and certificates that bore my name but were never really mine. You remember that clock which was always stuck at half past four? We thought it was always half past four on the bus home until Rachel pointed out that the hands were stuck in time. Shakespeare's were Rachel's undertakers, you know? As I looked up, I suddenly realized the hands on Shakespeare's clock had been fixed. The hands were no longer on the six and on the four. Time had moved on but I suddenly knew I had to turn back. Looking up at the clock I remembered that I had left the two watches in their gift wrap beneath the Milton department store table. At your feet.

It was this coincidence that led me finally to the truth I had not read on the wall for years. As Rachel had told me: I had mental glaucoma.

**

I like to think that Sebastian the waiter did what he did for me not because it was Christmas or because I had given him a sizeable tip but just because he was a good man. At any rate he came rushing up to me on my return to the department store restaurant and breathlessly said, 'The lady you were with?' I nodded. He said, 'Wait.' And he rushed to behind the counter and withdrew my jeweller's gift bag saying, 'She placed this in the waste bin. In error, I must be thinking.'

You weren't to know the gift bag contained two expensive watches. In retrospect I probably bought watches as retirement was on my brain. Maybe you didn't keep the gift bag safe because you really didn't want to ever see me again. Why didn't you ask the waiter to just keep the bag behind the counter in case I returned for it? I didn't know then. Well, I do now. It was an act of kindness. What's the loss of two watches when one has to cruelly confront the truth? You didn't believe I could, did you?

**

Carrier bags littered the arms and gloved hands of Christmas customers. I felt hungry and light-headed from the red wine on the rocks we had drunk before midday. I had eaten no breakfast, and resolved to buy a sandwich before boarding the overground train for home. On to the mainline station, through turnstiles, a powerful aroma of fresh coffee pervaded the air. I quickly bought a cheese sandwich and a flat white. As I gave the kiosk girl a twenty-pound note, I noticed that my train was leaving in three minutes. I didn't wait for the change but bolted for the platform ... the hot coffee scalding my fingertips, my ticket in my mouth, my cheese sandwich shoved into the top of my handbag. I missed the train. I might have done things differently if I hadn't missed the train. I sat down on the platform seat and checked the jeweller's gift bag. It was then that I saw the blue envelope.

36

Paul Witherington
Caveat
Madingley
Cambridge

May Day, 1985

Dear Daniel,

The last letter.

The letters began with Madingley. They will end with Madingley.

You have always insisted the letters came to you via Paul, always via your wife's brother, you coward, about 'our little secret', you huge flightless ostrich. I am gone now. This sealed letter for Paul to forward to you will only be posted when I have flown the cage of this decaying shell. In your future, your smooth square fingers touch the outer edges of this sapphire blue notepaper. There are so many shades of blue. I know them all. I am Patricia. In your future, I am gone. I am an anachronism.

But now, which is my now, the patch of world I inhabit grows darker inch by inch. There is a rectangle of azure blue sky. It is six minutes past eight, azure blue turning cobalt.

Slowly. This evening I sit. On slate grey days or on hot, stifling, breath-stopping days, I can only lie. We knew it was coming: immobility. Even the rage is immobile, but I have spent life preparing for this. We all do.

The bedroom window is at right angles to a brick wall. There are five hundred and sixteen bricks on this wall. The bricks are not terracotta new. Nothing in this life has been new for a long time. The bricks are the colour of dirty granite.

On the opposite bedroom wall I study chestnut-speckled grains on a sandy yellow wallpaper. You once said the colour of the hair on this head was chestnut. This head … it hurts. You were being kind. You are a good man.

There are fifty-eight thousand and sixty-seven chestnut-speckled grains on the sandy yellow wallpaper – and there is a clock. The deathwatch beetle sees me ebb and flow and she has placed an old clock on the wall opposite to remind me of the minutes I am losing, like the life I am losing, like the life that is oozing from this shell. It is the kind of clock that appears on school hall walls and it reads eight-eighteen. If you count the chestnut-speckled grains around its circumference, the circumference of this bloody clock, you will find one thousand and seventeen. Give or take a grain. If you count the days since I have seen you, you will arrive at three thousand two hundred and thirty-five, including two leap year days. It is eight twenty-two. I write: slowly.

Let us switch on the light and remember, Daniel. Let me lead you down that corridor, light up … Daisy will shortly be seven. The brass band plays marching tunes in the gazebo. No one knows we are here. Only strangers see us: think we are a small unit of a family.

What do we do when we meet in the Municipal Park? Why, we smile. Your lips move upward to greet us, your eyes down to take in her being from hair to toenails. This is the centre point of that hot summer. In the autumn of 1976, the government will appoint a Minister of Drought and we are very thirsty.

You are taking photos of Daisy. She is wearing blue plastic sandals and a strappy yellow sun top. As the three of us share two ice creams, you express concern about her delicately, freckled skin which is producing a pinkish tinge: slowly. Doctor Daniel. We try to persuade her to cover up with a Mickey Mouse tee-shirt and Daisy laughs when you beg her, on your knees, to do so. You dance with her; your straight back, your prehensile knees in time to her toenails and the beat of 'Land of Hope and Glory'.

You say, 'I have missed so much time with her. She is perfect.' Lost time. Perfect.

Now you are commenting on the gap in Daisy's front teeth. We inspect our own. Teeth from our teeth. You tell me she is beautiful and later spoil the moment by saying your fiancée is too. You must not speak about them in closely connected sentences. It is against the rules and I think you only mention her because of the dreadfully black guilt.

Daisy has blue eyes. 'Daisy blue'.

Now you are wiping the remains of a chocolate flake from the corners of Daisy's mouth. Here is my pretend story: we are a family. We live in a neo-Georgian detached house with a whitewashed front and this morning I asked you if you would like a change of cereal from your usual. We are celebrating a birthday today and you are not getting married in September. I pretend we are going to a pizza parlour ... or do they call it pizzeria? ... This fucking head pounds. This head is now a bowl of rice pudding and it will not attach itself to the chemistry examination paper.

Those fifty-eight minutes on the park bench in the rose garden belong to me. I own that time. I own nothing else of you. Time is the only thing we own. I can replay those minutes in this head – this fucking head. It is eight thirty-four and the rectangle of sky is turning midnight blue. Slowly.

When Daisy was born, I was sixteen years and sixteen days old. She was born to 'Bad Moon Rising'. August. 1969. Trouble was on the way. I am now thirty-one years, nine months and one day old. If I die in September, Daisy's birth would have been the centre point of my life and Daisy will then be the same age as I was when I was having our baby.

Listen … the breeze is singing our story.

I am losing more inches of light. Darkness creeps across the eiderdown. I give you this enclosed photo. A photo of the way she is today: a red gash on her chin through nervously and persistently sucking her dry bottom lip. Fifteen and changing quickly. Fifteen and rehearsing to be a woman. Fifteen and fucking nuts.

She keeps losing babies: your wife.

I imagine her to be 'Alice blue' and Icelandic. Vertical lines and distant lovemaking; open air dinners à deux – al fresco – and haunting melodies. Let me hazard a guess: the corners of your rooms are uncluttered, clinically white empty spaces.

I live in those spaces. Where are you both going on this coming, hazy Bank Holiday weekend? Snatching away days in some Mediterranean port, linking arms on cobbled streets, salty sea air clinging to your silky suntanned skins – oh beautiful people? Now you are considering purchasing some piece of memorabilia. You are debating its long-term worth, mentally viewing which space it will occupy in your home and I am with you. I invisibly and silently fill that clinically white gap which separates you. I live in the white lie which separates you for I am the past. The nasty inescapable past. Give it a name: Patricia.

Patricia the voyeur. She watches, through the window, from across the street, from the balcony overhead, the third uninvited guest walking beside you. She observes your closeness and your wife's edging away from you. A minute retreat of one or two speckled grains. Patricia is that speckled grain. Patricia is that silence which falls inexplicably but definitely on 'a red wine with ice' evening.

I hated watching you touch her when I was fifteen. When you had touched me.

And Daisy. There will always be Daisy: Patricia diluted down the years.

Daisy: our little secret. Our secret grows, Daniel. Everything grows around me: Daisy, and the deathwatch beetle's nails whilst I die as fast as I see others grow. Where do you keep the memorabilia of Daisy, Daniel? Where do you keep the photos you took of her on that scorching summer's day? Snapped during the fifty-eight minutes which I own. Which space in your home is occupied with the accumulated photos of a growing Daisy? Where do you keep the annual Father's Day cards I signed for you: the handmade card of a lunatically long-legged daddy? Danny Longlegs, I called you. Remember? The ones I sent to you and not to Benjamin. Are we in the garage, or the basement or are we in the loft, Daniel? Blotted out. In the loft? … Of course. You see. I know.

All those letters in which you told me about your 'Alice blue' wife. You could have stopped. You always held the ace. 'Witness power': the 'steel blue secret' you held tightly against me like a garrotte. You were the silent witness. We each kept our secrets.

But whilst I die our secret grows. Wherever you have buried our secret, it will drip out, ooze. Get too big for its blue plastic sandals and one day it will burst upon your life.

Patricia knows. Patricia can see into the future. It is eight forty-seven.

Jayne is the deathwatch beetle: shiny, scorched-haired slug who types out some silly stupid novel about clocks. During the day she taps away in the corner of the bedroom. Tap, tap, tap. Tapping out the letters of a story I have been dictating. I always dictate. She taps the alphabet in a different order every day. This has been Jayne's mission: to type up the story I dictate. I have a mission to get these secret sapphire blue pages to you. I will get this letter to you or die: ha ha, ha ha – to that brother-in-law of yours. Paul Messenger Witherington. Everyone has a function: to steal, to ring bells, to deliver. I write your letter in Biro.

Tap go the letters and thud go the stick fingers of the clock. Only the deathwatch beetle and the stick fingers of the clock disturb the silence. When she comes, it is to observe breathing. Has Patricia ebbed yet?

Jayne, fat, gauche, blubbering Jayne always needed me. Need. Does an insect need? I have observed her the way one might observe a shiny purple black beetle on a white page. Which way will this move? If I fasten it with a pin, will its legs bleed? Do insects bleed? Entomology is interesting but I tire easily. She tells me I stole her schoolgirl diary and exposed in song 'her love' for you to a busload of adolescents. Imagined wrongs. Memory is an unreliable thermometer of the truth. No sooner had Jayne and I resumed contact than she moved into this house and filled any spare space. It is hard to shrug off a beefy beetle. She is trying to square the circle of the past. She smiles and says, 'Oh, Patricia, you smell of sweet vanilla.' Jayne Thornhill: my half-sister: spawned from my father's wretched sperm and Margaret Mole-Faced Crawford. I am glad that hairy-chinned woman lost her job. I was so clever at listening quietly behind closed doors. I knew this story since Sunday School.

This head … I can attach this head to nothing. This head will not do as it is told, because it is probably no longer mine. It has a mission of its own.

Mother said that I was a perfect child but Father said the devil lived inside of me. He insisted I do things on time: finish my food on time, get dressed on time, be ready on time, get homework in on time, go to the lavatory on time, speak on time. Clocks ticking, time to make haste, clocks thieving, no time to waste. Catch cold clocks out. I like to drag my feet.

When I did not do things on time, he would make me sit and watch the clock all day and I sat and I watched the clock all day. 'Counting the clock that tells the time'. He said that 'time was the only true purgatory'. He made me live in hell. I would drag my feet and just sit. Sit and watch hell: watch the clock. So one day I drew a bloody clock in Biro on his new wallpaper. I discovered hell that day. And hell with Reverend Vickers every day after that. Maybe I am in hell now. Who knows? God knows. Maybe Father knows. He thought he was God. Where Daisy reminds me of you, the deathwatch beetle reminds me of him: Father not God. It is why I have hated her so. Like father, like daughter. She looks like him. She who escaped all that and now she is forcing me to face the very thing I do not have: Time. Like he did. She whines, 'Time for breakfast, time to sleep, time to dictate.' Time is the only thing I have and the only thing I do not have. The deathwatch beetle languishes at the edge of Patricia's moniker, paddles on Patricia's shores, skirts Patricia's vast ocean. As I dictate the novel, she rushes to make Patricia's mark in the sand; a keen eye to pick up Patricia's glossy pebbles; Patricia's words washing over her bulbous toes as she attempts to net them.

The beetle has served her purpose here. Social services would have scooped up Daisy had there not been permanent care and I cannot abide those bloody socials or medics. They do not serve. They dictate. The beetle was convenient. The beetle is also daft. I do not want Daisy left with her. I want you to take care of Daisy. She and this letter are the legacy which trails after: left to you.

I protected you, Daniel, all those years. I told no one of our 'Daisy blue' secret. Your wife kept losing babies. She should have taken greater care.

You protected me with that other 'steel blue secret'. It is four minutes past nine and I am gone but the deathwatch beetle knows you are Daisy's father, Daniel. She found your letters to me. You have no 'silent witness, steel blue secret' to hold over me now.

On Christmas Eve 1968, I had eleven minutes with you, give or take a few fucking seconds, ha ha, beautiful boy that you were. You never raped me. That is your key. The key that you hold. I loved you and had sixty-nine minutes with you if we count our time together in the Municipal Park in 1976. You have been there in the spaces of this life, just as I have been in yours. It is no matter that we have not shared cereal bowls, we are important to one another.

Your wife. Was she worthy of study or analysis? I do not remember. Paul's sister. The blonde berg. She dances on the edge of memory. She takes up scant space with me. She stood behind me in school lines. Was I the Vixen or the Venison

264

between the Thornhill and the Witherington? Ha. Ha. Ha. I had my eyes on my hated half-sister Jayne Thornhill's back in front of me. I am not interested in back stories.

Oh, look. The midnight blue rectangle has turned black. The bedside table lamp casts shadows across the chestnut-speckled grains and meanwhile, the lump in the head grows. No one can hold it back. Listen … listen … the deathwatch beetle has resumed tapping.

Take care of Daisy. I am now stopping a hole to keep the wind away so who gives a fuck? My dying wish is that you take Daisy. Help me. Help me. M'aidez. M'aidez.

Nine-seventeen. I have spent seventy-one minutes writing to you. Enough of this interior monologue. I die by degrees. Put out the light.

Always, Tricia

**

December 20th 2005

Danny,

A soft down of snow carpets the platform at Winchmore Hill. I'm Cambridge-bound.

The words carry me into an unknown whiteness, for the snow keeps coming and I'm propelled into the future on a roll. We have lived too long in the past.

Tricia, Danny. 'Always, Tricia'. Her final contraction. A woman who had never been known to use a contraction, leaves her own name as a final and special one for … 'Daniel'.

I write on the flip side of her sapphire blue paper.

Danny ... who is Daniel? I don't know Daniel. These people are known to me as Patricia and Danny. These new names change identities. Danny, knowing what I do now, you are as alien to me as this new name.

For once, Jayne was the silent one. Her silence gained her authorship of a novel and an adopted daughter called Daisy. I travel further up the line. The train pushes me into the dark, winter afternoon and as I look into the swirling clouds of snow, the train window reflects two bouquets of flowers: red roses and white lilies. One bouquet sent to a funeral in late May1985. The other, on the same day, sent to another kind of funeral: the funeral of my womb. The sweet sickly aroma of the white lilies pervaded our home so soon after receiving my medical results, when we were grieving our childlessness. The fragrance reminded me of sickly sweet vanilla.

A florist's mistake, easily done; switched addresses. Not meant for my eyes.

I write on her back.

I watered your grief that year. 1985. I thought it was for us; for arrival at a barren cul-de-sac. I know now it was for the severed contact with your daughter. Jayne must have found this letter and kept it from you. How we all underestimated Jayne. For Patricia, the silent pact was dead but how could you take ownership of Daisy?

Feeling cheated. It spreads from the stomach to the sternum. I am now going to make you feel that way. I am going to give you information which will make you feel cheated.

'Tricia' says that her sixty-nine minutes with you belong to her. I am questioning every single one I spent with you. It's like having lost a watch – or two. Did any of those minutes belong to me?

Where was I on that hot summer's day in 1976? Was I at a silly wedding dress fitting? When you returned from your 'family outing' did I rush to kiss you and tease you about the shade of my frivolous wedding dress? Or did that 'family outing' take place on another day? The day we were posting the wedding invitations, quarrelled, made up and posted them all the same?

Patricia lived and lives in the spaces between us for a reason of which I was unaware. I always thought the space she took up in our lives was because you never supported me in the police statement I wanted to make when I was fifteen. You were behind me on that open bus platform. You saw it all. Now I know why you remained a 'silent witness'. Patricia would have blackmailed you with her pregnancy. And after all, like I am now, you were Cambridge-bound.

Silly me, for as the train gathers speed I can hear someone singing my story clearly now. *'The loft floorboards are dangerous. Don't go meddling and sniffing over old ground.'*

You insisted that we became ex-directory soon after we married. How often did you see my brother, Danny? A lot more than I did. I can see the pity for me in my sister-in-law's eyes as you collect your letters. I see now what is written in Lydia's sidelong glances. Silly me. Not to know. Not to guess. Helpful Paul.

Who are you?

It all begins to make some other sense. The past is beginning to make perfect sense. This is the 'steel blue secret'. You were standing right behind me on the open platform of the bus. You saw Patricia push Jayne as the 366 bus swerved on the corner. You saw Patricia lean in with all her weight on Jayne which sent tiny Rachel, my friend Rachel, at the front of the platform to her pavement death.

That's why Patricia kept silent about her baby's paternity. Silence for silence. That silence left Jayne with the weight of guilt on her back.

I write on this bitch's flip side.

You paid up. All those financially challenging years in the late seventies' recession when you had a general practice before starting your political career. And suddenly in 1985 we could afford so much more. It creates a picture which I never knew existed.

Tell me, Danny. During the length of your political career, did you ever stick your neck out for anything in which you personally believed? The only thing I remember you doing was introducing a tramline.

Is the truth worth knowing, Danny? Because I am about to deliver my own garrotte.

Your secret is in the loft? The locked suitcase? All those Father's Day cards … those building society books … firing in the dark … I'm leading up to something … all those photos.

I am getting the story right. Now, I am getting the story right. I was the only one, the only one who could get it right.

You are wrong. You are so wrong.

Danny, *who does she look like?* Me. Daisy looks like me. And Patricia hated what she saw in her own daughter. The truth is in *my* suitcase. All those photos of me and Paul. Paul and the gap in his front teeth. Blond and *green*-eyed. I'm looking at this photo of Daisy and she has green eyes, not blue. How many times did Patricia need to convince herself of the colour blue? What Patricia saw in Daisy was an amazing family likeness to Paul and his sister. Me.

When I look at this photo of a fifteen-year-old, I see not you or Patricia, but my brother. And Patricia and Paul knew.

Because blackmail was Patricia's thing.

I am thinking. We are at Royston; almost at our destination, where our dog was cremated. I'm thinking about our streamlined, white vacuum of a house and thirty-seven years of marriage. I am getting off the train and I know what I am going to do.

Your wife

37

Dear Jayne,

A double-lipped Daisy smiled up at me, strawberry-haired, a promise for the future shining from her fifteen-year-old, clear green eyes; a half-child budding into womanhood. The photo had been taken over twenty years ago. If Patricia had not enclosed the snapshot would I ever have realized that my brother was Daisy's father? Did Danny feel cheated by that loss of time with this Daisy who he believed to be his daughter? Or did his political career necessitate it? Switching on my mobile phone, I got into the cab. Danny would be trying to phone and if he did now, I was not sure what I might say. I checked for messages and was surprised he had left none but then almost immediately the mobile rang. Danny, probably Danny. 'Hello.'

'Hello, Shelley?'

'Mum?'

'I've been trying to get you all day. I'm on my electric scooter,' my mother said. Her voice sounded joyful. 'It's snowing and I'm on my electric scooter. I'm on my way to the End of the World.'

'Where?'

'The End of the World. It's a new shopping complex. I don't know why I've never learnt to drive. All those years ...'

'Mum,' I suddenly said. 'Why did Paul sell your car that winter after he passed his driving test?'

There was one of those crackling pauses on the mobile line and then she said, less joyfully, 'I can't remember all those years ago. He probably needed money for something. I'll phone you when I get back from The End of the World. I've Christmas shopping to do and I'm having a ball ...'

The unwrapped watches read five o'clock. I had been travelling for three hours. The double-sided letter, written on sapphire blue paper, with the photo of a fifteen-year-old Daisy, were placed back in the crumpled envelope. I pushed the envelope into the pocket of my fun fur coat: the same envelope, Jayne, that you must have harboured in your pocket earlier today and stored for all these years.

The lush, open-curtained drawing rooms which lined the Witheringtons' avenue heralded Christmas, with floor to high-ceiling pine trees dressed in warming reds and purples. Parcels packaged with lost time ... I tried to picture Danny's face as I imagined giving him, on Christmas morning, not the watch but the sapphire blue envelope with the two letters, back to back: one from Patricia and the one from me. There was no sense of satisfaction but there was suddenly an idiotic sense of guilt, when I realized that I would be arriving at my rich sister-in-law's house without any presents for my three nieces. A sense of normality still lurked somewhere in my soul.

The cab pulled into the sweeping driveway and I paid the driver. As my boots scrunched into the snow on the pathway, I felt totally exhausted. I had planned the conversation with Paul, but not what my future might be. As far as I was concerned, I was still travelling forward into a shroud of whiteness which should be melting shortly. A lump of newly-laid snow fell from the knocker to the doorstep with a soft thud.

It was Paul who answered the door. As soon as our eyes made contact, I remembered the way Danny had looked at me when I told him I was meeting you, Jayne. He had looked half-angry, half-scared. Danny had been scared that you would open up his Pandora suitcase of worms. You didn't. How could you possibly know that my brother was your niece's father? You are thinking my husband is Daisy's father. And so would I, had it not been for Patricia's enclosure of Daisy's teenage photo. My world was shifting, changing shape, as the past began to take on different meanings.

'Hello, Paul,' I said. 'Put the kettle on. I've brought a little piece of Patricia to you.'

I only had to say her name. That was it. But for Paul's blond hair salted white-grey, he could have been twelve, me ten, him reacting to some recently discovered misdemeanour. He looked defensive. And he looked like the photo of Daisy.

Lydia called lightly from the hallway balcony. 'Shelley? What a surprise. Is Danny with you?'

I looked upward, past the towering Christmas tree's apexed star. Strains of the latest boy band thumped down towards me as my three nieces called down in a line. 'Auntie Shelley. Merry Christmas.'

Aunt. Yes, I was. To Daisy now. And as I looked up at them, I saw three Daisy photos: at twelve, at fifteen, at eighteen. We aren't an extended family who surprises one another by random visits and Lydia was descending the stairway past her three daughters looking slightly concerned, exchanging a sideways glance with her husband. As Lydia looked towards me with customary pity, I wondered how my

272

sister-in-law would cope with this news. But Paul acted quickly. 'Lyds, I need to talk with Shelley in my office. Will you bring some coffee and sandwiches through?'

Lydia obeyed. Paul was obviously dealing with a sister who had discovered her husband was a cheat and a liar. Lydia disappeared with discretion and Paul opened the study door which led off from the hallway. The study was thick and deep with burgundy. Every one of the books, many of them reference books on Law, had its own place on the wall-to-wall bookcase. I sank into the burgundy armchair, pulled off my boots and let my toes make tram lines in the soft-piled burgundy carpet.

'Can I take your coat?' he said.

My fingers tapped at the blue envelope inside my pocket.

'I'm cold,' I said, my eyes fixed firmly on my brother.

'This is a pleasant surprise. How can I help you?' he said as if he was speaking to a client. There was that tiny gap between his front teeth. How could Danny have missed that? Daisy was so like my brother. He did not sit. His green poker-player eyes remained on mine.

'I know,' I simply said. No one had ever had the courage to tell me the truth and yet everyone around me seemed so scared by what I might know, or might discover: Lydia, Paul … Danny, even you, Jayne, in the restaurant. Were you all scared of what I might *do* with the truth? Why? I had done nothing with any kind of truth in the past.

'What do you think you know?' Paul said, still standing.

There was an important question to ask. Swallowing hard, my throat dry from the long journey, I said, 'Did he ever feel anything for her?'

Paul's laughter was immediate. It sounded like a snort of relief. I had asked in the third person. It meant Danny. Did

Danny feel anything for Patricia? I needed to know this first; before I said any more. It was important.

He folded his arms and smiled, a little condescendingly I thought. 'It was a cold arrangement during those years. His communication with her was short, business-like, to the point. He made it absolutely clear there was to be no emotional input.'

So what about all these letters between my husband and dead Patricia Vickers addressed to Paul Witherington? I didn't ask. I let my brother carry on. 'He was seventeen when all this happened.' My brother sounded like a barrister. He was a barrister.

'And she was under-age,' I said.

'You've always needed to loosen up, Shell. It was a quick adolescent fuck for which he paid dearly in later life. But that's all it was. Really. No need to worry yourself. Go home now and enjoy Christmas. Quick fuck, that's all.'

Danny had felt nothing for Patricia? I now wasn't sure of that either. My brother was protesting too much.

'Benji paid a very high price,' I said.

My brother looked at me quickly. Something had changed. Why had mentioning Benji caused him alarm? Whatever the colour of lies, no one should have to live with them. The colour of these lies was not white and I was beginning to feel some pity for a girl, for my *niece,* whose birth was surrounded by lies. I looked at my watch and remembered. Daisy could be giving birth now and still the lies continued. 'Why did you let Danny believe the lie? How could you do that to both Danny and Benji?'

'Oh, speak in proper sentences,' he bit back.

But before I could tell him I was no longer a teenager and he couldn't pull rank, the study door opened. I kept my eyes firmly fixed on my brother. This time the colour drained from his cheeks. He was reaching into the drawer of his desk and pulling out a set of car keys. Lydia was lifting a tray of porcelain coffee cups, jug and mince pies from a hallway table.

'I don't think we're going to have time for refreshments. I've got to get Shelley back home to Danny.' Paul and Lydia exchanged a look of understanding.

I stared down at my toes on the burgundy carpet. I understood now, too. I could make things unpleasant for other people if I told the truth. But I was thirsty for a truth which had been denied to me all these years and the words of Patricia's letter burned in my head. 'Not so quick, quick, Paul,' I heard myself say out loud. 'I'm not sure Shelley wants to get back home to Danny.'

Lydia looked embarrassed and guilty. The 'safe house' to receive and pass on letters could only have happened with her collaboration. She went to pour the coffee, looked as though she had second thoughts and left the study, closing the door behind her and I wanted to shout after her, 'How could you have kept this from me all these years, Lydia? What you *thought* you knew? You were my friend. You were there soon after I received those clinical returns in 1985. Were you there at all?' There wasn't time to say it. Lydia had closed the door behind her.

'What lie was told to Danny?' Paul said quickly as soon as the study door was closed.

'How long have you known Daisy is your daughter? And I want the truth.'

'What are you talking about?' Never admit guilt. I had heard my defence barrister father say it again and again. Never admit guilt.

275

'Answer my question and I'll answer yours.'

He leaned back on the desk and sighed, picked up a pencil and jiggled it between his forefingers the way he used to when he was a young boy lying. Or when I saw him wigged and in court. 'We could never be sure of the truth with Pat.'

'Pat'. Patricia had now become someone else.

'The truth was anathema to her. She preferred to flirt with a range of possibilities. The truth resided somewhere else, never with her.' He shook his head and threw the pencil on the desk. 'For good reasons, nobody knew who Daisy's father was.'

I was thirsty and ... faintly irritated. He was still avoiding the truth. Or not admitting guilt. I got up and poured the coffee from the slim white jug. 'But the proof was right in front of your eyes. You just needed to look in the mirror.' Then I thought for a moment. 'Did you ever *see* your daughter?'

He hesitated, gave a little courtroom chuckle as if I was given to hallucinations and then said, 'Pat served time ... not long before she died. Drugs ... I ...' He scanned the bookshelves, 'I made things easier for her, although,' he quickly added, 'I'm sure the drugs were medicinal.'

It was all fitting into place. A 'Get out of Jail Early Card'. I was thinking back to 'Pat's' letter which had given me so much information. Patricia had been stopped from communicating, or I guess receiving money from Danny shortly before she died in 1985, the year things got so much better for us financially. '1985,' I said. 'The year Danny took his seat in Parliament.'

Danny Diego, one of the youngest MPs in the House: so much to lose by being connected with a woman who had served time for dealing in drugs; so much to lose by financially supporting a woman for years who had given birth to a child when she was just sixteen. 'You made things easier in return for what, brother?'

He didn't reply.

'No more communication with you or Danny,' I said. 'What a very good brother-in-law you have been to my husband. So when did Patricia tell you Daisy was your child?'

He did that chuckle again as if I were leaping to a huge assumption. I passed him a white porcelain cup and saucer, noticing an unusual slight tremor in his hand as he took the coffee from me. I went on. 'Because she did know Daisy was your daughter. Daisy stared her in the face for fifteen years with your eyes. And she never could stand the sight of me. So looking like me couldn't have helped much either. And then of course I was married to the boy she wanted to have as Daisy's father.

'She told a number of boys they were Daisy's father. Underage casual sex resulted in a lifelong pay cheque. But I saw her all right.' He took a sip of coffee. 'For Danny's sake. Not because I was any way involved.' And then he added, 'And for you.'

'Why did she go to Danny in 1976?'

He gave a barrister sigh and scratched his forehead to give him time to think; took a sip more of coffee: more time to think. He moved to sit on a straight-backed burgundy chair, placed the coffee cup on his desk and ran his fingers through the still ample head of hair. 'Pat wanted money. She had been on a trip to Africa the year before. She had left Daisy with her reverend father and returned penniless. He shrugged his shoulders. 'She tried Danny. You were getting married that summer. He...'

'Needed to cover his back,' I said.

'You've spoken to Danny about this?' he said.

'No. *Patricia* mentioned meeting Danny in 1976 in her last letter to him.' I looked at Paul over the porcelain rim of the coffee cup. 'I have been asked to deliver her last letter to him.'

'Someone else knows about this?'

'The woman who phoned Lydia for our landline number.'

'Someone phoned Lyds for your number?' He didn't know.

'The fat girl,' I said. Then added. 'Not so fat now. Beautifully groomed. Beautiful in fact.' And I meant it, Jayne.

He shook his head again. 'She knows about my involvement? I mean helping Danny out of a fix.'

You see. Still no admission of guilt.

'No. Only I know.'

'I can count on your silence?'

38

It was a long ride home and for a long time we barely spoke. Patricia. Tricia. Pat: different people in the same clothes. I looked at my brother at the wheel of his Mercedes. I now had four nieces. Then I realized. Daisy was also your niece, Jayne. So preoccupied with the revelation about my husband and brother I had forgotten to ingest that you were Patricia's half-sister. Big bold Reverend Bartholomew Vickers was your father too. Shit, Jayne. Was that why Patricia had hated you so much and made your school life one huge misery? But Patricia had mentioned your birth mother's name in the letter. Something flashed before my eyes: a coach on the motorway ahead of us; the slush. I pulled out the blue envelope. Took out the letter. 'Margaret Crawford,' I said aloud.

'What's that?' Paul said quickly looking at the sapphire blue writing paper. Had he recognised 'Pat's' handwriting scratched out in blue Biro and obvious ill health?

'Margaret Crawford,' I repeated. 'You remember who she was?'

Paul shrugged his shoulders, indicated to move into the fast lane.

'Dad told us she got sacked,' I said.

'Who? Where?' he said, pushing hard on the accelerator.

'The bus conductress. Sacked from the buses. In Milton. Dad told me to button my lip when I said that Patricia pushed

279

Jayne on the bus. Did Dad know you got Patricia, oh sorry, 'Pat' pregnant?'

No comment. Solicitors advise 'no comment'. But then I spoke again. 'Why didn't Patricia threaten you with the paternity of Daisy? What hold did *you* have over her?'

There was this long pause. For about ten miles until I said, 'You told her she could count on my silence about her murdering Rachel … And Danny promised that too …Oh, my God.' I blasphemed softly. 'Dad gave you the advice.'

Eyes ahead. No comment.

My mobile phone rang. It would be Danny. We had been on the motorway for at least half an hour and he would be mad with worry. Danny did worry for me. I felt sure it would be him, but it was my mother again. She talked, I listened. She talked at length. 'Don't go worrying about the past,' she was saying. 'What's done is done. Let it be.'

'That was Mum.'

'What did she have to say?'

'She says that she's been to The End of the World and back on her electric scooter.'

'The end of the world?'

'It's a shopping complex.'

'Further than Charing Cross then?' He said this as if to fuel some sibling closeness, but I pulled down the sunshade and checked my smudged eye make-up in the Merc mirror. 'You sold Mum's car that spring to pay off Patricia, didn't you? And Dad told you to do it.'

I placed the blue envelope back in my fun fur coat pocket. I wasn't having much fun. It was all coming together. 'You walked out on Mave at Charing Cross because you discovered she was still in contact with Patricia, didn't you? You knew Mave and Patricia had always been good friends.

Mave was a gossip. That was all too close for comfort, wasn't it?'

His knuckles were white on the steering wheel. I looked at the car clock. 'You may have a grandchild by now.' It was another twenty miles on before I said, 'I bought you and Danny watches for Christmas. Leather for Danny, gold for you.'

He allowed himself to give a half-smile.

'Are you smiling because you know I can't prove anything?'

He said nothing.

'The past is another country, isn't it, Paul?' I said. 'And besides the wench is dead.'

'You've misquoted Marlowe.'

'How little I knew my brother and my husband,' I said.

As I was falling asleep, I thought on you and Patricia as sisters ... I thought of how, if one could, with one push on a bus, destroy the lives of those one hated, would one do it? Patricia did. She did.

As I woke up, Paul was pulling into the carport. Danny wouldn't be in bed. He would be waiting up for me. But the house was dark and unwelcoming. Danny wasn't at home.

39

Jayne (53)
December 20th 2005

Dear Shelley,

So this was what happened on the evening of the day you walked out of the department store, leaving your gift-wrapped watches. I drove straight to the hospital in the midlands where we lived. He was already there.

'Hello, Danny,' I said.

'Hello Jayne.'

'Danneeeeey ...' Violet jumped up from her seat in the hospital corridor and threw her arms about Danny's neck. 'Daisy is having a baby tonight,' she said, smiling broadly.

He was standing there with two dozen downturned white roses in his hand, their petals almost touching the corridor floor, looking just as I had seen him in the odd television interview.

'I'm sorry,' I said looking up at him from my seat. 'Violet always greets people as though they are old friends even if I simply know their name.'

'Miss Dee,' he said, biting into a kiosk sandwich, he's obviously 'a man on the go', 'there's no need to apologise.'

I was at once embarrassed for a number of reasons. Your husband was no longer the boy with whom I had been

282

infatuated. He was a man in his early fifties, still attractive, and just as confident of his ability to play with affections. Affections were footballs to Danny Diego and I was suddenly taken aback by his reference to me as Miss Dee. I had, of course, used Patricia's Christian name and Danny's surname as a quasi-macaronic pseudonym for that bloody book *Girls in a Line,* as Daisy had referred to it, which was unlike any of my other Rose Good's Young Adult romantic novels. (He obviously had not read any of those.) He must have been aware of what I had done with the pseudonym 'Tricia Dee'. I saw it in his flirtatious, blue-speckled eyes. In that moment, I realized that the fifteen-year-old in me had not completely died and I flushed overwhelmingly. He still had a good crop of dark hair.

He passed me the two bunches of white roses and took hold of Violet's hand, gently pulling her back down to a seat. Danny Diego was now seated, shoulder to shoulder, him in his big sheepskin coat, between Violet and me, finishing his sandwich. We were bunched up, the three of us, but then Danny Diego has never had any respect for one's personal space. He still smelt of nicotine – possibly a more expensive brand than in his youth and I was still, it seemed, as mesmerised.

'What must I do with these?' I asked, looking down at the flowers and then at the shiny, gold wedding ring on the hand that was holding Violet's.

'You could try putting them in water,' he said.

'I'm not sure that the nurses will allow flowers until the baby is born,' I said. 'They've asked me to come outside the room whilst they carry out some tests.'

'Daisy's all right?' He looked genuinely concerned. 'She's a *primagravida.'*

283

'And I'm a *Darned Sindrum,*' Violet said.

'Yes you are, Violet,' your husband said. 'And downright beautiful with it, I would say.'

Violet giggled. And giggled. Loudly.

'Violet,' I said. 'Shush, Lovely.' Then I looked at your husband and said, 'I'm sorry, I didn't mean to be rude about the flowers.' The roses were wilting and weighty.

'They're for you,' he said. 'I have a card somewhere.'

'Me?' Danny Diego was giving *me* roses?

'Thank you for contacting me,' he said.

I blushed slightly. I had contacted him initially on Daisy's behalf. I suppose I was twenty years too late. And I had placed Patricia's letter to him in the garbage that very day. Bundles of guilt. Oh, my. Violet took both bunches of roses from Danny and I said, 'She's my daughter.'

'And thank you for looking after mine all these years,' he said. He had folded his arms and was looking up the corridor.

'I'm sorry we didn't keep in contact,' I said. 'Watch those thorns, Violet.' She was prodding the petals with her forefinger. I looked at Danny and carried on. 'I obviously found your letters to Patricia but thought it …'

He interrupted me; maybe it was the mention of her name or maybe it's because he punctuates dialogue with his own full stops. 'Life's complicated,' he said. 'And it was all a long time ago.'

I had remained silent all these years and I wanted to explain that it was impossible to be silent now. Daisy had caught up with it all. Of course, it would have been difficult for me if I had contacted him in 1985. I would have felt duty-bound to have given him Patricia's opened letter and her request to have you both adopt Daisy. Would you have done so, Shelley? Patricia had been so hot on dates in her letter to

284

Danny, I could no longer question his paternity.

He rubbed his eyes with his large hands. His wedding ring shone out from his left hand and I remembered Edwin's thick gold band. I never removed it when he died.

'You always apologised too much,' he said. 'You were the archetypal people-pleaser. You haven't changed, Miss Dee, Miss Good or Miss Thornhill.'

I felt awful. Everyone wants to change and I didn't want to be the Jayne Thornhill of his schoolboy, bus-top adolescence. I wondered there and then in the hospital corridor, rubbing shoulders with Danny Diego, who was rubbing his eyes with fatigue, if I had just been trying to escape the fat adolescent I once was by taking on these other names. 'Mrs Tips,' I said. 'I'm Mrs Jayne Tips.'

He didn't look interested. And then he said, 'Is Daisy having an epidural?'

'Oh,' I said, quite taken aback. 'I wouldn't suppose to be that intimate to know.'

The hospital corridor was filled with the roar of his laughter and then Violet's laughter for Violet loved to laugh and copied anyone who did so. She was very clever at imitating people's laughter. It's a wonderful knack I wish I had possessed. And I never knew anyone who could laugh quite like Violet. It felt surreal: to be here with your husband when I had only left you, Shelley, hours before. How strange our lives had become so inextricably entwined as a result of being in a line.

'You always had this old-fashioned way of speaking,' he said.

I felt foolish. 'Does your wife know you are here?' I said.

'No,' he replied. Then added, 'Thank you for being discreet.'

I frowned in astigmatic confusion and he said, 'Daisy told me you wouldn't say anything to Shelley. You haven't have you?'

I shook my head and thought, well, I almost did.

'I need some time before giving Shelley this news.'

It did occur to me that he had had something like thirty-six years already. But I simply asked, 'How long have you known you had a daughter?'

'Since the beginning of time,' he said.

The beginning of time. I was wondering who exactly Danny Diego was. I didn't ask there and then how he felt about the lovely Benji coughing up as Father for all these years. It wasn't the right moment. I would bide my time. There was a long silence in the hospital corridor as I reflected on Benji and what all this was going to eventually mean to him when Danny reached into his sheepskin coat pocket and pulled out a card. He gave it to me.

I read. 'A rose for a Rose,' I said. 'Thank you.'

How I might have been in La La Land had he given this to me as an adolescent but I was looking at the loops and curves of the vowels and consonants. For some reason Daisy's school exercise books bobbed across my mind: Daisy at fifteen writing 'Daisy Jacobs' on the cover. Then my mind bobbed along to Patricia's front room: to Benji standing beneath the murdered stag and its antlers at the funeral: Benji looking at the florist's card and throwing it on the mantelpiece. Do florists always sign bouquet cards? Benji knew then. Maybe he always knew. I would of course never have forgotten your handwriting, Shelley or Patricia's, or Mave's or Brenda Baker's. Schoolfriends never forget each other's handwriting: all those exercise books, all those examination papers. It's just that I had cleanly and conveniently forgotten Rachel's.

'Daisy says you're going to be retiring up here?' I said, putting the card in my jacket pocket. I could check it against the card sent in 1985.

'To be close,' he said. 'Shelley and I are going to be part of my daughter and grandchild's lives. At long last I can have the family I always hankered after.'

You had no idea of what your future was about to bring. I realized there and then in that hospital corridor that your husband had drawn a map of your future all for you and without your knowledge. He nodded to me in his sheepskin coat. I had only ever recalled him in a blazer.

40

December 20th 2005/Just Before Midnight

Present at the birth of Patricia and Danny's grandchild: it felt surreal. Danny stayed outside and played a form of card games with Violet. So Daisy's baby was born to the falling snow on December 20th 2005 and the shrieking of 'Snap'. Daisy had always told your husband, since their first meeting in September that she would contact him when she was in labour and that he could arrive and look after Violet so that I could be present at the birth. I would, of course, phone Benji as soon as the baby was born.

Daisy had never talked about her own baby's father but then her family seemed to be at a loss where fathers were concerned; there were just too many not doing an awful lot. Not least my own, with whom I had only exchanged a few sentences at Patricia's funeral. Anyway, I was just pleased that at thirty-six Daisy was having a baby. This had always seemed important to me and these days, I sighed, having a baby as a single parent did not seem as extraordinary as it was thirty-odd years ago.

Daisy had always told me that she had been present at the birth of Violet and so she wanted me present at the birth of her baby. In fact, when I had told her I was her aunt, she embraced the idea, more because, as she said, 'Violet is my cousin. We are blood-related!'

Well, I'm not very good at blood, or physical intimacy, I suppose, and the birth took a long time. I tried to refrain from looking at my watch. Daisy had insisted that the hospital clock be removed from the wall and special permission from the matron needed to be sought. I had been very busy. Danny dutifully ran off for coffees and egg and watercress hospital sandwiches and I said, 'Bear down,' many times, as I had seen it all on the weekly soap operas although the midwife kept saying to me, 'Not yet, not yet, don't exhaust her.'

The baby seemed to be born in a dream-like bubble. Just before midnight the midwife asked me to check my watch as the baby was being born. I looked at my watch and almost missed the vital moments. There I was at Patricia's grandchild's birth as I had been at Patricia's death. It was synchronicity. Here was Patricia, thankfully diluted down the years. When everyone was washed up, Danny and Violet were ushered into the private hospital room. Violet greeted the newborn baby, *de rigeur,* as though she had known it all along and she kissed Daisy so much I had to say, 'Violet. Daisy has just given birth. She's exhausted. And no, Daisy nor the baby feel like playing 'Snap' now. I do think you've snapped yourself out, Lovely.'

Then Daisy said, 'Jayne, I want you to name her. I want it to be your choice.'

'Oh, my,' I said and I looked out of the hospital window. I couldn't believe it. Here I was, with my expanding family: my Violet and my Daisy. Cousins but closer than siblings. They adored one another. And here was Danny Diego who looked set to become part of our lives as I was expecting you to do the same, Shelley. It didn't turn out the way I expected at all. But then of course neither do good novels.

I looked out on the drifting snowflakes and was about to open my mouth to voice my thought when Danny spoke. 'Tricia liked flowers,' he said. 'She christened you Daisy,' he said looking at my niece in her hospital bed and then looking across at my daughter he said, 'and she christened you Violet.'

Violet gave a huge grin and nodded saying, 'Violet.'

Then he looked at me. 'And you are a self-appointed Rose, Miss Good,' he said. 'I think Tricia would like our grandchild to be called 'Poppy'. Yes, Poppy for remembrance. What do you think, Daisy?'

Daisy looked at me beside the hospital bed and passed me her baby saying, 'What do you think, Auntie Jayne? It's your choice.'

This tiny being in my arms was my great-niece and I instantly fell in love with her. I then spoke to Danny saying a word that had been, up until now, fairly foreign to my lips. 'No,' I said. The name which sprang to my mind in that midlands hospital as those snowflakes fell was, I felt, a more fitting name and one which would please me and not your husband. 'Rachel,' I said softly looking down on someone I hoped would become a big chunk of my life and Violet's. 'We'll call her Rachel.'

'Rachel,' Daisy said as softly as I did. 'What a lovely name. Hello, Rachel.'

Your husband's face was as white as the snowflakes falling on the midlands street below and that teenage intoxicating feeling of being with him again began to drift away.

'I think I need to go and have a cigarette,' he said.

41

Shelley (53)

Dear Jayne,

That same evening, I know it was that same evening, Paul and I sat in the drawing room, me cross-legged on the floor in my fun fur coat, surrounded by removal crates and watching the melting snow. Danny had left the rake propped up against the garden fence. All this raking over the past: the need recently to let the gardeners go, the move to a cheaper home in the midlands to help finance another small family. Daisy was *having a baby*. I remembered you had said that, Jayne, in the Milton department store restaurant. Daisy was *having a baby*. It was all making perfect sense. Danny was now elsewhere, I knew. Just as he had been for most of our lives together.

Stripped of the personal bric-a-brac, it was hard to believe this had once been home. The home was withering to a house before my eyes: the continually re-painted white walls now bleak and lonely. Paul looked displaced and I told him to go home. Dawn would soon break through. The frozen past was now moving, right back to when Danny had chucked me and then got back with me again after 'the incident'. It had all been connected with Patricia's pregnancy. After 'the incident' she had no hold over him for he possessed the 'steel

291

blue secret': the silent witness right behind me on the 366 bus.

Danny had left a note. Another half-truth: 'Called to the midlands on business – back tomorrow'. But I knew he had received a call from Daisy at the same time you had, Jayne. This was why there had been no phone call from him and no message left on my mobile voicemail. Eventually I must have fallen asleep again for I was awoken by a faint tapping sound at the window. I thought it might be a bird but it was still dark. Suddenly I saw Danny's face at the drawing room window. He was smiling. It wasn't the lecherous, early-morning silly alcohol-induced grin, it was his genuine and warm lopsided smile. His key was in the lock. Paul woke up.

'It's Danny,' I whispered to him.

'You can't prove anything,' my brother whispered back. 'You're making an assumption.'

I went to the sitting room door and placed my forefinger to my lips. 'Paul's asleep,' I whispered. I expected him to ask immediately why my brother was in our sitting room but Danny's thoughts were elsewhere. He quickly took hold of my hand, pulled me close into him and whispered in my ear. 'Shelley, I have the most wonderful news.' He hadn't been drinking, he was high on his own adrenalin. He kissed me lightly on the lips. 'It's a miracle. I have such a story to tell you about something which happened to me when we were kids. It's going to change everything for us … for the good.'

I let go of his hand and fingered the creased, sapphire blue envelope in my right pocket. I had never imagined that he might be so free from … guilt. He took my left hand and said, 'Come into the kitchen so I can tell you the whole story and let Paul sleep.'

My heart was pounding as I stood in the cold, packed-away kitchen, stood stirring pasta in a large saucepan for he was starving, had been at the hospital all night. I stood in my fun fur coat, adding herbs and spices and chopped tomatoes, listening to his story, occasionally turning to watch more snow melt and slip from the hedgerow. His eyes shone. This was the happiest I had seen him in years and he was promising me a new beginning and the family we had yearned for during our marriage. I touched the blue envelope in my right hand pocket every now and then as I prepared sauce and listened to his words. This was Danny's story. This was the story of a Patricia, who, in her own words, would be diluted down the years, but present nevertheless. A hornet which has, no, *had* the power to sting years after its death for a hornet loses its power some hours after death. And as I listened to Danny's story, for once, I also listened as carefully to my own feelings. I realized that I felt angry towards all the people in my husband's story: my brother, father, mother, Lydia, Patricia and you, Jayne. I felt angry with you until you told me the full saga of your own story. So angry that I felt like lifting the pot of pasta and throwing it at the bare, white walls. Instead I threw the occasional piece at the tiling to see if it would stick and I listened on and on into his story. He told me it all, as I had read it on Patricia's sapphire blue paper. His now unveiled words slipped between the polished spoons and tiny crevices of wood upon the kitchen table. I stared hard at the veins and arteries on the table before me: veins and arteries which carried life to the very heart of the kitchen. They looked blocked. The surface had carried too much silence. And then I had a vision of a school desk, where a fifteen-year-old had dug deep those words with the needle of a compass for all the world to see: I DO LOVE DANNY DIEGO xxx. The 'V' had been hard to negotiate, I remember:

the kisses the first of many. I stared hard too at those large hands and yes, the square smooth fingertips which were lifting pasta from the white bone china plate to lips I had kissed and cherished: lips that were giving me his story. This was a story which was packing away the past into removal crates so that our future could be played out elsewhere. His lips were wiping away the silences which once existed between us.

'Thank you for finally telling me your story,' I said, still in my fun fur coat for it was cold in this white-walled kitchen. I now knew that Patricia had taken a lot more of my husband's life than sixty-nine minutes … 'but I'm afraid you have opted too late to tell the truth.'

He said nothing but looked straight at me.

'Do you think you can take a prize for silence,' I said softly, 'and return that prize to me when you have nothing left at stake?' Words from the past echoed around the white-walled kitchen. 'When you have had your successful political career, when you are retiring?'

'Who cares about the past now, Shelley?' he said.

'I care,' I said. 'Tell me this.' And I took a small mouthful of pasta and touched the blue envelope in my pocket which contained Patricia's letter and mine to him. I touched it like it was some kind of talisman: some escape into the future. 'When you were eighteen you covered for Patricia, didn't you? You saw her push Jayne Thornhill and you let Jayne live with that so you were off the hook and that saved your future.'

He placed the spoon on to the white bone china plate and pointed at me with the fork. 'No. You see even if Cambridge and my future hadn't been at stake, I still wouldn't have been a witness for Jayne,' he said.

'Why?'

'Because people like you and me go quietly by.'

'Go quietly by?'

'You and I are the kind of people who let things go by.'

'But you're a politician.'

'Exactly,' he said. 'You'll never get anywhere in life if you speak your true mind. *You've* never spoken your mind. You've taken everything on offer.'

I was stunned. It was another brittle stab at my core. 'But I tried. I tried to tell the truth.'

'I didn't,' he said and threw the fork on to the kitchen table. 'And there's no difference.'

At that moment, my brother walked into the kitchen and the two men embraced. My husband took some beers from the fridge and shared them and his story of his new grandchild. 'Because Shelley knows now,' Danny said but Paul wouldn't look at me.

They both lit up cigarettes and laughed and joked together and for all the world I could have been back on the top of the 366 bus, but this time excluded from the inner circle and of course Paul had his car in that last year so always drove home. I just kept throwing bits of pasta on the kitchen tiles and the bits stuck. I looked out beyond the camaraderie of these two men and saw my brother's Mercedes. The car.

Then I had the final piece of the jigsaw.

42

Epilogue
And Finally Jayne (Older and Wiser)
Mothering Sunday, 2020

Dear Shelley,

And so here I am: standing before the threshold of my old school: Milton High School for Girls. We are twenty-two minutes early. We: Daisy and her daughter Rachel, my daughter Violet and me. Although as I watch them get out of Daisy's car, I will keep a social distance. Rachel is about the same age as when we lost her namesake ... Violet is all heart-shaped like the leaves of her namesake, Rachel is strangely smooth and dark like her own, promising to be as rich in thinking as the Rachel we lost to a pavement, even though she isn't remotely connected by blood. The old school buildings are still here but new ones have been built on the playing fields. They are square buildings with clean, strong lines.

The last time I was here I was perched on a stacking chair at the back of the school hall in 1971, watching you, Shelley Witherington, emerge from the inner sanctum and take your head girl prizes in exchange for silence. I believed you had lived all your life in the inner sanctum. Now I know better. As I stand facing the entrance doors, I am watching my daughter Violet move towards me up the crescent as though she is on her catwalk. Although my daughter's life has been restricted, it has not been diminished and it has been far happier than mine, for much of my life here was wretched. Violet, I can see, is dressed today in lavender and I can smell a similar fragrance. She wears a lilac shift dress which Daisy, I'm sure, has made. It's modern, chic and up-to-date. Violet's probably chosen the design from one of Daisy's catalogues and Daisy would have painstakingly altered every centimetre to suit Violet's fashionable tastes. Daisy has embroidered swinging godet inserts she calls them and accentuated them by lace trim. As you know, Shelley, Violet made the decision to move in with Daisy and her partner and Rachel years ago. It made sense, what with Violet modelling so regularly for Daisy Day's fashions. It's hard for Violet to understand that she cannot hug me on this strange Mothering Sunday.

Daisy raises a hand and waves towards Benji. Violet copies Daisy. Daisy is waving at her dad who has parked outside the boys' school. He's carrying a shovel. 'Benji,' I say, keeping my social distance as we enter through the school gates. I've got to know Benji and his family well over the years. I like Benji. He has always seemed to me to be the only person I knew who has never lied; never kept quiet to save his own back; always so honest. Benji. And he was just so good when he learnt that he wasn't Daisy's biological father. What is in blood, anyway? Possibly he had always suspected.

'Benjiiii …' Violet enjoys the last syllable and Daisy pulls Violet back and explains that she cannot hug Uncle Benji.

'Hi, Dad,' Daisy says easily and I watch the cherry blossom blow from the trees like confetti.

'Hi, Grandad,' Rachel says. 'What a day.'

Yes. What a day: some forty-nine years on. I think I might cry too but my attention is diverted. I watch you walk up the crescent towards me. Look, you still skim pavements. You are accompanied by your husband who is also carrying a shovel. As you approach, I would like to give you a hug, but I can't. You never were a hugger anyway. 'Shelley,' I say. This is a beautiful idea but I don't have time to tell you this, to thank you for the planning as Violet shouts, 'Shelleeeey …' enjoying that last syllable and seeming to get a hang of this new social distancing.

Daisy simply says. 'Aunt Shelley.'

You smile and I say, 'Daisy, Shelley, you grow so alike.'

We come the back way to the gardens: Daisy, Rachel, Violet, Benji, you and me: an odd little group to gather on a spring Sunday. Your husband with sapling and shovel in hand leads. He knows the way, leads with the authority of one who almost owns, but as we pick through the path I recall how we have trod here many times before as teenagers. You fall back on the path and whisper to me, 'Danny didn't come then?'

'Did you expect him?' I say, noticing that the old prefabs and senior school toilets (I mean *lavatories*) have disappeared. Do you still care about Danny? I suspect something in your whisper that does care still … a little. Thirty-odd years of marriage is a long time.

You shake your head; shrug your shoulders. 'Once he knew Daisy wasn't his …'

We are almost expecting some kind of official ceremony: some speech. We gather beneath the six-foot Kilmarnock willow and stand six feet apart. The Kilmarnock is the one you planted, Shelley, and received the Garden Prize for, in the late spring of 1969 even though nothing at all could be

298

seen on your patch but that Miss Harefield-Mott said was such a good idea. Greg and Benji begin to dig. We feel the nip in the spring air and huddle in. I'm thinking this is a daisy day, the clouds drifting across the cerulean sky. We plant the tree: the black walnut which, with help, will grow strong in this open position. I look at young Rachel between Daisy and Violet and I look into the future and see our lost Rachel's tree, which will have twisting branches and a big broad trunk and the well-protected plum-shaped fruit it will yield. You gave me the choice, Shelley, and this was my choice for the two Rachels: dark, fine-grained and productive. As the digging over old ground continues, I recall the wisps of dark curl on the back of her neck, the knob at the top of her sturdy spine, the smoothness of her young limbs and the way she helped me with my maths homework and I remember holding on to the bus rail for my life and being unable to catch her by her scarf to prevent her from falling.

I look at you. I look at Daisy. I suddenly recall looking at you all those years ago in the department store and wondering what was so familiar about you. I thought then that it was the fifteen-year-old in you. But there had been something else and of course, it has been staring me in the face for twenty years previously in the shape of Daisy: the clear-eyed greenness of the eyes, this strange mix of you and Patricia. For Patricia is there in the set of Daisy's mouth. But I knew little of your brother until you told me he was Daisy's father. You asked me to tell Benji.

**

Now you ask if we can go somewhere quiet and you take me to the school hall, via the dining room corridor. I am

299

observing the mosaic corridor floor where my heavy school sandals have trod. This corridor was once filled with the smell of semolina and square, yellow carbolic soap. It still smells indescribably of school. But this is no longer the school hall. 'Where is the stage? Where are the honours' boards with the gold embossed letters of your name, Shelley?'

'We took them down years ago,' you reply. 'Further education colleges have no need of honours' boards.' And then you add, 'Nobody reads what is on the walls anyway.'

'No.' I give a small, knowing smile. 'It's all changed,' I say.

'Yes, it's all changed,' you say. 'Staff offices now have windows on to this reception area.'

The old school hall is transformed to light and airy and, where our form rooms once fringed the school hall with upper balcony and Biology lab, now there are untidy staff offices with computers and large windows. The windows could do with a clean. The balcony, where once Miss Harefield-Mott spotted me waving at a first former and hauled me out publicly for double detention whilst spitting saliva, has, like the prefabs and senior school lavatories, disappeared. But old geography still lives on in my head.

'No inner sanctums here then as we used to call it,' I say.

'Or traffic light entry.' You smile. You're showing me what used to be Greg's office before he retired, telling me about his 'open door policy'.

We stand facing where once the old school stage used to be. I think on past performances which are more immediate to me than the present. There is a grey, graveyard silence; there are sounds but these are echoed memories. The school clock is no longer on the wall. 'What I did to Patricia was

300

unforgivable,' I suddenly say aloud. 'I made her continually face the one thing she did not possess and that was time: I placed a clock on her wall and let her listen to its beating. I had watched the hands of the school clock slip around quickly in terror and my heart had beat in synchronisation. I wanted to make Patricia feel the same.'

'I know, Jayne,' you say. 'I read her letter, remember?'

It was the panic I felt when I saw all those watches in the jeweller's: clock faces, time faces. There were images on the polished, parquet flooring: images of rulers ground into my back; tufts of marmalade hair; splintered knees and mouths with pink dummies; ink-stained hands and eyes; the humiliation I felt between my legs when my angst-ridden words had been published; bus stops and lavatories and whitewashed walls; my mother's plastic gloves and soap-sudded dreams vanishing with the raising of Miss Harefield-Mott's perfectly plucked eyebrow. Patricia Vickers was the sum total of my fears and the May day she died I expected those fears to die with her. But they haven't. They have lived on in the classroom of my head and I have been living my own brand of coma. What a waste.

'I'm glad the waiter gave you the letter I intended for the bin, Shelley. It led us to the truth.'

You nod and give a half-smile, seeming as though you want to say something but you don't so I carry on. 'Patricia wrote that we die by degrees but Shakespeare also said that wounds heal by degrees. An irrational contradiction Rachel would say.'

'Well if ever there was a contradiction it was you proving to be Patricia's half-sister.'

'Do you know the sum total of conversations I had with my birth father was one? The Reverend Vickers did little more than ask me my name. But Patricia's last words told me that I hadn't had to live with him. Maybe I was the lucky one.'

'When you wrote that book *Girls in a Line* why did you use that pseudonym: Tricia Dee? How could you?' you ask.

'When Violet was born at Patricia's house, I found my old school diary. I found Danny's letters to Patricia, and I found Patricia's writing. I used some of her writing and traded it as my own. I lied.' There. I said it. For the very first time. 'I stole Patricia's words,' I said, as if to make it absolutely clear. 'The abbreviation of her name was some kind of token. Silly, I know.'

But you shake your head. 'Not hers,' you say. 'Patricia could never write like that. It was Rachel's.'

I look at you in bewilderment. *Rachel's* writing? '*Rachel's* words?'

'I asked Rachel's family if I could help trace some of their family members who were lost during the Second World War. Her mother gave me some of Rachel's old diaries. Benji had 'lost',' and you gesticulate the parentheses here, 'some of her writing and diaries from her family.' You raise your eyebrows. Then you add, 'More like got lifted on the top of a bus by Mave and given to Patricia for cold storage. But there were always pieces of your book which reminded me of something. Rachel was precocious in her use of language and some of it is quite clearly adolescent and even pretentious. Rachel would have come to realize that.'

Here was I, Rose Good, standing in the old school hall, feeling … silly and fifteen once again. The polished parquet flooring is the same. The walls have changed but the floors remain the same. 'But Patricia said …'

'Oh, she lied about everything.' Then you add, 'It was

Patricia who stole Rachel's words.'

'But there was such an understanding, such an empathy with my feelings … you remember how things were for me here …'

You nod.

'I thought that only Patricia, only the perpetrator of those deeds could understand …'

You shake your head. 'Rachel,' you say. And you repeat her name.

'Will you publicise this?' I ask.

'You want *me,*' you say, 'to remain silent?'

'No. I can't expect it.'

'There's a time to speak and a time to be silent. Rachel would have said it was divine retribution. You were reaping what she sowed and you had paid dearly with your guilt but maybe there's something we can do for her. Will you help me to put Rachel's writing together?' you say. 'I can do the history – Rose Good can add the flourish and put her name on the spine.'

'But it won't be me,' I say. 'I would just be the cover that sells the goods.'

'I know all about that,' you say.

**

The college caretaker wants to lock up on this special anniversary. So we meet Benji and Greg in the old school crescent. We watch as Daisy, Violet and Rachel take the spades back to Benji's car.

You couldn't help yourself, could you, Shelley? You had to say it. 'Benji,' you say. 'Did you queue? Did you stand in a line?' you ask.

Greg sighs deeply, leans on his shovel; seems to know what is coming next. I don't. I'm confused. Why are you speaking this way to Benji?

'A line?' Benji asks but I can see his heart beating a little faster.

'When the three of you took Patricia in Paul's car that Christmas Eve?'

Paul's car? Christmas Eve? There is this heartbeat before Benji asks, 'Who told you?'

'I worked it out,' you say. 'My brother said there were *good reasons* why nobody knew who Daisy's father was. You always knew Daisy wasn't your daughter, didn't you, Benji? What have you been doing all your life? Paying a debt?'

'I told her I loved her,' Benji says softly.

'But you didn't,' you say. 'That was just to make her feel better when you raped her, wasn't it?'

He pauses. He goes to speak; stops himself. Then starts again as if trying to find the right words. 'I could get pissed on a wine gum, you know?' And he looks up expecting to raise a childhood laugh. He looks like the eighteen-year-old schoolboy in the school crescent. But no one is even smiling and his hair is grey. 'Danny went first. He didn't rape her. Patsy wanted it.'

'But she didn't want you or Paul,' you say without a question.

'No.' The word and his glance fall lightly to the ground like the cherry blossom.

'And that's why the three of you never asked for DNA tests. There were good reasons for not knowing who Daisy's father was. And the reason why the three of you 'saw *Patsy* all right' through those years, wasn't it?'

'It was our joint responsibility,' Benji says.

'Whoever the father was …' you say.

'Whoever,' Benji says.

'The court would call it joint enterprise,' you say.

Further up the crescent Daisy slams the boot of Benji's car shut and walking towards us I see our three girls in a line, hand in hand.

Acknowledgements:

Marcel Proust, Christina Rossetti, George Santayana, William Shakespeare, Logan Pearsall Smith. 'Do They Know It's Christmas?'/Band Aid, 'In My Room'/The Beach Boys, 'I'm the Urban Spaceman'/Bonzo Dog Doo-Dah Band, 'Bad Moon Rising'/Creedence Clearwater Revival, 'Red, Red Wine'/Neil Diamond, 'Build Me Up Buttercup'/The Foundations, 'Blackberry Way'/The Move, 'Stuck on You'/Lionel Ritchie, 'Where Do You Go To My Lovely?/Peter Sarstetd, 'Silence is Golden'/The Tremeloes, 'Dear Lord and Father of Mankind'/John Greenleaf Whittier.

And thanks to:

Barbara Pavey, Janet Rolfe, Patricia Sentinella and Chrissie Thomas for reading raw drafts.
Jane MacKinnon for her brilliant eye for detail.
Gill Hartley for all the gardening stuff.
Kirsty Jackson: my editor and publisher at Cranthorpe Millner for taking this on.
My husband Syd for his patience.
My school chums who travelled with me during my not-so slim adolescence but ultimately my far-too-slim an adolescence.

BV - #0031 - 141021 - C0 - 197/132/18 - PB - 9781912964635 - Matt Lamination